CROOKED
V.3

EDITED BY
JESSIE KWAK

EDITOR

Jessie Kwak

COVER IMAGE

Photograph by sandr2002 on DepositPhotos

Cover design by Jessie Kwak and Robert Kittilson

ORNAMENTAL BREAK

Elements by Freepik and Good Ware from www.flaticon.com.

PUBLISHER

Bad Intentions Press

Portland, OR, USA

For more information, please visit: jessiekwak.com/crooked

CONTENTS

INTRODUCTION

Welcome to CROOKED V.3!

This third installment in the *Crooked* anthology series brings you ten more stories of space crime. Jobs will go wrong. Backs will be stabbed. Mayhem will break out.

And things will *definitely* explode.

You're gonna love it here. I promise.

The goal of the *Crooked* anthology series is to introduce you, the reader, to authors who are currently writing sci-fi crime stories. Many of the stories in this collection are set in larger universes, which means that if you read something you like, you'll find plenty more in that author's catalogue to keep you busy.

To help you discover work you'll love, I'm trying something a little different than most anthologies. While you can certainly read the stories in order from beginning to end, I've also included "Pick Your Poison" prompts at the end of each story. Whether you finish a story and think, "Hell yeah, I want more of this!" or "Let's try a different flavor of sci-fi crime," use the prompts to find your next story.

Or, just turn the page.

Whether you're picking up this anthology because you like the premise or to read a story by an author you already love, you're sure to discover a new author or two you'll dig.

Don't forget to follow the links at the end of each story for goodies, giveaways, and even more stories from the seedy underbelly of the Science Fiction shelf.

And if you want even more sci-fi crime in your life, head to jessiekwak.com/bad-intentions to pick up your copies of *CROOKED V.1* and *CROOKED V.2*.

Have fun out there,

Jessie Kwak
October 28, 2024

LOVE OF MINE

A EURYNOME CODE: SHADOW HOST STORY

BY K. GORMAN

1

"Babe, I think I'm in trouble."

With those few short words, it felt like a pressure cap had been unscrewed from her head. Soo-jin kept herself still, expression closed, attention ostensibly focused on the holopoint in front of her as her mind whirred to process her girlfriend's tone, her words, the context, and all the fucking background that had led up to them.

Around her, *Huli Jing*'s bridge hummed quietly. She and Giselle were the only ones on board. Zan, her first officer, had gone out several hours ago. Alone, she'd kept the ship in silence, the click and whir of the dashboard computers and low background drone of life support the only sounds she could hear. She listened to them idly, her jaws clenching together so hard, her teeth hurt.

Giselle had been distant lately. Quiet. Irritable. More combative when they *did* speak. They'd had spats before —hells, they were *both* firecrackers, and they shared a very short fuse sometimes.

But this time had felt... different. Not one of their normal spats. Something bigger, and she had no idea what'd caused it.

They usually slept together, or at least in the same bed. Hot-bunking it if their schedules grew askew. Or, if they'd had a real hot spat, then—

Well, Soo-jin always took the couch. Giselle had a thing with her back. The bed was better for her.

But lately, Giselle hadn't been coming to bed at all. In fact, she'd barely been on the ship. And there'd been this strange distance to her, this distraction, where she only half-listened to their conversations, or checked out of them completely.

Soo-jin had thought she was about to break up with her.

But, maybe—*maybe* it wasn't that. Maybe it *wasn't* something she'd done, or not done.

Maybe it had nothing to do with her at all.

Maybe she was about to find out.

"Trouble?" she asked lightly, feeling the silence stretch before she tried to massage it back into place. "What kind of trouble?"

Giselle hesitated. "There's these guys. I... owe them some money."

Something in her voice—a quiver, like a fragile, shivery bird—made Soo-jin finally look over.

She caught sight of Giselle's face, and—

Rage splintered her nerves. She was out of the seat and by Giselle's side in a heartbeat, hands shaking as she touched gently around her jawline, coaxing her to lift her chin.

Giselle cringed but did what she silently requested,

tilting her head up and back for Soo-jin to see, blue eyes slipping down and to the side in shame.

Her girlfriend had a gorgeous face. A gorgeous *every-thing*, really. Bombshell blonde with a side of whisky and aggression. Full of curves, with a strong, bold jaw, prominent features, and eyes as blue as the Novan sky.

The eyes were still blue, but one was rimmed with red, the surrounding skin swollen into an angry mix of red, pink, and purple.

She hadn't noticed it when Giselle had walked in. Giselle hadn't paraded it, and Soo-jin hadn't looked.

Gods, she hadn't even *looked*.

Too fucking caught up in her pity-me act to give even a basic shit about the woman she supposedly loved.

She lifted her fingers from Giselle's jawline and slid them into her golden hair, soothing.

"Where are they?" she asked.

Giselle pulled loose of her touch, shaking her head, again hiding the bruise from sight. "No. Don't. You'll make it worse."

"Oh, yes. Definitely. I'm going to be a real big fucking problem. For *them*." She bared her teeth, hissing a swear from the back of her throat and breaking away to pace a small, angry line up the aisle and back. "Let's see how much *they* like shiners. I'll give them a matching fucking set."

A soft hand on her arm stopped her.

"No. You can't. It's—they're bigger than that." Giselle sucked in a breath. "We have to do this the right way."

The 'right' way? In Soo-jin's opinion, the 'right' way involved repeatedly introducing her fist to their faces until they fucked off. Whatever loansharking debt repayment shit they'd trapped Giselle in—it was likely jacked up bullshit.

But Giselle's words stopped her short.

'We.' She'd said '*we.*'

She wasn't intending to leave. *Not* shutting her out. In fact, she was actively including her in her plans.

Elation sparked in her chest, and relief flooded in like a drug. She chewed her tongue a moment, a mix of giddiness, indignation, and protective anger melding into some hormone-ridden surge that sent her bouncing.

Everything was fine, then. They just had to solve this problem. And Giselle, apparently, had an idea about how to do that.

Fantastic.

She sat back in her original seat, crossed her legs, and leaned forward.

"All right. What did you have in mind?"

2

'Pay them a fuckload of money and fulfill her obligation' was apparently Giselle's grand plan.

Not as fun as Soo-jin's idea, but perhaps she'd give the fuckers a few shiners during the handover. Or sometime afterward, if she haunted enough dark alleys near their HQ. Giselle owed money to the Indigo Kids, a higher-class establishment than typical street-level loan sharks and, apparently, she'd already paid a good two-thirds of the money off. All she had left was forty-thou on the loan and thirty-three for the interest.

Seventy-three thousand credits. Enough to get a person to and from Enlil about four times on a mid-tier transport. So, not an eye-watering amount of money, but not something Soo-jin had lying around. Especially not when she flew a vintage hundred-plus-year-old dropship that liked to suck money down the repair bill toilet.

Literally, too. The septic system was the latest thing she'd had to special-order some bullshit for—which was even crazier since it hadn't even been part of the original model.

But she loved her ship. *Huli Jing* was worth every credit.

And so was Giselle.

Zan, her first officer, had returned from wherever they'd been. They watched her pull a load of old maps and scrounge equipment across the floor of Mess with a raised brow. "We going somewhere?"

Right. Everything had happened so fast—and in the middle of the night. Zan had been out when she and Giselle had schemed their plans.

"Yeah. Sorry. I know it's short notice." She turned to them with a cringe, wiping dirt-smeared dust off her sweaty hands, then pulling the netlink out of her pocket to flick through its menus. She sent a file Zan's way. "Here. Just finished the outline."

Zan brought their own netlink up and read through it.

The former soldier had been with *Huli Jing* over a year now—six months longer than Soo-jin had been seeing Giselle, actually. Tall, with a lanky, muscled frame, they'd embraced the post-military life with a passion for atypical styles and elegant fabrics. Often, they looked as though they'd stepped out of some fantasy setting where musclebound rangers got manicures between bouts of kicking ass.

They'd dressed simply today, and more modern. Geometric. Soo-jin's mind twinged, the look reminding her of some fashion movement she vaguely remembered reading about, but she dismissed the thought before it could fully form, focusing instead on their face and inwardly bracing for impact.

As *Huli Jing*'s only other employee, Zan worked for a forty percent split of the cut. More if *Huli Jing*'s systems didn't need anything stupidly expensive.

The file she'd sent them outlined her appraisal of a scrounge site close to the ass-end of the asteroid belt.

Fortunately for them, orbital mechanics were working in their favor. It'd only take a couple weeks to get there. Even less to get back.

Zan raised both eyebrows when they came to the end of the file. "That's quite the payout."

"Yes."

"What's the catch?"

And there it was. She'd known this was coming. Zan was many things, but they weren't an idiot.

Soo-jin hesitated, cringing. "It's not strictly... *legal.*"

"Ah." The eyebrows furrowed in concentration, Zan studying the file's details a little closer. "What's not legal about it?"

"The date. 82-Morgana doesn't qualify for scrounge for another nine months."

"Ah."

"Yeah. It's out of the way, and outside of patrol routes, so the chances of anyone being there are low, but..."

"But not zero. Got it."

The crew of *Huli Jing* ran a number of odd jobs, but their main business lay in scrounge. Not just normal scrounge, either, though they did that in a pinch—*Huli Jing*'s hull could fit a shocking amount of scrap metal when they were desperate enough, and genuine vintage wood sold for a fuckload on stations. Mostly, though, they searched for historic pieces.

Art. Ships. Weapons. Old beer cans were always good for a few bucks, but better when shined up and spaced out in auction listings. Colony stuff went for loads.

Niche colony stuff? Especially tied to historic or cultural figures?

Well, Soo-jin had one degree in engineering, another in archeology, a near-encyclopedic memory of random historical catalogs, and she loved using those things for extracting old, salvageable treasure from rotting, abandoned places. Every piece she found felt more like a rescue, especially when she got them all shiny and restored again.

Getting paid for that? What an absolute dream.

82-Morgana, an abandoned colony site in a medium-sized asteroid, had been on her radar for over twenty years, ever since she'd played an old video game that had used its story as a setting.

Over a hundred years ago, the story went, Niall Cook, who had gained fame and followers after demonstrating a bunch of spooky faith-healings and otherworldly-connections, took a loyal group of fellow Sol Cultists out to the asteroid—then an abandoned mining operation—where they could live and meditate in peace, undisturbed by the noise and 'thought pollution' of the inhabited worlds.

Several years into it, the tiny colony's O_2 sensors failed. They sent out an urgent distress call, but with so much distance between them and the nearest station, it took weeks for help to arrive.

When it did, rescuers found every single person dead. All in the same room, lying down as if they'd just gone to sleep.

Except for Niall.

Rescuers had found him next to the filtration panels in engineering, a broken breather in one hand, a pair of pliers in the other, reaching for the frame he'd likely just opened.

A horrific tragedy.

But a very *old* horrific tragedy, and Soo-jin's girlfriend *really* needed some money, so it was time to loot the shit out of it, fence that loot to some rich asshole on the black market, and pay off her girlfriend's debts.

If the Indigo Kids were lucky, she'd run it through a cleaning service first. However, since she doubted they'd given her girlfriend clean credits in the first place, she had a feeling they'd be unlucky.

Cleaning services were only for the *good* bad guys. Like her and Giselle. And Zan, if they wanted in.

Watching them, she wasn't sure if they would. Before now, their scrounge operations had always sat on the light side of the law. She might slip a few corners on the backend during the actual operation, but the salvage itself had always been legitimate.

This wasn't so much a step off the path as it was a leap.

It was a *lot* of money, however. And Zan, like her, wasn't exactly unfamiliar with the shadier sides of the law.

Their jaws worked for a moment, eyes focused on the data. Then they blew out a heavy breath, cheeks puffing in consideration. "You got a way to fence this stuff?"

"Yes."

"Cleanly?"

"I'll run it through the wash myself."

Zan grunted. "All right, then. Have you filed a flight plan?"

Soo-jin had been drawing breath, ready to defend the plan more, but stopped when Zan's words registered.

They were agreeing? *Already?*

"No," she said, hesitating. "I was waiting on you."

"That was wise. Where are you filing it for?"

"68-Lindon," she said. "It's adjacent."

"Go farther than that. Make a plan for skimming the belt sites. I'll help you." Zan met her eyes, eyebrows rising —a mix of concern and question. "Why the big hurry on this? *Jing* blow a nose cone or something?"

"No." Soo-jin winced. She hated admitting this— gods, it felt so unprofessional—but Zan had to know. They were business partners. Besides, she was pretty sure they'd understand. "Giselle owes money. Indigo Kids gave her a shiner earlier."

"Ah." Zan's head bobbed from side to side, weighing that. Then, they shrugged. "Well. Happy wife, happy life, right?"

Phew. They were cool with the job, then.

Soo-jin snorted. "We're not married."

"After this, you may as well be." Zan chuckled, a teasing eye roll fluttering to the ceiling. "Most people don't commit crimes together for at least a year."

"What can I say?" She shrugged. "Lesbians move fast."

"That you do. By the way, what's with the box outside?"

She frowned. "Box?"

"Yeah. Decent size, maybe two pallets. Ship parts label. You order a new refrigeration unit or something?"

Her brows furrowed.

Had she?

"Crap," she said, dropping the corner of the bag she was holding and heading for the door. "Let's see what Drunk Soo-jin gifted us with this time."

'Two pallets' didn't do it justice. The crate felt more like 'two coffins' stacked. With a heavy sigh and a pair of laser snips, she tore through the wraps and cut the security straps, scouring her mind for any memory of what she had ordered. The package was definitely addressed to her, and it was also definitely labeled as ship parts.

Was it a duplicate or something? No, she hadn't replaced anything this size since the coolant drowned its filtration unit last year. Extra side plating, perhaps? Something to do with her current sani repair woes?

No. All she'd needed were hoses and a new pressure regulator—all of which had arrived, and none of which was this large.

Sol's burned child. Maybe Drunk Soo-jin *had* ordered something. She liked to mix auction listings with whiskey, sometimes. It was how *Huli Jing* had ended up with the large, stuffed panda in the corner of Mess. Drunk Soo-jin had trouble reading measurements.

With a rip of splintering wood, she and Zan popped the top off, shoved it aside, and peered in.

The box was jammed with pieces of old black metal. Most of it was fairly thin, with occasional brushes of the stubbly rash she recognized in space-aged metal. Except for a few smaller rectangles, all the pieces appeared to be jaggedly triangular in shape.

She frowned. What the hells was this?

Maybe she *had* ordered extra side plating. Or top plating. Bottom plating?

She scoured her mind, trying to fit the shapes to some piece of her ship's hull.

If she'd ordered spare plating, why was it all so old and gross?

Beside her, Zan went still.

"Soo-jin," they said delicately, breath puddling in their throat. "Did you mail order a *Border Wars Mine?*"

Icy horror struck through her. Her pulse squirmed, the ghost of a memory rising like a faint, familiar wisp. She sucked in a breath, eyes wide with panic as they raked over the metal pieces in front of her.

No.

No way.

This wasn't a mine. These were clearly *ship* pieces. That was a strut, and there the meld for atmospheric seal, and—

Her encyclopedic memory for useless trivia kicked in.

Border War Mines had been built with ship parts. That was part of what had made them so scary—they could be mass produced from any ship-building facility. Ship parts, tempered with scan resistant metal, and coated with light-disrupting paint and bumps to disguise it—

To disguise it as aging, harmless space trash.

She looked down at the box in growing horror.

Her name and address sat boldly on the package label, damning her with the contents.

Sol's fucking child. I've finally fucked myself.

Maybe she could call customs and explain. Or Dockside. Or local enforcement.

No. No, no, no. None of them would believe a word she said. Not when a *Border Wars Mine* was involved.

SysOps, then. She had a friend there. Baik *would* believe her. He knew she didn't deal in munitions.

Wasn't he out, though? On some job?

Fuck!

Calmly—casually—Zan reached over and pulled the lid back into place.

"Why don't you go file that flight plan of yours," they suggested. "We'll want to leave before anyone notices us with this thing."

3

"We're in luck," Zan announced. "It's just frame and motor. Everything else is either missing or inert."

Soo-jin sagged into the couch with a loud groan, covering her face as several hours' worth of worry blew out of her. "Fuck me. Someone take my auction privileges away. I thought it was a *throne*."

Zan put their hands on their hips and surveyed the pieces with a considering expression. "We could make it a throne. How much welding do you want to do?"

She gave a hollow laugh. "Only enough to weld my hands away from ever accessing stupidly dangerous auction listings again. Gods, I almost had a *stroke* going through that departure gate. How in the hells did they *not* notice a fucking *bomb?*"

"Probably because this fucking bomb codes as ship parts." Zan chuckled. "Likely how it got through the mail, too."

She groaned, sliding further down the couch. "Thanks for checking it."

Zan saluted her with a wrench. "Aye, aye, Captain. And thank *you*."

"For what?"

"For providing a stimulating work environment. I haven't used my bomb disposal skills in years."

Ordnance had been their specialty, back in their military days.

"In that case, I'll order more bombs, just for you." She pushed herself off the couch, stumbling as the blood rushed away from her brain. She wasn't sure what, precisely, it had been doing there—the evidence scattered across the floor didn't suggest she was particularly *smart*—but a whooshing sound filled her ears as it fled and her vision filled to near-complete static for a few seconds.

With a more leftward veer than she intended, she headed for the small door that led to Engineering. "I'll go tell the honey."

Zan saluted again. "Happy wife, happy life!"

She gave them a half-hearted wave and slipped through the door.

The second it closed behind her—and the familiar background drone of *Huli Jing*'s Engineering closed around her—she felt her whole body relax.

Engineering always felt like a cave to her. Enclosed and isolated, its walls marking the inner shape of the hull and thruster displacements, rising to a ceiling that curved in on itself. Normally, she was leery of caves. She had a phobia of certain types of them, so she tried to avoid them. Exposure had helped. Doing scrounge work—it was hard to avoid caves.

Still, they weren't places she could relax in.

Engineering was different. It felt like a friendly cave, somehow. Like she'd spent so much time in it, had fixed or rebuilt so much of it, it had become a part of her family. Her mind had anthropomorphized it into some benign spirit, and she got a feeling similar to what some people felt walking into temples or churches. She hadn't had much luck with *those*—certain parts of her past meant they'd always feel alienating to her—but here? In *Huli Jing*'s Engineering? It felt like she *belonged*.

She spent a lot of time here. Fixing things. Maintaining things. Modern Science had yet to bless the populace with Faster Than Light capabilities—at least for its citizenry. She had some suspicions about its military R&D sectors—so journeys across the enormous amount of space that existed between places took a while. Not *years*, at least. Thanks to the G-force canceling effects of artificial gravity generators, they could push acceleration and deceleration rates well past the limits of unaided human soft tissues. Still, multiple weeks' worth of spaceflight grated on the boredom levels.

So, Soo-jin fixed things. Maintained them. Kept each one of *Huli Jing*'s many small fiddly bits well-oiled and well-inspected. It was soothing to her. Meditative. She lost hours to it, focused on one project or another.

On the way back, she'd have a bunch of dirty and rusted artifacts to occupy her time, but on the way out—repairs. Always.

Giselle found it meditative, too, albeit in a different way.

Soo-jin closed her eyes and stood for a moment, smelling the familiar smells, feeling the familiar vibrations in the floor, the taste of heat in the air, of ozone from the reactor. The collision drive and its many tubes were a subtle, soft glow overhead beyond the grating. And the coolant...

She let the room wrap around her, let the sensations

seep into her senses, drawing them in, breathing, searching...

The scent of jasmine caught her. Like a heeling ship, she turned and followed her heart to *Huli Jing*'s primary cooling system.

Within seconds, she caught sight of Giselle's silhouette, a warped shadow through the blue of one of the coolant tanks. Giselle. Her girlfriend. Meditating on the lid of the cooling hub, as usual.

A warm feeling filled her chest, and her heart curved her lips into a small, happy smile.

Suns. What had she done to deserve this?

Maybe Zan was right. Maybe she *should* marry this woman.

She considered that. What would it be like? Having a wife—having *Giselle* for a wife. Gods, the term itself felt so foreign. Wife. *Wife!*

She'd almost become one, once, back when she was barely legal and still in the hands of her cultist family. An arranged marriage. With one of her cousins.

She'd run the fuck away from that. Ever since, the term 'wife' had only been a joke. For herself, anyway. Lots of other people got to be wives, have marriages, settle down...

But not her.

Marriage, she'd thought, had been a distant dream. Long gone and slingshotting away from the System at an astonishing rate, strapped with the jet pack she'd set alight eight years ago.

Giselle had snuck up on her. A hot one-night stand that had led to another, then again the next week. On the third, they'd started getting brunch together, giggling as they whiled the morning away in Soo-jin's bed, or watched netdrama together on her couch.

Giselle had become familiar. Comfortable. An endearing body curled up against hers.

And, gods, she was a spitfire. And *very* hot. Soo-jin had followed her drunkenly, one ill-advised adventure after another, holding in breathless giggles as Giselle picked the lock on an old, rusted fire door, reveling at the ancient, obsolete machinery inside. The astonished look on her face when Soo-jin had pulled a bottle of whiskey she'd filched from a mobster's cart.

She treasured that look.

She hadn't been in love then, she thought, but definitely crushing hard. Riding the happy hormones.

No, it wasn't until months later that 'love' had come into play.

At some point or another, Soo-jin had taken to playing protector. And found Giselle doing the same.

They had each other's backs. They *trusted* each other.

She'd go to the ends of creation for her. Hells, wasn't that what she was doing right now?

Yeah. She was sunk.

And now that she thought about it—she *definitely* wanted Giselle as her wife.

But first, they had to solve her not-so-little debt problem.

As if sensing her presence—no, scratch that, *definitely* sensing her presence—Giselle's voice rang out from between the tanks, her warm tone underlain with rich laughter. "You going to keep lurking like a freak, or do I actually get to see you at some point?"

Soo-jin's lips curled even higher. She moved forward, rounding the edge of the tank. Giselle smiled up at her, legs crossed and back straight in her usual lotus position.

Crossing her arms, she leaned against the tank's frame and gave her girlfriend a slow, appreciative look.

"You know I'm a freak for you," she said.

Giselle laughed.

The happy warmth burst in her chest again. The sound felt like bells inside her, ringing happiness through her ribs. She gave a soft sigh, relaxing further.

"I'm happy to announce that we won't be blown up by my drunken auction purchase," she continued.

"Ah. No Fire Darts, then?"

Soo-jin winced. Fire Darts were, perhaps, the most terrifying part of a Border Wars Mine, though its other aspects made it a very close race. The entire *thing* was a nightmare. Assembled, it looked like some hellish, cyberpunk sea urchin. Two meters wide and tall and coated with scan-disrupting paint, each of its spikes held a localized shield-disrupting grav pulse blade embedded in its armor and contained demolition charges programmed to explode on contact. Once triggered, the rest of the mine would blow, flinging several thousand Fire Darts—tiny, self-guiding missiles programmed to find, chase, and attack—into the proximal space like a cloud of sparking embers. A combination of intelligent programming, nanomachines, lasers, and highly flammable accelerant gave the victimized ship many more things to worry about.

Soo-jin had been jumping at darting pieces of light for the past hour, thinking of them infiltrating her ship.

"No." Her cringe turned to a full grimace, teeth baring as her lips twisted in distaste. "Unless there's another package on its way."

Giselle snorted. "Good we got out of there when we did, then."

Giselle was smiling again. *Still* smiling. Her lips were infectious. Soo-jin found hers curling up again. Happiness lit up from inside, trapping her heart.

"Zan says I should marry you," she said.

Giselle burst out laughing.

"*What?!*" The word came out less like speech and more like a breathless squeal.

"It's true. They think I should put a ring on that finger."

Soo-jin detached herself from the coolant tank and slipped forward. Her gaze dropped as she approached, moving to where Giselle's hand flexed against her thigh. Giselle hastily shoved herself to the side as Soo-jin sat, making room, and sucked in a surprised breath when Soo-jin took up her hand and gently kissed it.

"And do you know," she murmured. "I think they might be right."

Giselle's expression sobered. She went still. Soo-jin kept hold of her hand. Giselle dabbed her perfume on the inside of her wrist. The scent of jasmine flowed into her, overtaking the humming machinery and chemical coolant scent in the background.

She used to hate the smell. Now, her mind latched onto it, tunneling down until Giselle was all she could see and smell.

"You must be a witch, to have captured my heart so," she murmured, making Giselle's breath hitch with laughter. It was a quote from a netdrama they'd watched last month, some sappy thing with a ridiculously happy ending. More seriously, and more quietly, she said, "Every time I hear you laugh, it fills me with joy."

Giselle stilled again. Around them, filtering coolant made the light dance. If she closed her eyes, it was like they were in a magical cave, surrounded by blue light.

The light glowed in Giselle's hair, spun gold taken by a glowing neon sky. The blue of her eyes seemed almost electric, pulling her in. Her lips were right there. Full, parted slightly, and so close. So *very* close.

Giselle licked them lightly, wetting them. "Soo-jin..."

There was so much more Soo-jin wanted to say. *So* much more. Instead, heedful of her lover's bruise, she reached out and pressed her gently downward, toward the cushioned mat they sat on.

"Shhh," she said, kissing her hand, then her shoulder. "Say no more, fair maiden. I know what it is you desire."

Giggling, Giselle let herself be lowered to the mat. Her eyes glittered up at her, electric blue, full of light and mirth.

"Oh?" she asked, breathless, one eyebrow rising. "And what is that? *Cunnilingus?*"

Soo-jin frowned down at her severely.

"No," she said. "A shitload of money."

4

Over the next two weeks, Soo-jin had some of the best sex in her life.

Then, sani broke for the fourth time, and she'd had to pump all the sewage out to fix it.

The entire ship had shunned her.

She didn't blame them. If she could, she'd shun *herself*. Unfortunately, the laws of physics required her to live with herself—and the stench.

Giselle *did* deliver muffins to her, though. *Twice.* While wearing an EVA suit.

It'd made her laugh both times.

And—instead of large amounts of sex—Zan had spent the last two weeks welding the Border Wars Mine together. It sat in three half-formed pieces in Cargo, looking about as menacing as a metal star lantern bound for some art festival. Zan and Soo-jin had been trading back and forth with how to best turn it into a throne. They also kept reassuring Giselle of its inertness, Zan even going so far as to fire a shot of electricity into one of the spike's defunct tips, demonstrating that its circuits were too corroded to detonate.

Soo-jin was... *almost* glad she hadn't been there for that one. However, her absence meant she'd been deep in the bowels of Engineering's underpanels, dealing with literal broken shit.

But they were here now. She could, for the moment, stop huffing sewage fumes.

Finally.

She strode out from the mostly-fixed sani, grinning as she trotted down the stairs and to the three-piece pile of EVA suits the others were putting on. Lidar had pinged 82-Morgana on approach, and now, *Huli Jing* sat in the shadows of its decrepit docking bay, one airlock extended and waiting for one of them to puff out there in a suit, fire up the ancient bay on a remote charge, and let them in.

Suns. Her antiquated ship's docking locks were old enough to actually *fit* this bay.

If the seals proved true, she might test that theory. But probably not for long. Unlike *Huli Jing*, 82-Morgana hadn't been diligently restored and maintained for the past eight years.

She didn't want to add herself to the colony's already-extensive death toll.

Ten minutes later, with the clunk and suck of seals engaging in the airlock, then the quieting hiss of vacating air, Soo-jin floated out her ship's extended back door, grappling for the handhold next to its lip. She clipped a cable to a ring on her harness, gathered herself in, and kicked off into the gap.

Her stomach squirmed toward her knees as she sailed into open space, the sense of danger lifting every hair on her body as she left the known sanctuary of *Huli Jing* behind. 82-Morgana's docks loomed in front of her, a jut of prefab concrete and metal hooded with rock. From this angle, it looked like it was frowning. And attempting to swallow her. Doors made of the same dark, space-aged paint mix that the Border Wars Mine tried to imitate loomed in front of her like a blunt, rectangular mouth.

A tiny piece of debris bounced off her helmet, the small scraping sound it made loud in her ears. As she closed in on the doors, she flailed for the handrail embedded in the sill, activating a burst of one of her suit's thrusters and keeping her body straight while she course-corrected.

Her hand connected. Then, so did the rest of her body.

She smacked into it with an inelegant scramble, thrusting her arm through the rail, and turned.

Behind her, *Huli Jing*'s back end loomed near the dock, askew in its alignment. Someone's helmet was visible inside the extended airlock, peeking through the porthole.

She couldn't see their face, but she knew who it was.

Giselle.

Her heart filled with a warm, buzzing sensation.

Suns. This 'love' thing felt good.

I'm going to buy that woman a million diamonds. A million trillion diamonds. And punch all the Indigo Kids' faces in.

She smiled at the thought, then busied herself with the dock.

She had an abandoned station to loot.

5

They got seventeen crates. Seventeen stacked, stuffed-to-the-brim crates full of old wiring, interfaces, and tools, along with the more *carefully* packed pieces of the temple and its contents.

The former would hide the latter on any 'randomly assigned' shakedown a bored patrol officer might decide to do.

It had been... spooky inside 82-Morgana. Haunting. It usually was in these abandoned places. People, even people like her, weren't used to the absolute silence an abandonment does to a place. Everything was always too quiet. Too vacuous. No air. No life support.

Creepy.

She loved it.

It also wasn't in bad condition. Even dormant, Morgana's reactor put off enough radiant heat that most of the colony's controls were intact. The farther they went in, the warmer it got.

There'd even been *air* past the inner seals.

Not that she'd trust it, given the colony's history.

Still, she'd enjoyed herself. Filmed the entire float-through—another thing she could sell, after extensive editing to remove any incriminating details of her crew or her ship—then got to work with a camera, a crate, a crowbar, and a multi-tool.

The work felt good to do. Slightly less good, given it was illegal and she wouldn't be able to sell it to any museums, but that was a quibble she quickly quashed.

She was a survivor, first. They all were.

Soo-jin let out a breath as *Huli Jing*'s engines engaged, carrying them away from the dead colony. She watched it drop away in the posterior feed, the bright blue of the engines casting its frowning face in stark relief for thirty seconds. Then, they switched off, and 82-Morgana became a misshapen silhouette against the stars.

They'd leave the engines off for the next eight hours, coasting back to their official schedule, then fire them again to course-correct for a different site.

Zan had mapped it out so well, their coasting path nearly aligned with their official flight plan.

Bless.

Now, all she had to worry about were government shakedowns and pirates.

She doubted she'd run into a government shakedown. Patrols were infrequent these days. That, however, made pirates *less* infrequent.

Huli Jing, however, was a surprisingly capable ship with an extremely capable set of engines.

She'd make quite a prize, but they'd have to catch her first—which would be difficult when she was blazing an ion trail faster than most non-military engines could keep up with.

So, really, there was nothing to worry about. They'd coast to the next spot, do their due diligence in scrounging it, and the next one, too, and be on their way to make bank.

They'd done it. Giselle was going to be free—and Soo-jin was going to be free to punch some Indigo Kids in the face during some premeditated drunken brawls.

Life was good. She could relax. And celebrate a successful run.

She cracked open a bottle of whisky. And several blunts. And celebrated until time blurred.

"I'm going to make you a ring," she said to Giselle a while later in her quarters, her tone a low murmur, slurring the words. She felt happy. Content. Like her entire body was a smile, the alcohol pounding nicely through her veins. It was like a fire. Sweet fire.

Everything was sweet right now.

"I'm going to make you a ring of iron and gold," she said, slurring the words again. It was a quote. Another netdrama they'd watched. She hoped she'd got it right. "On a bed of wood and stone."

Her workshop's bench was made of prefab—but she could pretend, couldn't she?

Giselle seemed to like the idea. She was smiling, too. She looked like a cat, she thought. A happy cat, laying on Soo-jin's bed. Looking at her with those electric eyes. Purring.

...Purring?

No. That was... probably *not* her girlfriend. The grav gen, more likely. Sometimes, part of its cycle seemed to hit that gray area between 'rumble' and 'vibration.' Usually, it set her teeth on edge.

Now, however...

She giggled at her brain's mistake. Then stopped

giggling when Giselle moved. Her girlfriend shifted her shoulders and reached out for her.

Smooth fingers traced over her brow. She held still, the feeling absolving through her. Tingles rushed her nerves. When Giselle moved closer, all she could see was her face, haloed by her golden hair and the lights of her quarters.

"I prefer a bed with you in it," Giselle murmured in her ear.

Then, she kissed her. Sweetly.

Everything was sweet.

6

Soo-jin slid awake. Drowsy. Confused. Blinking. Cold.

Something felt wrong. Like the breath had gone out of her lungs. Like she'd lost it. Or—like she'd lost something else.

No. Not some*thing*. Some*one*.

The other side of the bed was empty. Cold.

Everything was cold. Why was everything cold?

Where was Giselle?

She blinked hard. Felt around. The smell of jasmine lingered in the sheets, along with something else. A hint of smoke. Cold metal. The taste of ozone.

Her head hurt. Why was everything so cold?

In the next instant, something clicked in the room around her, like a spring had pushed a lock into its chamber.

Lights flashed on. Her ship began screaming.

Soo-jin jolted, flinching at the din. *Huli Jing*'s emergency klaxons were a shrieking wall of sound. Horror slashed her body into motion. She stumbled out of bed, tripping on the twisting sheets, and lurched for the auxiliary dashboard embedded into her desk.

Its screen flashed with errors and warnings.

LOW OXYGEN. LIFE SUPPORT FAILURE. CATASTROPHIC MALFUNCTION.

Fuck!

Moving on instinct, she shoved herself to the side and banged the emergency wall panel. It clicked open, and she nearly cut her hand jamming it in for a breathing mask. Struggling fingers fumbled the straps to her face, eyes wide and her mind coated with panic.

Giselle. She needed a mask. Where was she? Engineering?

Giselle went down there sometimes when she couldn't sleep. Meditated. Soo-jin fumbled for the second mask, then flung herself onto the Engineering door.

It wouldn't open.

Alarm spiked fresh across her mind. She tried again. Then she input an engineering override into the panel.

The panel flashed with a message:

WARNING: FIRE.

Her heart stopped.

Fire. On her ship. There was *fire. On her fucking ship*.

And her girlfriend was on the other side. No, not girlfriend—fiancée.

She'd asked for her hand last night. Promised her a ring. She remembered that. *She remembered that*.

In a flurry of motion, she bolted for the other door. This one opened, at least, if slower than usual. She sprinted for the bridge, the second breather clasped tightly in her hand, and—

And found Zan already sitting at navigation, cool as a cucumber, and not wearing a mask.

She surged forward. "Zan! There's a fire! Take this! You—"

"There's no fire," they said, watching the computer. "It's a Chaos Script. Your girlfriend loaded it into the system earlier. Then, she left."

Soo-jin stumbled to a halt. "What?"

The scene swam around her, as if everything was floating on water. She stared dully, brows furrowing as she tried to process their words.

She couldn't have heard that right. Was she hypoxic?

Probably. But that didn't matter. She had a breather now. She'd *get better*. But Giselle was—

Zan turned, and Soo-jin's mind shut down.

They weren't hypoxic. They were very clearly sharp and with it. They were also very clearly pissed.

Cold fury cut like a sober knife. A piece of herself unraveled, her mind playing their words over again and again.

Chaos Script. Giselle left. There is no fire.

"I—" A small noise fluttered her throat, then died there. It felt like it was choking her. For a second, she couldn't breathe.

"She sabotaged us," Zan said, turning back to the dashboard. Lines of code streamed down one side of their screen. The other side was taken by a different program. As Soo-jin watched, they scrolled. "She sabotaged us, loaded the script, and floated off to another ship."

Their voice was cold, but not calm. It vibrated with barely contained fury. They appeared to find what they were looking for in the scroll. With a flick of their wrist, they deleted several things.

The klaxons stopped screaming.

Silence fell so suddenly, it felt like she'd been hit.

Her ears rang.

Inside, it felt like her mind was breaking apart. Her heart was slower to figure it out.

It took her a few seconds to work her tongue.

"She—no. She didn't do this. She—"

Zan looked back at her, their eyes pitying.

"I'm sorry, Captain. She played us. And we fell for it, hook, line, and sinker."

7

Soo-jin watched the security feed over and over again. Giselle, bent over the open lid to *Huli Jing*'s coolant hub, pulling out an equipment bag, her meditation mat tossed to the side. Giselle, crawling into the underpanels by the reactor. Giselle, leaning so far over the collision drive's bumper, Soo-jin could only recognize her by the pants she wore, the shape of her body.

Giselle, leaving through the airlock, wearing an EVA suit she'd never seen before.

Numbness spread. It felt like some part of her mind had detached itself and was floating away. Fog rolled in.

This was real. Giselle *had* done this. She *had* played them.

She'd played *her*.

Soo-jin thought back to last night. What she remembered of it. The ring. The laughter. The kiss. The sweetness.

Giselle had been... *pretending*? All this time?

She'd strung her along.

The bruise. The lead-up. The way she had been acting.

Had she hunted her down, or had she simply grown close to her and seen an opportunity?

Soo-jin wondered if she actually did owe someone money. Zan was guessing at a second person, maybe a third. It made sense, in an odd way. You couldn't pull something like this off on your own, no matter how good you were.

Had one of them punched her? Had she asked them to?

Was she fucking them, too?

That doesn't matter now. It's over. She can fuck whoever she wants.

The dashboard on Zan's side blooped an alert, the tone loud in the quiet. The light reflecting off their face shifted as they brought it up.

"Contact. Short range comms."

Good. Since Giselle had apparently destroyed their long-range ones.

They'd managed to get the dashboard halfway out of the Script. It was still running havoc all over their main systems, but *Huli Jing*'s OS had a partitioned build, a double layer of protection away from prying eyes and inexperienced hackers.

She'd had it built to thwart government scrutiny on the more analogous parts of *Huli Jing*'s engine capabilities —the ones that didn't *quite* bow to current regulations but in fact blew them out of the water—but it had saved their hide on Giselle's attempt, too.

Partially, anyway.

Another bloop sounded. Longer and more insistent this time.

Zan's eyes rose to meet hers. "Ready?"

Soo-jin just looked at them.

"Right." They turned back to the dashboard. "I'll do the talking, then."

They accepted the call. Numbly, she stared up at the main screen as it switched over. The frail body of the holopoint cut through the air, both sharp and insubstantial. The blip between acceptance and connection seemed to linger.

Then, the holoscreen lit up, and Giselle was staring down at them, her face extraordinarily magnified on the feed.

"Hello, *Huli Jing*," she said brightly. "Let's talk about your predicament, shall we?"

Soo-jin's jaws clenched. She held herself still. Tense. Her entire body felt like pieces of rock, all lashed together.

The rock piece of her heart was cracked and bleeding. Unable to stop. All she could do was sit, tense, and feel the emotion seep out of her.

It felt hot. Like an infected wound.

"What do you want?" Zan asked.

A smile bloomed on Giselle's magnified face. "Straight and to the point. I always liked that about you."

Dizziness slipped through her mind. That smile that had once filled her with warmth made her guts wrench with revulsion. Bile hit the back of her throat. Bile, and remnants of the alcohol from earlier. Her head was light, having trouble focussing. She'd been like that for a little while now. Was that shock, or had Giselle slipped her something to make her sleep?

She watched the screen. Giselle's lips forming words. She could still smell jasmine. She wanted to scrub her entire bed down. She wanted to burn it.

"We want your ship, of course. Don't worry. We'll

drop you off at a safe location." The smile widened again, and Giselle beamed, as if it was a great joke. "We don't *kill* people."

"How the fuck—" Soo-jin said, the words leaving her mouth before she realized she was saying them, "—are you going to fence this ship? *Huli Jing* is a registered collection. She's not *subtle*. The second she hits any decent port, dockside's going to get a registration ping."

"Easy," she said. "You're going to sign it over to me!" She beamed again. "Consider it a wedding gift."

Anger surged. Soo-jin leaped to her feet, knocking over some part of the arm rest.

"You piece of fucking shit. You think you can take *my* ship? No. Fuck you. Fuck—"

Giselle's laughter interrupted her. "I suppose the wedding is off, then. Ah, well." She smiled again, leaning forward in her seat, propping her head up with one hand. Her exposed teeth had a predatory look, as if she was hungry. "This is my favorite part. Please, do go on."

Her... favorite part?

All of Soo-jin's anger snuffed out. She had trouble drawing breath.

Giselle read the look on her face.

"You aren't my first mark, Soo-jin. Suns, you weren't even the *best*. Just the best I could do at the time." She shrugged, as if to say, 'That's how she goes, sometimes.' "I'm going to miss you. That whole protective streak you had going? It was really sweet. You made me feel good, which is always a bonus."

Something inside her was breaking, leaking out. A fountain of hurt, drowning her. She struggled for breath.

"I'm not giving you my ship," she said.

"You have no choice. If you don't, I'll starve you out. I've rigged your systems to blow."

"I thought you didn't kill people?" Zan said.

"We don't," Giselle said. "That's a choice *you* make. It's out of our hands now."

"I see."

"I know you do. Straight to the point. As I said, I like you." She beamed a grin, then turned back to Soo-jin. "As for *you*—"

"Fuck you," she said. "You're *not* getting my ship."

Giselle laughed. "A little slow, aren't you, sweetie? It's over."

Soo-jin said nothing, only glared.

"You know, you were so easy to play. My favorite type. Damaged. Broken. A victim full of Daddy Issues. Mommy issues, too." She smiled. "Suns, Soo-jin. Is there any issue you *don't* have?"

"Fuck you."

"I believe I already did that. Many times."

"Fuck you. You're not getting my ship."

"Repeating the same thing won't get you what you want, no matter how much you say it. Zan, be a dear and talk some sense into her?"

"Don't worry," Zan said, getting up and heading toward the back. "I will."

"Good. Soo-jin is such a sweetheart. I wouldn't want you *both* dying due to her stubborn stupidit—"

The lights went, along with Giselle's transmission. The ship fell dark and silent, everything dying like a gasp of last whines.

The air stopped.

Huli Jing was dead.

A light flicked on in the back of the bridge. She

turned. Zan stood at the panel they'd been rummaging through, their netlink light in one hand, a thick bundle of wires in the other.

They'd been snipped cleanly, their ends angled in the same direction.

As she watched, Zan put the netlink and its light between their teeth and started taping each wire to the prefab underneath the panel, taking care to splay them so they wouldn't touch.

"I had enough of her talking," they explained, their voice slurring around the netlink in their mouth. "Now, let's find out what that bitch did, fix it, then find a way to fuck her up."

"We can't," she said. "She's going to blow up the ship."

They snorted.

"Bullshit. She *wants* the ship, doesn't she? She's not going to blow it up. Not after you did all that work restoring it. She won't get paid for a shell." Only one light still shone in *Huli Jing*, but it was enough to see them cast their eyes at the ceiling. "Come on. You knew her best. Where would she put this shit? What would she do?"

"I don't know," she said. "I—"

"Then help me look. We don't have much time. She won't blow us up, but she's not going to wait forever—and we're the ones without life support."

8

It took them ten minutes to find the first piece of sabotage —a well-placed signal disrupter on the back of the dashboard in Soo-jin's quarters. She stared at the small bug wrapped around the communications wire. *Huli Jing* was so old, she used insulated wires for her comms. It had been one of the only things to protect against signal jack attacks during her time of service.

This was one of the few places without insulation.

Giselle had *planned* for this.

Well, of course she had. She'd already told her that. In excruciating detail.

Gods. She'd been so... awful. So different. And yet —not.

She'd seen Giselle get like that before. She'd *seen* the crazy in her. Seen the way she'd swindle swine at a bar. Seen the way she'd sleight her way into a game. The way she'd hold a knife at her back while she smiled up at a mark, waiting for the moment she got close enough to stab it into his leg.

She'd seen all that—and she'd loved her for it. She'd *proposed* to her.

But—all she'd been was another mark. A more exciting one. Someone to have fun with. And *Huli Jing* was the leg she'd stabbed.

I'm such an idiot.

Gods, it hurt. Getting stabbed always did.

Feeling numb, she made a note of the disrupter, checked the lines for any others, then floated back out from under. So far, Zan was right. They *hadn't* blown up. Giselle *was* waiting. But she didn't want to tempt fate by killing Giselle's bugs. If their signals started disappearing, she'd know something was up.

Better to let her think she was crying in the dark. Or getting beaten up by Zan.

She moved on, continuing the search.

By the time Zan found her, forty-five minutes later, she was elbow deep in coolant tubes. The lid was off, and

Giselle's mat lay in pieces to the side. She'd taken it apart methodically, cutting it into smaller and smaller pieces. She hadn't found anything, but it'd made her feel good. She'd imagined she was cutting hair. Golden hair. Giselle's hair.

She probably was. Giselle had spent a lot of time on this mat. There had to be strands of it.

It still smelled like her. A bit less now she'd pulled the stuffing out, but the jasmine hung in the air, instantly recognizable.

The sound of boots stepped out on the walkway above her.

"We're in luck," Zan announced. "I spotted her."

Soo-jin stopped. Except for their lights, *Huli Jing*'s Engineering was pitch black. Talking to Zan was like talking to a spotlight.

"Yeah?"

"Yeah. She decided she wanted a look at our face. Caught her silhouette moving against the stars. I've got my scope on her."

A portable tracking scope. She'd seen it once. Apparently, they'd won it in a game.

They hadn't been a sniper. Their training lay in ordnance—which was why she'd had them go over the mine pieces for her.

Soo-jin stopped looking up at them. It was too bright. Instead, she stared numbly at the wall.

Then, she sighed.

"So, we can see her now. What does that change? She disabled the gun, you know. Stole a piece right out of it. It won't even load. I checked it. And—besides, unless we can disable every single one of her bugs, which we don't have *time* for—she can fry us the second we try to turn it on." She sank, fingers gripping the frame of the coolant vent. "It's *useless*. She played me, and I fucking *fell* for it."

Zan said nothing for a long moment. Their light held steady, too. She could feel it on her hair and shoulders. Could imagine the pity on their expression.

The light shifted away from her. Boots rang out on the ladder. Zan, climbing down to see her.

She cringed. But, instead of pity, their tone was pure, cold menace.

"No," they said. "She played *us*."

She looked up in surprise.

"To play with a person's emotions—that is a unique cruelty. Relationships require trust. You trusted her. We trusted her. That is what we are supposed to do with our friends. What she did? It's hateful. And we're going to make her *pay*."

The boots reached the end of the ladder and came down to her floor. She listened to them walk closer to her and stop at her side. She was trying not to cry, but tears had been sliding down, anyway. Hot tears, turned cold by *Huli Jing*'s slipping temperatures. Their streaks felt raw on her face, like they'd been dipped with something acidic.

"Are we?" She'd tried to make her voice sound strong, but it came out rough. Husky with grief and crying.

"Oh, yes. We are."

"I see. And I suppose you have a fabulous plan to get us out of this little situation she's screwed us into? Gods. She's been with us for months, Zan! *Months!* She knows *everything!*"

Zan snorted. "Bullshit. I've been here for nearly a year, and *I* don't know everything."

"She knew enough to screw us."

"To screw *you*, anyway. I kept my virtue intact."

She cringed, clutching the frame harder—and Zan sucked in a breath.

"Sorry," they said. "Bad joke."

"No. It's truthful."

She sighed. Gods, the truth hurt.

"Say," Zan said. "Remember the mine?"

She frowned. "Yes?"

Of course she remembered the mine. Apart from the mission, it was all they'd been talking about for the past two weeks.

What about it?

A small, mischievous smile curled the corners of Zan's lips.

"I may have... *misrepresented* how dead its circuits were."

Their words sank in. For a moment, she didn't speak, working out the picture Zan was painting for her.

Then, her mouth dropped open.

"The trackers?" she asked. "They *work?*"

"About half of them, anyway. I used a dead one for the demo." Their mouth quirked with wry humor. "I... didn't want her to worry."

She stared. No. Neither of them had. They'd been trying their best to comfort her, make her feel welcome on the ship. Capable.

And she'd played them.

Well, apparently, they'd accidentally played her right back.

"With *Huli Jing* dead in the vacuum, she's the only target out there," she said, realization dawning.

"Yep. And I bet there's a grav drive around we could stick in, let it go where it wants."

Oh, yes. She had about five of them lying around. All she had to do was cannibalize one of the grav crate motors.

Her mouth quirked up.

"It's been a while since I got to use *Huli Jing*'s drop doors," she mused aloud.

"Sounds like they need the exercise."

"Yes." She paused, a thought coming to her, then smiled. "I've also been looking for a place to unload all the sewage I've had to evacuate this week. You think we can fit some bottles inside the spikes?"

"Nah. Use bags. They'll shred on contact."

Silence reigned for several long seconds.

Then, Soo-jin started to laugh.

9

It took them three hours.

It would have taken them less, but they had to secure all the random shit in Cargo to the walls, then turn the place into a vacuum, *then* make sure the doors were working.

They were, but it had been a while. And ratcheting them out from inside the floor panels was an exercise in patience and stamina.

Even with her strength augments, her arms still ached.

Then, Soo-jin towed the mine to the opening, switched its grav drive on, then shoved it the rest of the way off with a pole.

Zan stayed on the bridge, tracking the other ship with their scope.

She watched the mine float out, a spiky nightmare obscuring the stars.

"This thing is a nightmare," she said through the comms.

"Yes," Zan replied. "I can see why you wanted one as a throne."

She didn't answer this time. Ahead, the mine's spiky form grew even smaller. She was losing its position.

As she watched, the scent of jasmine touched her tongue.

She and Giselle were the same size. She'd taken her suit. Hadn't realized until she'd put the helmet on.

Now, watching the mine go out, thinking about what it'd do to the other ship—it felt poetic.

Fuck. She still felt numb. And she still had a ship to fix.

She began ratcheting the drop doors shut again. If Giselle wandered toward *Huli Jing*'s underside and saw them open, she might suspect something.

Then again, if she did that, she'd get a face full of Shit-Loaded Border War Mine.

Soo-jin huffed a laugh into her suit, disturbing the jasmine.

"You know," she said between breaths, working the doors' manual release. "It's a shame those Fire Darts didn't arrive. I could have turned them into Shit Darts."

Zan snorted. "Maybe next time."

"Love of Mine" is a story in K. Gorman's Eurynome Code: Shadow Host *series.*

Want more?
Read Sanctuary's Flight
Captain Soo-jin Dokgo is no saint. Foul-mouthed and hot-headed, she trawls the system's outskirts, taking odd jobs, stripping salvage sites, and steadily washing her problems down in a cotton candy haze of clubs and alcohol.

But a message from an old friend leads to a job she can't refuse, and a mother and son need more help than any sane person can give them.

It's time to boot up Huli Jing's drives and show the system what she can really do. Because pirates are on their tail, and they're playing for blood.

Read for free:
kgorman.ca/books/sanctuary's-flight

Pick Your Poison
1. *Hell yeah, backstabbers gotta pay.* Head to "The Old Ship Job" by Arthur Mayor

2. *Keep it sapphic, but somehow dial UP the explosions.* Go read "Renegade Havoc" by C.E. Clayton in CROOKED V.2

3. *Dammit! Who can you even trust?* Keep going to read "Rogue Negotiator" by Audrey Sharpe

ROGUE NEGOTIATOR

A STARHAWKE ROGUE PREQUEL

BY AUDREY SHARPE

Author's Note: *I always write to music, and I select a different piece of music for each story, one that feeds the mood I need to get the words flowing. For this one, I circled back to the music I used for ROGUE, another of Nat and Isin's prequel adventures. If you'd like to experience this story the way I did, listen to the soundtrack for* Speed *while you read.*

"LET ME DO THE TALKING, ORLOV."

Natasha Orlov shot her muscular companion a dirty look. "I know, Isin." Like she needed the reminder. Unfastening her harness, she slipped out of the pilot's seat of her shuttle, *Gypsy*.

He stood up behind her, crowding her in the compact space. "I'm the negotiator. It's my job."

"And I'm the pilot. Back off," she growled through gritted teeth. She kicked her booted foot behind her for emphasis, connecting with his shin.

His pained grunt and annoyed huff gave her great

satisfaction, as did the fact he stepped back toward the co-pilot's seat. She'd made her point.

She took her time slipping out of her duster, hanging it on the peg behind the pilot's chair. She always wore it when she flew, but it was too conspicuous in a place like Dry Gulch, especially in the heat of summer.

And she wanted to be as inconspicuous as possible. She always played the silent role for the smuggling negotiations her boss, Mirko, conducted. Nat's petite stature and unassuming appearance made the players dismiss her as inconsequential, especially when seen beside the solid bulk of her employer.

Which worked out just fine for her. With Mirko drawing all the attention, Nat was free to lighten the pockets of those around her—a necessity considering how little Mirko paid her for piloting *Sphinx*, Mirko's freighter.

Profits from their smuggling operation had been few and far between during the last few years, which was the primary reason Mirko had hired Isin. He was a trained negotiator—or so he claimed—whereas Mirko was as volatile as a solar flare, either demanding or cajoling, depending on her mood.

It made her undependable and reactionary. Nat had seen more than one deal go supernova when her boss lost her temper and started spewing obscenities.

Which is why Mirko had remained on *Sphinx* for this pickup, sending Isin in her stead.

But as far as Nat was concerned, his presence was a lateral shift. In the week since he'd signed on with the crew, he'd managed to tick off every member of the crew except for Mirko. He hadn't shown the same tendency toward volatility that Mirko had, but Nat had serious doubts about his negotiating skills.

Oh, he clearly was educated. He loved showing off his extensive vocabulary. But he wasn't what anyone would call social. Or friendly. Every time she'd been in the same room with him, bitterness and anger had wafted off him like cheap cologne.

So did a patronizing condescension that drove her up the wall.

"We need to get moving."

She gave him a withering look. He could huff and puff all he wanted, but this was her shuttle. They'd leave when she was good and ready.

She sauntered into *Gypsy*'s cargo hold, Isin right behind her.

Being *Sphinx*'s newest crewmember hadn't stopped Isin from acting like he was the smartest person in the room even when he clearly had no knowledge or experience on a subject. He also enjoyed telling her what to do. Like right now. The flight down had been the longest thirty minutes of her life.

His height bugged her, too. It wasn't enough that he had a fancy education and Mirko raved about how brilliant he was. No, he had to be tall, too. The top of her head didn't even come up to his shoulders.

Which is why it was so damn easy for him to loom over her.

The only thing that kept her from planting her fist in his mouth every time he opened it was her understanding of the laws of physics. His arms, legs, chest—just about everything really—were all hard muscle twice her size. If by some chance she got a shot in, he'd flatten her the second he got a hand on her, no matter how quick and nimble she was.

But if by some miracle his negotiating skills actually resulted in a steady increase in funds, she'd find a way to put up with his obnoxious presence and pompous behavior. *Gypsy*'s sensor display had been acting up lately, and without the money for parts, she couldn't make the necessary repairs.

Today she'd learn the truth about his skills, or lack thereof. And hopefully she'd make a good lift or two in the process.

As she walked toward *Gypsy*'s back hatch, Isin settled his hand on her shoulder and pushed his way in front of her. "I'll go first."

She bit the inside of her cheek to keep from elbowing him in the ribs. Considering the muscle definition she'd glimpsed when he was doing push-ups in one of *Sphinx*'s cargo bays, she'd bruise her elbow without hurting him. "Fine. You can get shot or arrested when Razor's people don't recognize you."

He paused, his jaw tightening. "Shot?"

Her smile was sickly sweet. "Razor's not just a smuggler. He's also the sheriff in this town. He takes the safety of the residents very seriously." She was exaggerating, but Isin wouldn't know that. As a criminal himself, Razor tended to turn a blind eye to non-violent crime as long as it didn't negatively impact him.

Violent crime was another matter entirely. Which is why she'd left her Reiter pistol in her duster.

"Always a good idea to check the exterior cameras *before* lowering the hatch. As a rule, smugglers aren't trustworthy." She was laying it on thick, but she had a week's worth of angst to expel. And her target was right in front of her.

He glared at her. And didn't move.

Which made her wonder if perhaps he didn't know *how* to lower *Gypsy*'s hatch. Or check the cameras. He might be passing his ignorance off as arrogance.

His glare turned haughty. "Where are the cameras?"

She'd called it. Smiling to herself, she slipped past him, pulling up the images on the small monitor above the hatch comm. The cameras weren't top of the line by any stretch, but she'd positioned them to give her a clear view of the area around the hatch, just in case one of their customers got any ideas. *Gypsy* was the closest thing to family she had. She'd never leave her beloved shuttle exposed to potential thieves.

But the dry, dusty landscape didn't reveal any surprises. Not that she expected any from Razor. Mirko dealt with him on a semi-regular basis, which is why Nat's boss had chosen this as Isin's first test. Their employer wanted to see if Isin could get the notoriously tight-fisted Razor to come down on his price for the cargo they were picking up, something Mirko had never managed to do.

Isin moved closer, boxing her in as he peered at the images.

She tensed, stifling a growl. One quick jab to his solar plexus couldn't hurt too badly, could it?

"Looks clear." He straightened, but still took up *her* personal space on *her* shuttle.

"Oh, really? Are you sure?" Sarcasm dripped off every syllable.

He peered down at her, his lips pulling back from his teeth in a snarl.

She switched from sarcastic to patronizing. "Nervous about your first time?"

"Hardly."

The bitterness in that one word could have corroded steel.

Whatever. She didn't care enough to give it any bandwidth.

Getting to know Isin was never going to make her to do list. He was no different from the rest of *Sphinx*'s crew —a cog in Mirko's grinding machine, easily discarded or replaced. The only person besides Mirko that Nat spoke with on a regular basis was Hobbes, the secondary pilot who took over *Sphinx* when Nat went on delivery runs with *Gypsy*.

And the sooner they finished this pickup, the sooner she could ditch her unwanted companion. "Then let's get this show on the road." She tapped the controls to lower the back hatch.

He stared at her for a long moment, his dark eyes narrowed, before he stalked down the ramp.

She let out an exasperated sigh before following him, securing the hatch behind her. Round one had ended in a tie.

The hot, dry air of midsummer hit her lungs like a blast from an oven. Nat wrinkled her nose, fighting the urge to sneeze. What did it say about her that her body preferred inhaling years of accumulated grit and odors from the stale, recycled air on *Sphinx* rather than the dry but decidedly cleaner air of her desert surroundings?

She'd set *Gypsy* down on the landing pad, a fancy name for the stingy area that had been cleared of scraggly scrub brush and thorny cactus. Fifty meters away the backside of the two-story wooden structure that housed the Dry Gulch Mercantile faced them, the building laying on top of the orange-tinged dirt like a stocky reptile basking in the sun.

She spotted movement through the back window. A moment later the oversized warehouse doors rolled back, three figures stepping into view. Razor led the group, his two deputies behind him, armed with rifles.

She recognized both of them from prior visits. Razor's miserly behavior didn't extend to his employees, who tended to be loyal as a result.

Razor's shrewd gaze slid over Nat before locking onto Isin. His weathered face and grey beard marked his age, but his corded arms and defined pecs under his black T-shirt and vest told a different story. Razor didn't mind hauling the crates of merchandise he moved. He also dealt personally with anyone who acted up in his town. His hand rested lightly on the pistol strapped to his hip. "Where's Mirko?"

Isin halted, raising his hands slightly when the deputies lifted their rifles in his direction. "Mr. Razor?"

"It's just Razor." His gaze swept over Isin's button-front shirt and slacks, which looked ridiculous in this setting. "Who are you, city boy?"

"I'm Isin. Mirko sent me," Isin said in a decidedly pleasant and respectful voice Nat had never heard him use before. "I'd like to talk to you about the merchandise we're picking up."

She fought to contain her snort of laughter at the fancy-dancy tone. Most of the time he sounded like he had a stick up his butt. And was that the beginnings of a smile?

"Why?"

"I have a few things I would like to discuss with you,

if I may?" Isin answered, his expression friendly and relaxed. Like they were hanging out at a bar. Or a high-society party.

She kept from making a face. Mostly. Who *was* this guy?

Razor's deputies exchanged a look, like Isin had stopped speaking Galactic English.

She totally understood the reaction. None of the smugglers she'd met talked like this.

Razor looked vaguely amused. "What things?"

"Things better discussed in private." Isin's tone was almost apologetic as his gaze slid briefly to Razor's deputies.

Razor didn't follow his gaze. He studied Isin like he was trying to decide if he was simple or crazy. He tipped his head toward one of the men. "Check him."

Handing his rifle to Razor, the deputy approached Isin. Isin submitted to the thorough pat down without complaint, that weirdly calm expression still on his face.

"He's clean." The man stepped back, reclaiming his weapon.

"Alright, city boy. Let's have a little chat." Razor swept a hand, motioning Isin toward the warehouse door.

Isin inclined his head. "Thank you."

Thank you? She'd never heard *anyone* say those two words during a delivery run.

But he'd gotten Razor to agree to talk with him. Usually Mirko had to bring a bottle of booze or make a suggestive comment to get a similar concession.

Nat stayed on Isin's heels, following him into the warehouse. The clatter and scrape of boxes being moved, opened, and packed greeted them as they entered the interior. She counted at least fifteen people inside the warehouse space, none of whom gave them so much as a glance.

The temperature inside the warehouse was considerably cooler than outside. The sweat that had beaded on her forehead cooled against her skin. Razor was stingy with his smuggling clients, but he didn't skimp on the comfort of his staff.

Not that Nat was temperature sensitive. She'd spent too much of her life in miserable conditions to let a little heat bother her.

Razor led the way across the warehouse floor toward the far end where an open staircase led to his second-floor office. The vaulted ceiling and high windows in the rest of the warehouse gave the office a commanding view of the entire area, including the town's main street.

Razor was king of his domain.

"You have a list?" Razor pointed at Nat.

"Yeah."

Razor waved her toward the swinging doors that led into the mercantile.

Nat was more than happy to be relegated to a subservient role... until she saw the condescending look on Isin's face. He smirked at her before following Razor up the stairs.

Her teeth ground together. Maybe she could take him down a few pegs during the flight back. How would the jackass react to a loss of gravity? Or some barrel rolls in atmo?

Although with her luck, he'd lose his lunch and make a mess in her shuttle.

Not worth it.

Pushing Isin out of her mind, she stepped through the swinging doors and entered the mercantile.

The two register clerks glanced her way, but she didn't see recognition in their eyes, even though she'd seen them both before. Just the way she liked it. She never wanted to be memorable.

She nodded at them as she grabbed one of the woven shopping baskets. Pulling out her comm, she scanned the list of items Mirko had told her to pick up, each item marked with the price Mirko was willing to pay.

Nat grimaced as she compared that price to what she saw listed on the display for the first item she came to. She might need to test Isin's negotiating skills with her supply list, too.

She took her time winding through the long rows of merchandise, checking the items on the list while surreptitiously surveying the other customers. They all ignored her completely. Her lean figure made most people see her as an adolescent rather than an adult, and her nondescript brown hair and pale skin were commonplace, as were her clothes. It gave her an invisibility that worked to her advantage.

She also chose her marks with great care. She couldn't afford to get on Razor's bad side.

She immediately dismissed the harried woman with the two small children. The woman's threadbare clothing and gaunt face indicated she needed every credit she had. Nat never preyed on those who were struggling to stay afloat.

But she had no problem plucking a credit square out of the pocket of the overfed, insufferable man who'd just paid for his purchases. The pompous windbag was ordering around his assistant, a scrawny youth whose arms were already loaded with bags.

Her next mark was a woman wearing a surfeit of

jewelry that clinked when she snapped her fingers at one of the clerks. Nat divested her of an intricate gold bracelet as the woman strode out of the mercantile, nose in the air.

A few minutes later Nat snagged a second credit square from a man she'd overheard tell his female companion she wasn't pretty enough to wear the dress she'd pulled off the rack. The man then proceeded to buy an expensive shirt for himself.

All in all, a successful shopping trip. Except only three of the ten items on Mirko's list had made it into her basket. The rest were priced higher than Mirko wanted to pay, so Nat passed them by.

When she approached the register, the clerk gave her a pasted-on smile. They looked like they could use a stiff drink. If she wasn't with Isin, she might have offered to buy them one.

"Ready to check out?" they asked her.

"Yes."

She reached into her pocket for the credit square Mirko had given her.

A hand clamped around her wrist and squeezed.

Her heart leapt into her throat, her gaze snapping up. Right into Isin's dark eyes.

"There's no need for that," he said smoothly, favoring the clerk with a closed-mouth smile. "I've already arranged payment for all the items on Mirko's list."

Nat stared at him, uncomprehending. "What?"

"I gave Razor our list, and all the items are already boxed and waiting for us." He was using that overly pleasant voice again, but it didn't match the emotion burning in his eyes. "Come with me."

He tugged on her wrist hard enough to pull her off

balance. She stumbled as he practically dragged her after him.

"Let go of me," she hissed under her breath, not wanting to attract any more attention than Isin already had.

He ignored her until he'd pushed through the swinging doors into the warehouse, hauling her with him. "Just keeping your fingers where I can see them," he murmured, giving her a hard look.

She glared back. Had he really seen her make her last lift? Or was he bluffing to get a reaction out of her?

She yanked her arm, but he didn't let go.

Fine. She knew one sure way to loosen his grip. She shifted her weight to bring up her knee.

He must have seen the intent in her eyes, because he released her like her skin was white hot and stepped back. "You're a real piece of work, Orlov."

She gave him a megawatt smile. "Thank you."

His mouth tightened.

That only made her smile widen.

"Let's go." He jerked his head and stalked across the warehouse to where a couple of Razor's people waited beside a large pallet.

She strolled after him. Eight large crates formed the base of the pallet. That would be the Osirian firewater they'd been sent to fetch. The stuff would burn a hole in your insides, which is why it had been banned, but that didn't stop folks in the Rim from clamoring for it.

She didn't know how Razor had gotten ahold of the stuff, and she didn't want to know. All she cared about was getting paid when they delivered it to their buyer.

Two smaller crates were strapped on top. Mirko's supplies, apparently. She wanted to know how Isin had arranged that, but she didn't want to give him the satisfaction of showing her curiosity. If he'd paid more than Mirko had wanted to, it would be his hide, not hers.

Isin spoke with the two workers, sparing Nat a quick glance before leading the way out the warehouse doors.

Nat hung back as the two workers maneuvered the pallet toward *Gypsy*, Isin striding confidently ahead of them. Was it wrong that she was getting a perverse pleasure out of watching this scene unfold?

Because Isin couldn't open *Gypsy*. A fact he discovered when he reached the shuttle and placed his hand on the hatch controls.

His glare returned in full force, cutting across the distance between them.

She slowed her steps even more. "Problem?" she called out in a sing-song voice.

Razor's people glanced between the two of them as tension crackled like lightning bolts.

"Just waiting for you." The words sounded civil enough, but Isin's eyes promised retribution.

Bring it. She'd been threatened by far scarier people than him. Intimidating her wasn't going to work, even if he could flatten her with one hand. He'd have to catch her first, and she could hide on *Gypsy* whenever she wasn't on *Sphinx*'s bridge.

Which is why she took her time reaching the control panel and lowering the ramp.

Isin stalked up the incline the moment the ramp touched the ground. "This way."

Razor's people glanced at her, clearly uncertain who they should be taking direction from.

She leaned her shoulder against *Gypsy*'s hull. "Go ahead." She lifted her chin in the direction Isin had gone. "Just leave the pallet in the cargo area. I'll unpack it."

One of them nodded while the other pushed the pallet up the ramp. They returned with their empty dolly a moment later, making tracks back to the warehouse.

She didn't blame them. Isin was practically breathing fire.

He appeared at the top of the ramp, his arms folded over his broad chest and a scowl on his face. "Was that necessary?"

She pushed off the hull and strolled up the ramp. "Yes. Yes, it was."

"I'm the negotiator." He emphasized *negotiator* the way some people would say *king.*

She scoffed. "And I'm the pilot. Gypsy is *mine.*" She stopped in front of him, fisting her hands on her hips. "I don't take orders from anyone regarding my shuttle."

"You're impossible," he snarled.

"And you're arrogant," she snapped. "If it were up to me, I'd kick your sorry ass off my shuttle right now."

He flinched. Maybe. Or was that a sneer? "Good thing it's not up to you."

Definitely a sneer. "Mirko's not going to be happy if you overpaid for those supplies."

His sneer turned smug. "I'll have you know Razor sold them to me at cost. *And* dropped the price of our cargo by ten percent."

Her mouth popped open before she could stop it. She snapped it shut. "You're lying." Except he wasn't. As a professional liar herself, she knew the tells that gave a liar away.

Isin had told her the truth.

He tipped forward at the waist, bringing his face

closer to hers. "Unlike some people, I don't need to lie to get what I want."

"Must be nice to walk around with that silver spoon in your mouth."

Okay, that was definitely a flinch. His expression shuttered. "You're the pilot. So get this scrap heap in the air." Turning on his heel, he strode toward the cockpit.

She touched her hand to the hatch controls, sealing up the shuttle as her gaze narrowed on his retreating back.

Maybe a mess in the cockpit from a few barrel rolls would be worth it after all.

Her hand dipped into her pocket as she considered her options. Pulling out the two credit squares she'd filched, she displayed the balances.

Oh, ho! Jackpot.

Her mood improved considerably. *Gypsy* was *definitely* getting her sensor display fixed. And then Nat was going to treat herself to a cold beer and nice meal at the next restaurant she encountered.

Her gaze flicked back toward the cockpit as she contemplated her newfound good fortune.

To roll or not to roll?

It was tempting. *Really* tempting. Watching Isin's dark skin turn green and his eyes bug out was a moment she would love to see. But not enough to spend the next week cleaning every surface in *Gypsy*'s cockpit.

Still, she was a very creative person. And *Sphinx* wasn't a huge ship.

Her lips curved in a wicked smile. She'd find the best way to repay Isin's kindness. And he'd never see it coming.

"Rogue Negotiator" is a prequel story in Audrey Sharpe's
Starhawke Rogue series.

Want more? Read ROGUE
She didn't see it coming...
Having her shuttle blasted out of the sky by a Setarip
cruiser wasn't in Natasha Orlov's plans. Neither was
being stranded with a muscle-bound jerk. Or saving his
life. But space happens.

Read for free at:
dl.bookfunnel.com/yttr3ksqrn

Pick Your Poison

1. I love me a character who can talk—and fight—their way
out of trouble! Head to "Ransomeware" by Robin Jeffrey

2. A batshit crazy plan's better than no plan at all, I guess.
Go read "Highly Irregular" by Kate Sheeran Swed in
CROOKED V.1

3. Let's spend some time on the other side of the law. Keep
going to read "Second Breath" by Peter J. Foote

SECOND BREATH

A JUPITER'S EYE STORY

BY PETER J. FOOTE

DAMMIT, MORE KIDS. KEEP MOVING, KEEP MOVING, *keep... Crap.* Rosario struggled to keep her expression neutral as the school trip of Martian children walked close enough to trigger the holographic display for the eighteenth time today. Squaring her shoulders, hands clasped behind her back at parade rest, Rosario tried to tune out the canned presentation. *What I'd give for a big steaming mug of atole about now.*

As the excited chorus of youth reveled in the field trip to the spaceport of Peldaños, an area normally out of bounds, shouts of excitement turned sour as realization hit. The spaceport was boring.

I could have told them that.

Five hundred meters below the Martian surface, the mile-wide loading docks were technically part of the spaceport as they stored and transported goods and people through a series of elevators to docked ships above. But they just looked like a series of cul-de-sacs with shipping containers around the perimeter to Rosario, with moving sidewalks and electric carts transporting people and goods back and forth. Given the dubious honor of standing guard in front of one of the huge cargo pods which housed the two-meter square tub of super-charged microbe infused soil into which rested a dwarf cypress tree, Rosario wanted nothing more than to put her feet up, or better yet, do some real police work. *But oh no, instead of tracking down those gaspers stealing our air, let's put the so-called problem cops on babysitting duty.*

Thankful for the police interface visor that shielded her gaze, Rosario watched her partner from her peripheral vision and felt her jaw clench. Carlos Sanchez was an old-school Martian cop that was only on the force because he knew when to keep his mouth shut when superiors needed a timely confession and wasn't afraid to crack heads. He was everything she hated about the law, but after five years of waiting to walk a beat and get away from video surveillance, Rosario knew complaining about her partner would only make matters worse. And just as they got their teeth into doing something real, hunting down air thieves, the anniversary of The Slip arrived.

"Excuse me, is it true you're a slip survivor?"

Tuning out Carlos's snickering that came over her earpiece, Rosario flipped up her interface visor and knelt before the child before her, making sure her dress uniform covered her service pistol. Just on the cusp of double digits, the young girl wore her school uniform proudly with her name tag straight an inch above the zipper of her breast pocket. Even the ribbon in her dark braid matched the blue and gray of her uniform, echoed by the multitude of stickers on the data pad in her small hands. The rest of her classmates paused their behavior when they realized one of their own dared to speak to a police officer.

"No Maria, but my father was. He was a couple of

years younger than you are now. I'm sure you've read," Rosario tapped Maria's pad, "that when the builders were expanding the Ampato column of the city they hit an unknown pocket of ice and, with the heat from the construction, a piece of the rift wall collapsed, causing the slip. It was the single greatest loss of life since we won our independence from Earth." From a brief glance Rosario saw that she'd gathered a throng of listeners and continued her family's saga with long practice. "The dry facts are all part of the display," Rosario waved at the holographic reel that was now playing unwatched, "but facts aren't people. My dad was sound asleep in his room when the slip happened. The avalanche took out power, air, and communications. Can you imagine being alone in the dark with nothing but a 72 hour emergency pack to keep you alive?" Rosario saw the chaperone, little more than a kid himself move to cut her off from expanding on the gruesome details, but she stopped him with a cold stare.

Life isn't easy on Mars. Some people have forgotten that. Shielding these children now doesn't do them any favors.

Turning back to Maria, Rosario shared a rare smile and finished her tale. "My dad was on hour 80 of a 72 hour air bottle. His small size was the only reason he hadn't run out when help arrived. Do you know who rescued him?" Dark bangs shook over wide brown eyes. "It wasn't the police. It wasn't civil engineering. It was strangers from Reverie Station. The orbits were in alignment, so when the asteroid miners on Reverie heard the news about the catastrophe, they got into the ships and hurried to help. Rockhoppers spend most of their lives in dangerous situations like that, so they ignored orders from police like me and started digging through the rubble. They found my dad and 52 other people still clinging to life." Rosario stood up, blinking, wondering what made her open up. Clearing her throat, Rosario resumed parade rest. "To commemorate that selfless act, we, the Martian people, give Reverie station a tree every year, so a piece of us is always with them."

Not to mention the microbe charged soil and the cargo hold of hormone therapy and anti-radiation drugs that goes with it that's worth a king's ransom, but dad convinced the rest of the city council to do it, and dad always gets what he wants. But he and I agree on this at least, the tree is good PR for both sides even if only one in five survive the year on Reverie.

Other kids shouted questions and Maria tugged on Rosario's jacket, but her earpiece chimed, saving her from the flood of questions.

"Officers Sanchez and Vera. Orders from Central, I repeat, orders from Police Central," a monotone voice said, and Rosario knew that dispatch would sound the same whether reporting the baseball score or a nuclear attack. "Those gaspers you've been hunting tripped an alarm in the disused catacombs above the old Ampato column. Command has given you permission to proceed. Acknowledge."

Rosario and Carlos shared a glance before confirming the coordinates on their gauntlets. Rosario flipped down her visor and keyed her mic. "Acknowledged. Officers Sanchez and Vera proceeding to those coordinates." Still seeing a crowd of youth in front of them, Rosario paused and stared at Maria. "We have to go, but I'm sure you can finish the tour on your own, right?" Rosario winked and realized that her visor hid the movement, so she gave a weak smile and pushed her way through the crowd, feeling their eyes on her back as Rosario hurried after Carlos.

"ARE YOU SURE THAT'S SAFE?" Shift supervisor Rubén Aparicio's voice rang through Liam's helmet, causing him to lose his grip on the damaged aerial but thankfully an armored knee threaded through twisted aluminum and a safety line kept Liam from a kilometer long fall to the base of Tempe Mensa. His tools hanging from his belt strung the aerial, and as he felt the vibrations, he forced himself to not hear a death knell in their rhythm.

Not only does that crook skim ten percent of my pay, he tries to kill me! Liam thought as he scrambled to pull himself upright until he was once again safely straddling the collapsed aerial. He smoothed down the seal-it tape that held the empty middle finger on his right glove as he caught his breath. *Ok, maybe safely isn't the right word, but you can't beat the view.*

Forcing himself to take slow, even breaths, Liam relished the wave of cool air that brushed his face, helping evaporate the sweat on his brow as he distracted himself by admiring the City of Steps. Peldaños was an amazing achievement in engineering and determination that never ceased to astound Liam, but was so often overlooked by native Martians. Solar panels, agricultural bio-domes and the shuttles of the spaceport dominated the plateau, but it was cliffs that were the genuine achievement to Liam. Built as a series of connected columns, each column was a self-sustaining town in itself. Most of Peldaños was tucked within the cliff to protect it from radiation and storms, but that still left an array of light tunnels, observation blisters and social pavilions. It was an achievement now at risk of having two hundred kilos of radioactive waste scattered over it.

Liam did not know who screwed up, that was above his pay grade. But when the alert went out that a drone carrying radioactive waste had acted like Sister Florence after getting into the communal wine at the orphanage, Liam went running. What he found was that it had collided with a communication aerial, putting both at risk of crashing down the inhabited cliff, a call for volunteers went out as emergency services was caught with their pants down.

Why did I volunteer again? But Liam knew why, he couldn't help himself. Which is also why he was sheltering refugees in the old disused section of the Ampato column. As a climate orphan and raised by the sisters at St. Teresa's on Earth, Liam spent the first part of his working career as a zero gee welder, breaking down surpass ships and orbital stations. He had the skills and knowledge to transverse the dangerous aerial and connect the tow cable to the incoming shuttle. *Assuming the darn thing gets here before this aerial goes ass over teakettle down the cliff.*

"O'Fallon? Come in technician O'Fallon," Rubén's voice wheezed through the speakers in Liam's helmet loud enough that he turned down the volume.

"I'm still here and this would be a lot easier if you would stop shouting in my ear," Liam replied and carefully continued threading his way through the twisted aerial towards the bright green octagon egg that was the stricken drone. *Damn, those thruster struts are wrapped around the drone like pretzels.* Thinking of food made

Liam's stomach rumble, reminding him he'd been heading in from the solar-cell field for lunch when the accident had happened.

"But you can do it right? We don't know if it will hold until emergency response gets here," wheezing Rubén continued. "And if it falls, it will be partly your fault, O'Fallon. If you didn't lock your tool cage, another of the team could be out there with your portable plasma cutter. And while I have you, why do you have a barrel labeled hazardous waste in your cage?"

Damnit, they tried to access my cage again. Bracing his back against an aluminum crossbeam the size of his calf, Liam tapped a series of commands into his gauntlet and opened a secure radio frequency. "Queenie, you there?"

"Of course Tiger, where else would I be?" a cheerful voice sang out and instantly Liam felt a smile across his face.

"Did Rubén or one of his minions try to get into my cage again? Are you ok? I hate leaving you in there like a piece of equipment, but it's more secure than my room at the hostel. Heck, the screened-in porch at the orphanage is more secure than my room." Liam knew he was rambling, but his concern for his illegal AI companion weighed on his mind.

"They tried, but failed. I tapped into the security feeds and watched them, but those reinforced braces you welded to the door kept them out. You know if you made me more drones, I could defend myself and that would keep you from worrying."

Imagining a dozen football-sized mechanical spiders erupting from his tool cage to overrun his work supervisor like defenders of a castle made Liam smile, the blinking light on his gauntlet of Rubén demanding his attention erased it. Switching channels so that Queenie's nattering was still in one ear, Liam keyed his microphone.

"I lock my cage because you and your goons know I keep my earth whiskey in there, Rubén, and I used half my weight allowance to bring it with me, not that Martians know what decent alcohol tasted like. And if you couldn't tell, I'm kind of busy here." Liam crawled through the swaying wreckage until he was beside the trapped drone. While all the remote readings had shown that the radioactive waste hadn't been breached, seeing the unbroken shell of the green egg released a knot in Liam's chest.

"O'Fallon, if you cut me off like that again..."

Liam tuned out the supervisor's ranting and Queenie's description of what her hack into Peldaños security cameras showed her of normal Martian life, and started marking where the incoming shuttle and net could capture the drone so he could cut it free, when something in Queenie's report penetrated his brain.

"Say that again!"

"I said the shuttle is due in sixteen minutes. Are all earthers hard of hearing?"

Liam quickly muted his supervisor. "Say that again, Queenie, something about the air alarm I bypassed?"

While straddling a twisted aluminum beam, Liam pulled a pry-bar from his belt, popped the cover and let his fingers dance over the controls of the drone, Liam listened to Queenie repeat herself. When Queenie finished, Liam clenched his right fist, popping the seal-it tape that held the glove where he had a missing finger, making it look like he was giving Mars the bird. *Damnit! I told them not to take so much air at once, I could only fudge the safety margin by point two percent. The iron foot of Martian law will have them tossed out an airlock unless I do something.* Stuck between a rock and a hard place. Knowing that every second counted, Liam leaned back, gauged the distance between the drone and the relative safety of the plateau, and nodded.

"Queenie, I need you to focus. I'm going to give you some rough weights and distances along with photos of the accident, and I need you to tell me how long I need to fire the drone's thrusters to flip this twisted mess over. Ok?"

"You going for a ride, Tiger?"

Liam shut off the persistent voice of his supervisor and popped open the manual control panel for the drone and prayed that the risk he was about to take didn't put more lives in harm.

Minutes later, his harness cinched tight, Liam allowed some of the nervous energy that flowed through him to affect his voice so that his lie sounded believable and keyed his radio.

"O'Fallon to ground crew, something's gone wrong, the drone is active again, it's about to fire thrusters, I'm going to..." Liam broke the connection and stabbed the ignition.

Now I just have to measure 4.206 seconds in my head. Trusting Queenie with his life, Liam struggled to hold the button in as the captured drone tried to reach the sky.

Firmly trapped like a fly in a web, the stricken drone still had some fight in it. Twisted aluminum tried to straighten, but true to Queenie's projection, the aerial corkscrewed as it bent backwards and Liam found himself upside down with the Martian surface rushing towards him.

Three Mississippi, Four Mississippi, and Liam

released the thruster button. Liam felt the vibration of the drones' thrusters cut out, and with all the grace of an amusement park ride coming to a stop, the twisted framework groaned the last three meters before collapsing on the plateau, the drones casting unscratched.

Seeing Ruben and other members of his work crew skipping along the Martian surface, Liam shook his head, turned his back on them and stumbling, making for the nearest entrance to the city and the refugees.

✳

"Maybe we should wait for backup?" Rosario said, the respirator that covered her face muffled her words. When Carlos pulled his service pistol from the holster on his hip, she knew he'd heard her, but was choosing not to reply.

Darn it, if I hadn't let emotions get ahead of me, we would have a tactical team leading the way, instead we're lost in the dark.

Their interface visors abandoned for respirators, they had nothing more than the lights on their gauntlets and the narrow light strips roughly adhered to the cavern walls every hundred meters to guide them, Rosario knew they were in uncharted territory. Literally. *Like even my map is from before the Slip, half the tunnels are just gone and the other half were dug post disaster. We should have volun-told someone from civil engineering to lead the way rather than following these shifting dots.*

Staring at a forked tunnel where the map dispatch sent to her gauntlet showed a straight line, Rosario rotated the map until it made her dizzy, but what Carlos made her downright nauseous.

"These criminals don't deserve to be taken in and given a hearing. We can do this ourselves."

Past his prime and out of breath, Rosario wished that she'd heard him wrong, but knew that she hadn't.

Wheezing badly enough to fog his mask, Carlos continued. "Back when I was a rookie, we just sent gaspers for a short walk out of an airlock and waited for them to be discovered. And since most already had a criminal record, we used them to firm up our clear out rate. Everyone won."

Except for the people who just suffocated. Knowing that she no longer wanted anything to do with Carlos's idea of justice, Rosario looked at her incomplete map and decided. *My best guess is that the O2 thieves are that way.* Rosario adjusted the map to the right, so it pointed towards the floating red light that showed the tripped alarm. *And if we go that way,* she moved the hologram left, *we should meet up with reinforcements and Carlos won't try anything with a group of witnesses, at least I hope not.*

Nudging her shoulder so her 3D map spun, Carlos asked. "So, which way then? Justice doesn't wait." His fogged up mask did nothing to hide the cruel grin on his face.

Rosario steered them left and prayed they'd meet the reinforcements quickly.

Mierda! At first, Rosario thought she'd made the correct decision as the beaten gravel path through the derelict tunnel transitioned into smooth polycrete, and the lighting shifted from occasional haphazard glow strips to regularly spaced illumination, but when she and Carlos rounded a corner and saw the gaspers, she knew things were going to end badly. Wearing nothing but patched thermal suits and connected by a daisy-chain of airlines connected to a series of O_2 bottles stacked on a three-wheeled cart, Rosario realized that these weren't hardened criminals, but children, roughly the same age as those in the tour group she chatted with an hour ago. Rosario wondered if the criminals' ages would stay Carlos's hand. Maybe she wouldn't have to find out as one figure stood out from the rest. Dressed in an armored vac-suit, wearing a heavy belt of tools and sporting the clear stencil of civil engineering on the side of the helmet, Rosario breathed a sigh of relief. *Of course, the alarm would have shown up on their boards as well, and the crossed communications that should have told the repair crew to leave it to us might be a blessing.*

Then Carlos's service pistol rang out, and Rosario knew things were going to end badly. Whether Carlos intended his shot to be a warning or a kill shot, Rosario would never know, but when the bullet ricocheted off one of the O_2 cylinders before striking one gasper in the abdomen, it was the law, not the criminals that drew first blood.

"Hold your fire!" Rosario shouted and shoved Carlos as his second shot struck sparks against the polycrete wall. The pressurized but oxygen poor cavern made the rapport of the pistol sound like a damp firecracker, but did nothing to stop the lethal nature of the weapon.

Carlos stumbled, bounced off the nearby wall, but kept his feet under him. "Who's side are you on?" Carlos screamed, fogging his mask again, but not enough that Rosario couldn't see the rage in his eyes.

He won't be happy until someone is dead. How did this go so wrong?

Seeing the gaspers and the lone civil engineer try to flee, their connected air hoses getting tangled, Rosario wished she could put a stop to this. Turning to plead with Carlos that they should just arrest them, Rosario barely had time to blink as the butt of Carlos's service pistol connected with her chin, cracking her mask. Blinded by tears and the escaping warm air from her damaged mask, Rosario fell back on her training and twisted away, avoiding a second blow. Hastily brushing back her hair, Rosario clamped her left hand over the crack in her mask and willed her heart to stop attempting to rupture her ribcage.

Calm yourself, remember the training that's been drummed into you since birth. The cavern is pressurized. As long as you keep the crack covered, you should have more than enough air. The three short pulses followed by three long and three short again that vibrated Rosario's gauntlet confirmed an officer in distress signal was active and went a long way to getting her breathing under control. *That should get backup here faster, along with emergency services.* Thinking about the wounded gasper, Rosario got to shaky feet and surveyed the conflict.

What is that idiot doing? Rosario watched as the maintenance person, a man in his early thirties from her quick glimpse, put himself between the frightened gaspers, several of whom were attempting to aid their shot friend, and the armed Carlos. The pry-bar in his suited hands looked useless against the service pistol that drew a bead on his chest. Rosario briefly considered drawing her own pistol, but the idea of shooting her partner in the back, even to stop more death, was a step too far for her.

Instead, Rosario rushed Carlos, and put police training and countless hours at the gym to good use and wrapped her arms around her partner from behind and squeezed.

"Stand down Carlos, this is getting completely out of control!" Rosario screamed, the rushing air from her cracked mask made it hard to speak, but she knew he heard her.

"Traitor!" Carlos roared and fought against hold and fired his pistol, the shots chipping the polycrete tunnel and ricocheting into the shadows.

Barely able to see over Carlos's shoulder, Rosario saw the maintenance tech rush forward and, with a wild swing of his pry-bar, slap Carlos's service pistol from his grasp, where it slid along the floor back towards the gaspers.

Please don't make me shoot you, Carlos, please. Rosario prayed and put her youth and countless hours in the gym to good use to hold the older man. Even with her air escaping, Rosario felt she could subdue her partner until help arrived.

But a lifetime on the streets breaking up riots and cracking heads taught Carlos a thing or two as well, things that never made it into the police manual. Dropping one shoulder, Carlos used Rosario's attempt to adjust her hold to stomp on the inside of her left ankle.

Crying out in pain, Rosario instinctively released her hold on her partner, allowing Carlos to slip free just as the maintenance tech rushed forward again. But even as pain stabbed its way up her leg, she could see that the tech was no fighter and pulled her service pistol free, just as the tech swung his pry-bar again. But this time, he wasn't as lucky.

Stepping in like a skilled dancer attending a junior

high dance, Carlos grabbed the tech's forearm, and used their combined momentum to throw the tech towards Rosario. In a crash of bodies, the tech and Rosario stumbled to the polycrete floor, her service pistol flying from her hand.

"Get off me, you oaf!" Rosario wheezed, feeling light-headed, and pushed the vac-suited tech off of her. Between the escaping air and the stabbing pain that radiated up her leg, Rosario didn't like her chances, and when she saw Carlos bend down and pick up her service pistol, she knew things had just gone from bad to worse.

"You were never cut out to be a real cop," Carlos sneered and raised Rosario's pistol just as several faint thumps echoed throughout the cavern.

Through her cracked respirator, Rosario saw Carlos's eyes go wide, before he staggered and blood sprayed the inside of his mask. Dropping to his knees, Carlos raised the pistol a couple inches towards Rosario, but even wounded as she was, she could roll clear as bullets struck the polycrete floor. Reaching for the tech's pry-bar, and knowing it was no use against a gun, Rosario saw Carlos jerk again, and his chest turned crimson. Dropping the gun, Carlos clawed at his mask in vain before falling forward, dead.

ARE cops so addicted to fighting that they'll even attack each other? Liam thought as he struggled to get his head on straight, which wasn't any easier with the female cop under him poking him weakly in the ribs. Ah shit, her mask!

Rolling off, and briefly wondering why two cops

wearing their dress reds were here in the dark caverns of the abandoned city column, Liam pulled his roll of seal-it tape from his belt. "I don't know if you can hear me, but I'm not attacking you. I'm going to patch your respirator." Dark eyes met Liam's and he could just see her small nod. *Good, because I'd hate to do this with you fighting, as you look like you could break me in half.* Stamping down the rush of adrenaline coursing through his veins, Liam wasted no time tearing off narrow strips of tape and placing them along the maze of cracks. When Liam saw the fog dissipate from the inside of the cop's mask and her labored breathing became measured, he knew the immediate danger had pasted. A quick glance at her gauntlet air gauge showed flashing orange, which was better than red, but not by much. The blue flashing light on his own gauntlet told Liam that not all the danger was done.

"I hear you, Queenie, but I don't have time to chat. We need medical assistance at my location asap ok? Make it anonymous if you can, ok?"

"Ok Tiger, I can do that, but wouldn't the police tactical team headed your way have the equipment and training for an emergency?"

"Shit! Ok, forget that, just do what you can to scrub the digital records around this location," and without waiting for a reply, Liam disconnected and sat.

What are you going to do now? One dead cop and another... but Liam's musing was interrupted as the cop in question tapped his arm and pointed past him. *This will not be good, I just know it.* Distracted by the fight and aiding the stricken cop, Liam had completely forgotten about what had happened to the other cop. Looking over his shoulder, Liam saw who had saved him.

A small kid, only thirteen or fourteen, stood shaking

behind the dead cop, her air hose stretched taut to the air tanks the other refugees hid behind. The service pistol in her hands looked massive, and Liam idly wondered how she'd kept a grip while firing it.

Shit.

Knowing that she likely couldn't hear him, Liam held his hands out, palms facing the girl, and spoke to her as he walked forward.

"Kuri, isn't it? You like to draw butterflies, right?" Liam said in slow, calming tones as he struggled to remember anything else about the girl, most of his interactions having been more mundane, like seeing to everyday survival and hiding them until the transport off Mars was ready. "You're Sano's little sister, right?" Something of what Liam said must have traversed the thin air between them, as Kuri looked at the crumpled form of the dead refugee, her brother.

Liam felt a stab in his chest that he knew was nothing like what the young girl now felt. "I'm so sorry, but if you give me the gun, you can go join the others, ok?" and before Kuri could reply, Liam carefully slipped the weapon from her bloodless hands. "That's good, now you join the rest, ok? And I'll be right over to help in a minute." Praying that he just didn't lie to her, that somehow this mess would get sorted, Liam gave Kuri a tiny push, setting her on her way.

One problem down, now just... Shit...

Distracted as he was with disarming the girl, Liam had missed the female cop crawl to her dead partner. She'd taken the gun from his limp form, staining her hands in his blood in the process and trained it on his chest.

Liam fought the urge to move even though he wanted

to see what the other refugees were doing, but knew he needed to focus.

For the space of two breaths, the pair just stared at each other, before Liam ever so slowly placed his gun on the floor and took a slow step away from it. While some of the tension from the cop's muscular shoulders bled away, the gun never wavered from Liam.

Slowly pointing at his gauntlet, Liam waited for a nod before opening a short distance general frequency.

"I don't know what brought you here, but this isn't what it looks like," Liam started, but was quickly cut off.

"This looks like O2 thieves stealing air and killing a cop. None of you are walking away from this."

Taking another slow step away from the gun and putting himself between this female cop and the refugees, Liam wracked his brain for an argument that would do something before the security reinforcements arrived. "You're right, they are thieves." Liam saw the small jerk that went through the female cop as she heard the unexpected truth. "And you know why? Because those in power make the laws that you enforce. Do you know who these children—yes, I said, children—are?" Liam forced himself to take a few calming breaths as he saw the cop lean to look past him. Her shoulders dipped, but the barrel of the pistol never wavered. "They're the dependents of indentured employees who have fallen through society's cracks. The Mega Corps their parents signed up with had no problem finding transport for them, and were whisked off to the mines, processing plants or whatever, but the transport to Reverie Station for their dependents had a drive malfunction and is stuck here until it gets repaired. And because of your stupid laws." Liam stepped forward and when he saw the cop finger the grip of her pistol. He stopped himself from taking another step, but continued: "They are now illegals. The Mega Corp won't pay for their O2 quota. They can't contact their parents, and Martian law would turn them into wards of the state until they're eighteen. Forced to work behind closed doors for the state to pay for their food, water and air. That's not a life, so they stayed together and hid. Until I found them. They made a clumsy bypass off this old line and were stealing scraps of food to survive." Dropping his hands, Liam knelt before the cop. "Their shuttle will be ready in eleven more days. Can't you give them that? Take me in, say I shot him." Liam nodded at the dead cop. "Give them a chance."

"My job is law and order," the cop said, her voice heavy with emotion, but what emotions, Liam couldn't distinguish.

"Law and order are as warm as the atmosphere outside, but what about justice?" Liam said, crossing his hands on his lap.

Universe, if you're listening, I could use a favor.

"Reinforcements will be here in minutes," the cop said, and the barrel of her pistol dipped an inch. "All this will be out of my hands when they get here."

Come on. The universe answered, now come up with something. Remembering something the sisters at the orphanage used to say, the spark of an idea germinated in Liam's mind.

"We tell them the truth, or at least our version of it." Liam felt renewed excitement in his voice and hoped the cop did as well. "There was a single air thief, gasper, whatever you call them," Liam said, pointing at the dead refugee and prayed that Kuri would forgive him for desecrating her brother's memory. "He tripped an alarm, bringing both you and your partner and me. But the thief was dangerous. He took me captive, and in the struggle to save me, your partner there," Liam pointed at the rapidly cooling body, "got shot with his own gun."

When the female cop put a hand to her earpiece, he knew he was out of time, but he could do nothing but kneel there and watch as she was as still as a statue before shaking her head and giving a single nod to the voice only she could hear.

When she holstered her pistol, Liam felt a glimmer of hope.

"I can't give you eleven days, but I might know another way to get them to Reverie Station. But I'll need some help and a lot of luck."

"The sisters at the orphanage always said I was born under a lucky star," Liam said as he stood. "Name's Liam, by the way. What do they call you when you're off duty?"

"My name is Officer Vera." Pausing, she added, "Rosario. Now quit chattering. The tactical team is almost here and we have to get these kids out of here."

"Rosario is a lovely name," Liam said and hurried after her.

"This is a terrible idea. It's only been a day and half since I met you and you've made me a criminal," Rosario said when she saw Liam steer the electric cart holding the massive refrigeration unit around the corner. She spoke softly into the microphone of her interface visor so her new partner wouldn't hear her.

"It's your idea," Liam replied in her earpiece, using their secure comm line routed through Queenie, though who this mysterious person was, Liam hadn't explained to Rosario, only saying they were a trusted friend.

"That doesn't mean it isn't a terrible idea. I can't believe I let you talk me into this, Liam."

"The way I remember it, you needed little convincing," Liam replied, and before Rosario could respond, he added, "Sometimes it takes a criminal to do the right thing."

Her cheeks getting hot, Rosario forced herself not to fidget from parade rest, and kept her gaze forward. "Well, I certainly look better than you in those stolen spaceport coveralls you're wearing."

"So, you were looking?"

But before Rosario could think up a witty comeback, Liam brought the cart to a halt, the rubber tires squeaking on the polished floor. Rosario's new sentry partner left his station and stomped towards Liam.

"You can't park here, this area is off-limits for commercial use. We're the honor guard for the Slip gift and it takes off in an hour," rookie Jairo González said, his chest puffed up so much Rosario thought a seam might pop. "You need to..." But the rest was cut off as Liam slapped a datapad against the young man's chest.

"And this is part of it. I have the refrigerated medical supplies, I couldn't have brought them earlier, could I?" And before the rookie cop could answer, Liam slid up beside the young cop, threw Rosario a quick wink, and started paging through the screens on the pad faster than the eye could follow. "See? Right here, page 87, perishable medical supplies will be loaded directly before take-off," Liam said before snatching the datapad back.

"But, but... we weren't told," the rookie sputtered.

"I'll deal with this González," Rosario said and tossed

the young cop a credit chit. "Do me a favor and go find me a cup of atole. I need something to warm me up, and with my sore foot and all." Rosario waved her left ankle gently.

González looked from Liam to Rosario, nodded like his head was on a spring, saluted Rosario, and dashed away.

When he was out of earshot, Liam spoke. "That kid is a cop?"

"Rookie, top of his class, graduated last week. I'm nearly old enough to be his mother, and listening to him talk is exhausting."

Liam opened his mouth, paused as if rethinking what he was about to say, then said, "We'd better get moving. The shuttle above will call for this container soon." And without waiting for Rosario to reply, Liam hurried back to the electric cart, swung it around and, with a flashing light and backup horn to announce its arrival to all within a hundred meters, he backed the massive unit into the cargo pod.

Acting like nothing was out of the ordinary, Rosario slapped the controls to close the cargo pod door, effectively sealing them off from the rest of the spaceport. Rosario gave Liam a nod, and he quickly popped the hatch on the refrigeration unit.

But instead of a maze of pipes, compressors, and sealed vials, out poured people: the refugees from the cavern. Scared refugees. In the thirty-six hours since the incident in the cavern, Rosario had had a crash course from Liam about how the other half lived, and that knowledge sat like a ball of acid in her belly.

"I'm going to need your help," Liam said to Rosario and nodded his head towards the half dozen blinking children wearing O_2 masks and carrying small emergency bags. His tone turned soft as he directed his next words to the refugees. "You can take those masks off for now. There's good pure air here, thanks to this tree that will be your companion all the way to Reverie Station." Half the children stared at the tree, likely the first they'd ever seen in the flesh, and the other half stared at Rosario, in her police dress uniform and sidearm. "Don't worry about her, kids, she's the one who helped in the cavern, remember her? She's much prettier without the respirator, isn't she?" A couple of kids giggled as Rosario blushed. "Ok, maybe not much of a joker, but she's here to help you get to your parents. Right Officer?"

Rosario flipped up her interface visor and tried to smile reassuringly. "Ah, um... Right."

Liam rolled his eyes and went to speak, when Kuri, her air mask clipped to her belt and emergency bag tucked under her arm, turned to Rosario.

"Aren't you going to arrest me and toss me out an airlock? I killed your friend."

Rosario felt her mouth go dry and when she looked to Liam for support, she found him watching her along with the others. "No, I'm not. What Officer Sanchez did was wrong, and while I'm not saying what you did was right, I think I understand why you did it. Liam has shown me that the law might have forgotten that it needs to care for the weak as well as punish the guilty, and I think you've been punished enough."

When Liam smiled, the ball of acid in Rosario's belly lessened.

"Ok kids," Liam said, saving Rosario. "I see everyone has their emergency kits with enough food, water, and waste bags to tide you over until you get to Reverie Station. And while I wish I could go with you, I am sending along a friend." Liam pulled a box out from under the driver's seat of the cart and from it removed what looked like a metal football with legs. When he placed it on the floor of the cargo pod, tiny claws snapped twice, paused, and then snapped again before scurrying up a metal wall. "My friend Queenie is sending along one of her drones. The drone will make sure the security cameras don't see you, and will keep the cargo pod door to the rest of the ship locked until you get to Reverie. But you need to keep your hands off everything else in here, ok?"

"We understand," Kuri said, her voice sounding more mature than her years. The rest of the children moved behind her, their youthful faces serious.

Nudging Liam, Rosario said, "We should go. As you said, the shuttle will call for this pod soon, and then it's in the elevator to the surface."

"Right," Liam said and scanned the cargo pod as if looking for something to distract him from the parting. "I have a friend on Reverie Station who will be there when you land, and drive the cart off before customs shows up. Just keep calm and this will work." Liam opened his mouth as if to speak again, but snapped it shut and nodded. "Good luck."

Cycling the cargo pod door again, Liam and Rosario stood alone in front of the closed door, neither saying anything, their silent hopes sent to whatever forces might be listening.

"Is something wrong?" González said, returning, each hand holding a steaming cup of vending machine atole. "Why is the cargo pod closed? I wanted to see the tree one last time."

Rubbing her eyes, Rosario flipped her interface visor

down and replied. "Nothing is wrong. They're about to call for the pod. Our duty here is done. Go home, rookie."

"But I got you your atole..."

Shaking her head, Rosario turned away from the rookie. "I think I need something stronger than atole. It's been a long couple of days and my foot hurts. Go home," she repeated and waited for the young cop to walk away, still holding the hot beverages.

Liam and Rosario stood together, close enough that their elbows brushed.

"Well, I guess..." Rosario started, but Liam interrupted.

"I could go for a drink as well. Have you ever had Irish whiskey? I might know where we could have a quiet drink and watch the shuttle departure listings together?"

"No," Rosario said, but when she saw Liam's smile waver, she continued. "No, I've never had Irish whiskey, but I'd like to try it. Lead the way."

"Second Breath" is an origin story for Peter J. Foote's Jupiter's Eye series. Join Peter's newsletter to read his other books and keep up with Rosario and Liam's adventures.

Read his novel, Ghosts of Colossus, *for free:*
bit.ly/ghostsofcolossus

Pick Your Poison

1. *Doing crime for good? I'm in.* Head to "Fool's Gold" by Jessie Kwak

2. *Let's keep hanging out on Mars for a bit.* Go read "Martian Scuttle" by Andrew Sweet in CROOKED V.2

3. *Take me away to a planet far, far away!* Keep going to read "On Ignition" by Heather Texle

ON IGNITION

RELIANCE SINCLAIR BOOK 0.9

BY HEATHER TEXLE

CHAPTER 1

I CUT THE POWER TO MY HOVERBIKE AND STRETCHED my lower back. This was the seventh house I'd stopped at since landing on Remus-3 that afternoon. The sun had set well over an hour ago, throwing the row of single-story homes into shadow.

Three houses down sat a greige, one-bedroom home with two seedling trees trying to get a start in the front yard. It was a new development area, and every building looked the same. I worked as a claims investigator, and that particular one was being rented by a client of my company after her own home had been destroyed a few weeks ago. The house was dark, and the client's low altitude vehicle was nowhere to be found. She hadn't returned home from work yet, or else her LAV would be parked on the small landing pad in front of the house. There wasn't room for it anywhere else.

Heat from my bike rose, mixing with the already humid air. I plucked at the knit fabric of my powder-blue shirt to keep it from sticking. They had only opened the planet to colonization four years earlier, and the weather patterns hadn't stabilized. What had started off as a cool, drizzly day had flipped to a scorcher in a matter of hours.

I brushed at my dress pants, making sure no insects had stuck on them during the flight. Between the rain that afternoon and the sweat threatening to soak through at my armpits, my professional image was suffering a hit.

It was a quiet night. A delivery drone buzzed by overhead, no doubt taking advantage of the clear skies. Dozens of them zipped about with tiny flashing lights, dropping off construction materials to the building projects all around the city of New Baia. On this street alone, I spotted two houses being 3D printed. The cranes supporting the bulky tubes that poured the regolith cement rose above the rooflines, although they were silent and still at the moment.

I scanned the sky for anything larger than a drone. Hopefully the client hadn't gone out for dinner or to see friends. I didn't want to wait all night to talk to her.

Over the last three months, twelve clients in the area had doubled their fire coverage. That wasn't suspicious, as they lived in an up-and-coming neighborhood. Property values were increasing. However, of the twelve, five of their houses had burned down soon after and they'd all collected hefty settlements.

My boss wasn't thrilled, so she sent me to make sure everything was on the level. Insurance companies didn't believe in coincidences, and neither did I.

"Open a comm to Felix," I said, tapping the cuff on my forearm to wake it up. It operated by scanning the neural impulse signals sent from my brain to my hand and translating them into code its processor could read. I held my index and middle fingers pressed together and made a sharp, jerking motion to the side to launch the holoscreen projection. A semitransparent window lit up in front of me. A few seconds later, the metal, feline face of my ship's avatar filled the main screen.

"Aren't you done yet, Reliance?" he asked. "The dust from that resort project is getting all over everything. I already sent the hull cleaning bots out twice, and I don't even want to look at my filter readings."

"Sorry, buddy, it's going to be a long night. One client slammed the door in my face, one wasn't home, and I still need to track down two whose forwarding addresses didn't check out."

"Fine, but I want a maintenance overhaul when we land someplace civilized. My cleaning bots can't reach everywhere, you know."

He had a real thing about cleanliness, and experience had taught me it didn't pay to argue. I wondered if that came more from the standard ship's protocol or his cat personality program.

"I confirmed the five houses that burned down are total losses," I said, steering us back on topic. "Not even the walls are still standing. How hot does it need to get for regolith to melt? If there's a manufacturing defect, we could transfer the cost to the construction company."

Felix had heterochromia eyes—one green and one blue. The green eye glowed brighter as he processed the data. "Approximately one thousand, four hundred kelvins, depending on the exact composition."

"In Celsius, please." Damn cat. He knew I hated conversions.

"Approximately one thousand, one hundred degrees Celsius."

"Was that so hard?"

"Not for me."

If I didn't love him so much, I'd throw him in the nearest scrap heap.

"Any new messages from Jarrett yet?"

"Not since you asked sixty-three minutes ago."

My stomach clenched. "Let me know when there is."

A year ago, I'd resigned my position as agent from the Department of Enforcement of Criminal Affairs—otherwise known as DECA. My partner had turned on me—even tried to kill me. Everybody loved him, though, and I didn't have any proof. Stars, I didn't even have a motive. Smearing a fellow agent's name wasn't something my coworkers took lightly.

The only one who stood by me was my best friend, Jarrett. A couple of months ago, I asked him to use his skills as digital forensic investigator to look into my old partner. He'd agreed to, but I think he only did it to give me a sense of closure, not because he believed there was anything to find.

It had been two weeks since we last talked, and he hadn't returned any of my comms. He often got so absorbed in a project that he tuned out the rest of the galaxy, but the guy was practically glued to his cuff. Jarrett should have reached out by now.

I pushed the worry down to focus on the case at hand. "Felix, show me the file for this client again."

Felix's hologram disappeared, replaced by a stack of files my company had sent, my notes, and a few documents I'd saved while researching the case on the weeklong flight to the Remus system. I made an exaggerated tapping motion with my index finger to open the first file and aerial scribed through the document. The client's holo appeared, along with the personal details recorded at the time she signed the insurance agreement.

Jorja Reed had light-brown hair, a round face, freckles, and a small gap between her two front teeth. She looked kind in the photo—the type of person who would smile and scoot over at the lunch table so you could sit next to her. Her salary as a human resource consultant easily covered the mortgage on the modest two-bedroom home that had burned down and the eight-year-old LAV she had insured with us. My preliminary research hadn't revealed any connection between her and the other clients, other than that they lived in the same neighborhood and used the same insurance company.

I aerial scribed to the next document. It was a map of the area with geomarkers on the locations of the five burned houses in red and seven additional ones in blue, showing the clients who had increased their fire coverage in the last three months. Felix had run it through several analysis programs, but we hadn't been able to discern any kind of pattern. As usual, research only took me so far. The answers would come after I talked to everyone and pieced their stories together.

As if on cue, the rumble of a small-engine LAV filled my ears. Wind tossed my coffee-brown hair around my face and into my eyes as Jorja Reed landed on the parking spot beside the house she now rented. She cut the power and spent a minute gathering her things from the passenger seat. The gullwing door popped up, and she climbed out hauling a large purse and gym bag. From the way it threw her off balance and caused her shoulder to drop, I gathered it was heavy. Weights? Or a portable anti-grav pad for low-impact aerobics? From this distance, it was hard to tell, but a trip to the gym would explain her late arrival.

Now was my chance.

Before I'd even swung my leg over my bike seat, a short, muscular man stepped out from the far corner of her house.

Stars-all, I was losing my touch. How did I not notice him when I did my initial fly by?

He wore a mishmash of navy blue and lime green and walked with a cocky swagger. As he drew closer, I caught a neon glow circling the back of his shaved head from ear to ear.

Blockers. Highly illegal and favored by gangs at the outer edges, where DECA was understaffed and over-worked. The devices were surgically implanted with tita-nium plates to anchor the tubes in place, and they were a pain in the ass to remove. When activated, they created an electronic dead zone that extended several meters around the wearer.

Something in the way he moved set me on edge. I hunched down close to my bike to keep from being seen and slipped my hand under the flap of my crossbody bag. My palm slid around the handle of the blaster holstered inside. I didn't have any authority on this planet—or anywhere else in the galaxy—but I sure-as-the-void wouldn't sit here and watch him hurt her.

Jorja spotted the man and drew up short. Her head turned toward her front door, then back to her LAV. Both were too far away to offer any safety. Her fingers clutched around the strap of the gym bag, clenching and unclench-ing. She didn't run, though.

I paused, evaluating. She recognized the man.

Neither of them seemed to have noticed me. No

surprise given the distance. I stood motionless so as not to draw attention to myself.

They exchanged heated words, but I only made out the general tone, not the conversation itself. Jorja gestured toward her home. Her voice rose, and I caught the words, "I can't," before the wind snatched away the rest.

The man lifted the front of his shirt, revealing a flashy, blue-steeled blaster tucked into his pants.

I eased my weapon out of my bag and leveled it at his chest. Center mass. His blocker shouldn't be effective this far away, but I couldn't risk turning on the blaster yet. Its power cell emitted a distinctive, high-pitched whine that would draw their attention.

Adrenaline flooded my body, and I worked to even out my breathing and hold the blaster steady. Blood pounded in my ears. My vision tunneled until I blocked out everything except the two people arguing twenty meters ahead of me.

Shit. I didn't want to shoot a man. Not again.

Jorja's hands trembled as she tossed the gym bag over to the man. He stooped to pick it up, never taking his eyes off her. The shit-eating grin on his face tempted me to pull the trigger.

"Go!" Jorja yelled. Her frame shook with the force of her words, and she punctuated it by jabbing her finger at the street.

The man gave her a jaunty salute and walked off toward a skyracer hoverbike he had parked at the opposite end of the block. He strapped the bag to his bike, turned off his blocker, and fired up the engine. It kicked to life with a flare of sparks, sinnalite exhaust coughing out the rear tailpipe in a smoky haze. It shot up to the nearest skylane and burned air, heading east.

Jorja ran up the steps to her front porch, waved her cuff at the door reader, and slammed the door behind her once she was inside. Every light in the house flashed on.

I had a quick decision to make. I could either stay and talk to Jorja or I could follow the asshole who robbed her. Talking with Jorja was the smarter option. Chances were, she wouldn't pull a blaster on me. In fact, she might shed some light on what I'd witnessed. It was possible it was unrelated to the fire claims I was investigating, but that would be one heck of a coincidence.

I tapped my cuff. "Open a comm to Felix, audio only."

"Reliance?" he asked.

"Change of plans, and I'm going to need your help."

CHAPTER 2

My hoverbike purred to life. She was a Cymbeline SR9, cherry red, and tricked out as much as I could afford after selling my house on Brione-5, cashing in my retirement plan, and putting a down payment on the *Soteria*. The hoverbike had been the one extravagance I'd allowed myself, and on days like today, she was worth every credit.

"Give me a map of New Baia." Felix accessed the city's network, found a current map, and sent the visual to the visor display in my helmet. A little pulsing dot showed my position. "He was heading east. What's out there?"

"Not much." Felix's voice shifted from my cuff to my helmet speakers as I shoved the protective gear over my head. "Some temporary housing for construction crews, a public transportation hub, a medical clinic, grocery stores, two schools, some restaurants ... then you hit the edge of the city and it's all new agriculture fields being planted."

None of that helped me narrow down where he might be going. "Let's try something else. He was flying a skyracer—a Frischling Dart. Grab three separate audio samples from my cuff's microphone and enhance them. See if you can identify the sound of his bike."

I punched the throttle and shot up to the skylane, almost colliding with a delivery drone. It shrieked a warning and swerved left. I leaned to the right and narrowly avoided getting hit in the shoulder by one of its rotating propellers.

"This would be easier without all the alarm bells sounding," Felix said.

The stabilizers kicked in, steadying the erratic wobbling that threatened to buck me off the bike. I turned east, following the man's path, and accelerated as fast as my bike would go.

"Try it again," I said, then shut up to avoid causing interference in the recordings. It was almost fully dark now. Houses flashed by below me, and their warm, glittery lights outlined the residential blocks like a map. I swiveled my head, searching for signs of the skyracer.

"Got it!" Felix's voice blared in my ears.

"Great. See if you can triangulate where the sound is coming from based on the readings. I know it won't be precise. Just get me a direction."

Ten seconds later, a second pulsing dot appeared on my map. I dropped out of the skylane and veered forty-five degrees to my starboard side. Flying outside of the designated air travel routes meant I risked running into unregulated flight devices, but it would also let me make up the space I'd lost with my slow start.

The dots drew closer, and I rolled my wrist on the throttle to increase my speed.

I dodged a hovering traffic monitor drone and spotted the bike not far ahead. He'd dropped from the main skylane to ground level. I followed him down, easing back until I was a block and a half behind him, keeping pace beside an older-style LAV. It was a six-passenger model, and the bulky frame provided decent concealment.

We'd only gone two and a half kilometers from Jorja Reed's home, but it was a lower-class area of the neighborhood. Houses were single story, older, and built out of simple mycelium forms. Yards looked overgrown and unattended. I peered into the windows of several as I passed, and more than one house appeared vacant.

My brow furrowed. They couldn't be more than four years old, given the age of the city. Why did the owners leave, and why hadn't anyone moved in?

The guy turned onto a quieter street that didn't have any traffic for me to hide behind. I slowed to put more distance between us.

Something about the guy's skyracer seemed familiar. It was painted electric blue with bright-green swooshes along the sides, the same color as his blocker tube. I had an eye for hoverbikes, but I'd had no reason to take note of this one.

"Felix, scan the recordings from my bike cameras since we arrived. Tell me if you find anything matching the Dart's description."

"You don't ask for much, do you?"

If I could thunk my helmet against the handlebars without tipping the hoverbike, I would have. "Find it in the next five minutes, and I'll bring you back an extension cord to play with—one of those long, slinky ones you like."

"Fine, but only because it sounds more interesting than the stuff you usually have me do."

Dang cat. Everything had to be a freaking negotiation. Sometimes I wondered if he understood I was the captain, and he was the ship's avatar. Scratch that. In his mind, the ship outranked the captain. Obviously.

Soon, the residential buildings shifted to businesses—a used LAV sales and repair garage, a corner grocery mart, a vice store, and a pawnshop with a sign flashing *WE BUY GOLD AND JEWELRY* in the window. The first two were dark; the second two looked to be doing good business at such a late hour.

A minute later, the guy landed his skyracer in a side lot by a bar. By the time I did a slow flyby, he'd dismounted and was already giving the behemoth of a bouncer a manly sort of handshake-shoulder bump-back slap kind of greeting. The bouncer had a blocker, too, but hadn't activated it. My guess was it would have interfered with music pouring out the open windows.

I parked at the end of the lot, waiting to see if he was staying or just dropping off the bag. The LAVs nearest me were all souped up with illegal mods and sinnalite boosters welded underneath their thrusters. I counted nine hoverbikes, each one painted a flashier color than the next. Thin strips of clear, flexible plastic littered the ground. I dismounted my bike and picked up the closest one. A neon-green diamond was stamped on the top. Packaging for a strip of narcotics tabs, with the gang's mark. Users would score drugs inside, take them on the way out, and toss the little backing strips on the ground. Sometimes criminals were clever, but not often.

There was a steady trickle of people entering and exiting the building. It wasn't a dance club, but it wasn't a typical neighborhood bar, either. I'd worked as a DECA officer for a decade—long enough to recognize a gang hangout when I saw it.

Five minutes passed. It looked like I needed to go in if I wanted more information.

My powder-blue shirt and black dress pants were far too professional for this crowd. I'd stick out like a zit on a first date.

I opened the side compartment over the portside thruster on my bike and pulled out my leather riding jacket. Safety-wise, I should have worn it earlier, but the heat had been down-right sweltering. I laid it over the seat and dug in the compartment for my crossbody bag. Inside that was my pocketknife.

A few awkward cuts later, and I had turned my pants into shorts. I rolled the hems to hide the jagged cut lines and tugged on the ends until nothing too salacious showed. Then I tucked the bottom half of my shirt up under my bra to turn it into a crop top and adjusted the fabric to smooth out the wrinkles. The material bunched in the back, but my jacket would cover it. I unclipped my hair and finger-fluffed the brown strands into a messy style to get rid of the helmet hair. To top off the look, I cranked my lip pigment pen from my usual shade of peach to an eye-searing ultraviolet that pulled out the blue in my top.

When I spotted two women heading for the entrance, I timed my walk to arrive right behind them, wanting to look less conspicuous as part of a group.

The square-jawed bouncer smiled at the ladies in front of me. "Tulia. Hettie."

He nodded and let them pass.

I attempted to slip in with them, but he took a half

step sideways, using his substantial mass to block me. The smile vanished from his lips, and his eyes traveled the length of my body. They paused at my hands and hips, no doubt checking for weapons. Hopefully he wouldn't search my bag.

He jerked his head, granting me access inside.

I scooted past him and stepped through the door. Inside, the bar was dimly lit, loud with music and chatter, and smelled of stale beer. A long bar ran along the right wall. Two bartenders poured drinks—a twenty-something man and a woman who looked about ten years older than me, but they'd been a hard ten years. Eight people sat at the bar with drinks in hand and another dozen relaxed at tables scattered around the room. On the left was a trilliards table with a large group watching two men play. Most wore at least one article of clothing in neon green and had blockers wrapped around their heads. A few sported other body mods, as well. The man with the gym bag stood in the middle of the group, talking to the only person sitting. The shot caller?

I diverted my gaze and sat on an empty stool at the bar.

The female bartender worked her way down to me. She had teal hair in an asymmetrical cut that emphasized her sharp cheekbones.

"What'll it be?" she asked, wiping her hands on a rag.

"Lonnie Powell whisky. Neat."

She scoffed. "Does this look like a place that stocks that fancy shit? We've got standard Earth imports and a local potato vodka that burns like sinnafuel going down."

"Any whisky will do."

She poured me a drink from an unlabeled bottle in

the well and set the glass of straw-colored liquor in front of me. I held up my cuff, looking for a reader to pay.

She arched an eyebrow. "LTs only."

"Ah." I dug out a few bills of legal tender from my bag and placed them on the bar.

"You don't look familiar. What brings you here?" she asked.

I shrugged one shoulder and sipped the whisky. It tasted watered down. "I'm in town for work. Thought I'd grab a drink and see what New Baia had to offer. I heard a girl could have a little fun here."

"Heard from who?"

My brain scrambled for the name of a local business. I didn't want to tip her off that I worked for an insurance company without knowing how all of this connected. Per usual, I'd jumped in without a plan. Better to be vague than caught lying.

"Some women at the resort. I'm interviewing for a job there, and to be honest, I didn't catch everyone's name. Kylie? Mylie?" I picked two of the more popular names in this segment of the galaxy.

"Rylie?" the bartender asked, sliding the LTs into the pocket of her apron.

"Maybe?"

Her lips pressed into a thin line. "Hmph."

I couldn't tell if it was a good hmph or a bad hmph, but she moved on to serve another customer.

A loud *clack* sounded from the trilliards game, followed by a few cheers and even more grumbles. I slid my gaze to the table while taking a sip of my weak drink. A skinny guy with a hook nose and low ponytail sunk his last ball into a pocket on the lowest table, winning the game. His opponent still had two balls on the middle level and three on the highest, so it was a sound beating. LTs changed hands from loser to winner and between spectators.

Trilliards wasn't my favorite, but Jarrett had made me play a few rounds with him over the years. Our favorite bar in Clava had a couple of tables. You could have fun knocking the balls around, but to excel at it required a solid understanding of physics. I could do it, but it wasn't exactly what I called *fun*.

A woman challenged the winner. She arranged the balls into a diamond on the top tier of the table. The hook-nosed guy switched to the shortest of his three cue sticks and broke. One of his balls dropped to the second level, so he shot again.

My gym-bag guy slapped the shot caller's shoulder a few times and walked to the back of the bar. I spun around, pretending to search for something in my bag while I watched where he went. He opened a door marked EMPLOYEES ONLY, disappeared for a few seconds, and came out without the gym bag.

The hair on my neck prickled with awareness a second before a shadow blocked out what shitty light filtered down from the grimy overhead pendant.

Turning around, I found a man leaning sideways against the bar beside me, his chest a hairsbreadth from rubbing against my arm. I crossed my leg and used the movement as a pretense to scoot my ass to the farthest edge of my stool.

"Hey, sweetheart," he said. The stench of hard liquor on his breath carried over the short distance between us. "Heard you were looking for a good time. Tonight's your lucky night, because they call me the Party Machine." He drew out the last word like *muh-sheeeeen* and pumped his hips on the last syllable. "How about I buy you another drink?"

He raised a hand with two fingers held up to the bartender.

"I need to use the restroom," I said and extracted myself from his presence.

Halfway across the room, I glanced over my shoulder. He'd already downed the first shot the bartender had poured and was lifting the second to his lips as he worked his way to the next woman at the bar.

The single restroom was down a short hall and across from the employees-only room. I stepped inside and ran my hands through the sonic hand washer in case anyone followed me.

I waited another minute, then cracked open the door and peeked out. No one was looking my direction, so I slipped across the hall and into the opposite room.

Not wanting to risk someone seeing a light shining under the door, I tapped my cuff, launched the holoscreen projection, and aerial scribed the command to turn on its external light. It only illuminated a small space in front of my hand, but it was better than nothing.

I shone the light around—a desk, two folding chairs, a stack of boxes filled with liquor bottles, and a cheap wire rack spanning the length of the back wall. More wooden crates lined the bottom shelf, along with a couple of pails. The next level up had open crates, and the one above that held five mismatched bags, including the gym bag the guy had taken from Jorja Reed.

Even though I doubted anyone could hear me over the music, I kept my steps soft as I weaved between the chairs and around the desk. It would be too easy to bump into something in the dark.

The shelf of bags was at eye level. I pulled Jorja's bag forward, noting a piece of orange tape on the end with the address of her old house scrawled across it in scratchy handwriting. Inside were stacks of legal tender, neatly bound with banker bands.

My lips pressed together in a thin line as I moved down the row. The next bag also had an address taped to the end, and I recognized it as one of the burned houses I'd visited this morning. It was stuffed to the top with LTs. Each of the other three contained the same. Four empty, crumpled bags were shoved behind the last one.

Moving down to the shelf below, I shone my light into the first crate. Blasters. About a dozen—mixed models, scuffed, and missing a few charge packs. The other box held a mix of knives and illegal tech. I pulled out an electric telescoping baton, watching blue-white sparks dance at the end when I snapped it open.

I pressed the button to retract the baton and placed it back in the crate. This must be a stash house. Well, stash bar.

But why wasn't there more security? Or even a lock on the door?

Probably because I was the only person stupid enough to snoop through the local gang's stuff. Smart, Reliance. Real smart.

I sniffed, and my nose scrunched in self-defense at an acrid, chemical smell. Bending down, I peered into the open pail on the bottom rack. It was three-quarters full of small, yellow pellets.

My brows drew together. Sinnalite pellets were a regulated substance. They should be stored in heat-and-static-resistant containers because they were highly flammable and, once ignited, burned hot and long. A special chemical foam was required to kill the flames. There was enough to burn down an entire apartment building.

Or several small homes.

I let out an audible groan as realization dawned. The gang was coercing homeowners to take out large policies, using sinnalite pellets to burn down the houses, and then extorting the insurance money from the policyholders. That was why the houses burned hot enough to melt the regolith walls and incinerate any evidence.

Some of the addresses on the bags I recognized as belonging to our clients, but not all of them. The empty bags implied the extortion had been going on for a while. How many people had lost their homes? Their life savings?

I didn't have the authority to arrest anyone, but I could record what I saw and show it to my boss. She could take it to New Baia's DECA office. There was no guarantee she could convince them to launch a full investigation, but maybe they could recover the money and return it to the homeowners. It wasn't an optimal solution for the insurance company, but my boss would appreciate stemming the tide of future losses.

I launched my holoscreen projection and had aerial scribed to the visual recording application when the door swung open, startling me.

"What the ... Who's in here?" came a gruff male voice.

My heart rabbit-kicked against my ribcage. I spun around to see the stocky silhouette of the man I'd followed.

"Lights," he said, and the room flooded in bright white light. It only took a second for him to take in the scene and draw a conclusion about my presence. A slow smile crept across his broad face. He lifted his shirt and drew the blue-steeled blaster from where he'd tucked it in at his waist. "I don't know who in the void you think you are, sugar, but you chose the wrong cookie jar to steal from."

CHAPTER 3

My breath hitched as I raised my hands in the air. No glow emitted from his blocker, so him pointing the muzzle of his blaster at me wasn't an idle threat. There was no way he would miss at this close range. Best-case scenario, I'd be incapacitated if it was on the low setting. If it was on high, I'd be nothing more than a pile of smoking brisket.

"Whoa," I said, fighting to keep my voice calm. "Nobody's stealing anything. I was looking for the restroom and got turned around. How about taking your finger off that trigger?"

"How about you—"

While he was still finishing his thought, I shoved my hand into my bag, drew my blaster, and flipped the power switch on in one smooth motion. The high-pitched whine reassured me it was charged.

"Drop your weapon." My years in the Department lent an air of authority to my voice that left no room for debate.

The guy was fast. I had to give him that. He slammed the palm of his hand against the titanium plate of his blocker. Green light flared around his head, and the whine from my blaster died. Raised voices from the bar told me he'd killed the electronics out there, too.

Shit.

I lunged for him, dropping my blaster to the floor and hoping to catch him unprepared. Ground fighting wasn't my specialty, but I'd trained for it. Most fights ended up there anyway, whether or not you wanted them to.

My left hand shot under the man's gun arm and grabbed the cloth behind his elbow as I twisted and slid to my knees. My shoulder rammed his torso before I dropped my right arm to wrap around the inside of his leg.

He brought his fist down hard, striking my spine between my shoulder blades. The shock of the impact bowed my back.

I grunted but didn't let go.

As his hand swung down for a second blow, I straightened from the knees and pulled on his arm at a downward angle. The sudden movement threw him off balance, allowing me to take his full weight on my shoulders. I completed the firefighter's carry throw by rolling forward. He landed flat on his back with an impact that shook the floor. I followed the motion through, rolling over his prone body and onto my feet.

The guy recovered quicker than I expected. He'd held onto his blaster through the throw and swung it in my direction. Then he hit the side of his head, this time killing the blocker. His blaster hummed back to life.

My hand flew to my side, but my blaster wasn't there. It was right where I'd dropped it on the other side of the room.

As if in slow motion, I watched his finger squeeze the trigger. I threw my weight to the side and dove behind the desk for cover. My hip slammed into the rack, making the cheap wire frame shake. I risked a glance and saw two of the weapons crates had slid to the edge of the shelf.

I kicked the nearest leg—once, twice. The rack rocked forward, and one crate toppled over. Knives and weapons rained down around my bare legs but thankfully missed skewering me. Music blared in the bar again, covering the cacophony of noise. It only took me a second to locate the electric baton and snap it open. Raw blue energy pulsed between the two prongs at the tip.

It wasn't a blaster, but it would do.

I drew my feet underneath myself in a crouched position behind the desk. My pulse pounded in my ears, and my lungs burned with the need for oxygen. Too many days in space took a physical toll on my body.

"How about we make a deal?" I offered. "You go back out to your friends, and I'll leave through the rear exit empty handed. We both walk out of here like nothing ever happened."

"I have a better idea. How about I shoot you right now, then get my friends to help me dispose of your body?"

Sweat dripped down my neck. Was it my nerves, or was it getting hotter in here?

"I think I like my plan better," I said and chanced a peek around the edge of the desk.

A bolt of energy shot past my face. I snapped my head back to safety and surveyed the damage. It left a smoking hole the size of a trilliards ball in the wall above the pail.

My eyes widened. It wasn't the wall that was smoldering. Light-gray smoke wafted up from the pail of sinnalite pellets. The idiot must have hit it with that first blaster shot and ignited the fuel.

Even as I watched, orange and blue flames licked up over the edge of the pail. Heat radiated from it at an alarming degree. We only had a few minutes before the entire room went up in flames.

"Hey, crack shot. This place is about to go up like a solar flare."

"One problem at a time."

His footsteps drew closer. I lowered myself onto my belly and slithered under the desk. Luckily, my ass had ended up in the chair cavity, giving it ample room to move. However, my chest and shoulders found the gap beneath the drawers a little less accommodating. I took a shallow breath and wedged myself deeper.

A pair of lime-green shoes drew level with my face, and my fingers tightened on the baton. He pivoted around the desk and shot at where I'd been crouched a moment earlier.

I lashed out with the baton, striking a bare patch of skin right above his ankle. He howled, jerked twice, then crumpled to the floor. I poked him with the baton—turned off—but he didn't move.

It took me thirty seconds to wiggle out, because the guy had had the nerve to fall face-first along the length of the desk. I had to scooch back, then shove him aside to squeeze out. The flames were half a meter high, and a thick layer of smoke clouded the ceiling.

A quick scan with my cuff confirmed the guy still had a pulse. Yippee.

I grabbed the duffle bags of LTs off the rack and chucked them through the open door. Then I flipped the guy over like a pancake, looped my arms under his armpits, and dragged his heavy ass to the bar.

No one appeared to have heard the blaster shots over the music or noticed anything out of the ordinary.

"Fire!" I shouted and waved my arms. "Everybody out!"

A few people nearest to me raised their eyebrows, but

nobody moved. Most probably they hadn't even heard me over the thumping of the music. I looked for a way to grab everyone's attention and my eyes snagged on the unconscious man on the floor. I smacked him across the side of his head, activating his blocker. The music died.

That people noticed.

Using an empty chair as a step, I vaulted onto a table, kicking over two glasses of beer.

"Hey!" a dark-haired woman protested, but she shut her mouth when I snapped open the baton. It wouldn't hold a charge while the blocker was on, but it was still a formidable weapon.

"Sinnalite fire! Everybody out the front!"

A loud crash from the back room punctuated my words, and when black smoke billowed into the hallway, people got the message. I waved the baton for effect until they got their asses in gear.

I jumped down from the table and lifted the guy by his armpits again. "A little help?" I asked a passing couple, but they didn't stop. Thick smoke poured from the door. Those in the back coughed at the chemical fumes and shoved the people in front of them. The gang members at the trilliards table tried to come my way, but the tide of people was against them.

I was the last one out of the bar, unless I counted the unconscious guy, whose feet exited after me as I dragged him across the threshold. The cool, fresh air soothed the burning in my smoke-filled lungs. After a few deep breaths to reoxygenate my blood, I ran back inside.

※

An hour later, I straddled my hoverbike while waiting for the DECA officer to give me the go-ahead to leave. He looked annoyed at having to take everyone's statement. As the lowest rank here, he'd be stuck filling out reports all night. I smiled. Insurance investigations were rarely this exciting, but at least there were fewer reports.

His superior had grilled me for fifteen minutes straight, even after I gave him the bags of LTs. I guess deference went to the unconscious party. Then the guy woke up and confessed everything in a fit of rage. They'd had to slap a pair of augmented restraints on him to keep him from fighting his way out. Unfortunately, his buddies had cut their losses and run as soon as they'd exited the building. The officers would have a void-damned time rounding them all up.

During all that, the fire department arrived to put out the flames. After I explained about the sinnalite pellets, they called in a specialty vehicle that carried the chemical necessary to extinguish it. They provided me with the contact details for the head of their arson investigation unit, and I left a message for her to reexamine our client's homes with this new information in mind.

The officer finished talking to the female bartender and gave me the "all clear" wave. I nodded, slipped on my helmet, and fired up my hoverbike. Even though I'd only left the Department a year ago, it felt like a different life. The quicker I got back to my ship and off Remus-3, the better.

Heavy clouds rolled in, threatening to rain, again, but otherwise the ride home was uneventful. I reached the *Soteria* and had my bike secured in its rack in the cargo bay before the first drops fell.

Ash and soot coated my hair and clothes. I debated

heading straight to my bunk and taking a shower—I'd even splurge on a hot water one, because I didn't think all the sonic showers in the Alpha Bohn-ri system could leave me feeling clean after tonight. In the end, I climbed up the ladder to the bridge on the top level and collapsed into my captain's chair. A hidden emergency bottle of Lonnie Powell whisky was calling my name.

Felix sat in the copilot's chair and watched me pour two fingers of amber liquid into a glass. Subdued lights from the console made his iridescent black scales shimmer blue and purple. I knew he was evaluating me for signs of stress and poor mental health. He was the ship computer's avatar, but they'd also programmed him to be a social companion on long trips through space. I reached over and pet him between his ears to reassure him I was okay.

Then I tossed back my drink and let the liquor burn the grime from my throat. I leaned back, rested my feet on the console, and shut my eyes. It had been over a year since I'd seen real action like that—not since I'd left DECA.

And seeing the officers—talking to them—had left me unsettled.

I hoped they would follow up on the case, arrest the gang members for extortion and arson, and return the legal tender to the homeowners. However, it was just as likely the gang had paid off one of the agents and everything would get swept under the rug. I'd done what I could. Tonight, I'd file my report with my company. Then it would be out of my hands.

"I found it," Felix said.

"Found what?" I asked, still staring at the back of my eyelids. All the smoke had given me a headache, and it was hard to concentrate.

"The skyracer. You were right. It was parked next to one of the client's houses you visited today. The blue one that increased their insurance last week. You knocked on their door, but nobody answered."

"The house on Antiquities Avenue? Hopefully they hadn't given the gang any money yet, but I'll add their names to the list of potential victims for the local DECA office."

"So, can I have it?" His speaker crackled in his best imitation of a purr.

"Have what?"

"The extension cord. For finding the bike?"

I opened my eyes to find him kneading his metal paws into the scratched fabric of the chair. "Ah, shit, Felix. I forgot to stop."

His paws stopped working the seat cushion. "No cord?" The last claw pulled out with a loud snap of torn thread.

Void-damn-it. "It's been a really long day, buddy. I'll get you one at our next stop. How about I bring your favorite charging pad down to my bunk tonight, and you can recharge down there with me?"

"Two."

"Two?"

"I want two cords at the next stop."

"Deal."

Felix's tail coiled around his front paws in a satisfied motion. His green eye pulsed brighter. "You have an incoming comm. Rel, it's from Jarrett."

My boots hit the floor. About damn time. "Put it through."

Felix's green eye pulsed, again. "It's text only. Encrypted."

"Well, decrypt it," I said, impatient.

My pulse raced. I'd rather talk to Jarrett in real-time. Remus-3 was on the outer edge of colonized space, but they had the latest subspace relays set up. The communication delay would have been minimal.

"What's taking so long?" I asked when the words didn't appear.

"He put it through three levels of encryption," Felix said. "I'm trying one of the decryption programs he installed now."

Another minute passed. My fingers drummed on the console.

"Got it. Displaying on the main holoscreen."

The message was brief, only taking up two lines across my screen.

MEET ME IN THE BRIN MARKET AT THE MELON STALL. EIGHTEEN HUNDRED HOURS.

TELL NO ONE. WATCH YOUR BACK.

"That's it?" I asked.

"That's it."

Brin was on Andaress-4. It was Jarrett's hometown. It didn't make any sense. Why the heavy encryption? Why wouldn't he just ask me to meet him at his apartment? And why did I need to watch my back?

I pulled up a star chart and plotted a course. The market was only held on Saturdays. If I left right now and pushed the *Soteria* to maximum warp speed, I could make it.

All traces of weariness vanished. I shrugged into the straps of my harness and clicked the buckles shut. Something was wrong. Something was very wrong.

"Felix, initiate the preflight check. We're going to Andaress-4."

Hang on, Jarrett. I'm coming.

"On Ignition" is a prequel story to Heather Texle's Reliance Sinclair series.

Don't Stop Now!

Dive deeper into the world at heathertexle.com

★ The story continues in *On Impulse*. Find out what caused Jarrett to send such an urgent message to Reliance and how much it cost him.

★ Read Reliance and Jarrett's adventure to take down Lady Ilymechina in the *FREE* prequel *On Instinct!*

★ Be the first to know about new releases, deals, and upcoming events! Find bonus content like book club questions, inspiration boards, and more!

PICK YOUR POISON

1. Love it! Now, let's go infiltrate a top secret facility. Head to "Proof of Life" by MJ Blehart

2. I want more stories about badass women who aren't afraid to stir up trouble. Go read "Terminal Sunset" by Erik Grove in CROOKED V.2

3. Uh oh. Who's that ominous figure in the corner? Keep going to read "Mad Dog" by R.M. Olson

MAD DOG

BY R.M. OLSON

Toothpick didn't take his hand off his pistol as he ducked into the small tavern. He'd lived on Blackrock long enough to know that would be a bad idea in a place like this.

Outside on the street, there were ghosts. In a place like Blackrock, ghosts were unavoidable—the combination of cellular damage from faster-than-light space travel and the past trauma that created them were ubiquitous here, deep under the surface of the small moon that served as the pirate port. And inside the taverns, the people were as vicious and deadly as ghosts, and just as likely to kill you.

His eyes caught on a figure in the far corner nursing a drink. He sighed.

He'd almost hoped he wouldn't find her.

He made his way across the dingy tavern towards her and pulled out a seat at the bar, close enough for conversation, but not close enough that he'd look like he was intruding on her space. From what he'd heard, that wouldn't be wise.

"What'll you have then?" A pretty, sharp-faced

woman stepped up behind the bar, looking Toothpick up and down in an unimpressed fashion.

"A beer'll do for me, thanks," he said.

He watched the woman beside him from the corner of his eye.

She wore a long oilskin coat with the hood pulled up so her features were in shadow. There was a glass of rum, mostly empty, in front of her, and from the looks of it, it wasn't her first. Her posture bore the weary slump of someone who'd just come in from a long space-run, but he'd heard the stories. He was smart enough not to underestimate her.

The barkeep returned a moment later. She slid a glass of beer across the counter to him then turned back to her work, but he noticed she murmured something to the woman before moving on.

Toothpick raised his eyebrows. Abigail wasn't known to play favourites in her tavern.

The woman drained the rest of her glass and turned to him with a wry smile. The movement pushed back her hood, and he saw her face for the first time.

Her black hair was pulled back in a sailor's ponytail, her face the weathered brown of someone who'd spent most of her life among the stars, the radiation aging her skin beyond her years. She must be younger than him by half a decade—late twenties, maybe—but there were lines on her face that were all too common here in Blackrock, the sort that came from pain and suffering and privation and months or years of living on the sharp knife-edge of survival. Her gaze was cool and perceptive, but there was a shimmering heat of anger under it.

"You're looking for me, ain't you?" Her voice was low, with just the hint of amusement to it.

Toothpick nodded noncommittally. "Could be, yeah. Got an offer for a woman goes by Mad Dog."

She grinned, something sharp in the expression. "Well now. What sort of an offer might that be?"

"Ain't my offer, this is from my captain. He wanted to offer you a place on our next run. Sent me out to track you down."

She raised her eyebrows, still grinning. "That so? What's the job, and what's the cut?"

Toothpick hesitated. But in the end, he'd been sent to pass on the offer. What she did with it afterwards was her affair.

"Job's a quick grab-and-run, I been told. Merchant ship coming off the Wolf Sector and headed for the Level, and Captain thinks it'll be worth our while. Said he needed someone who was a hand with weapons, since this ship's armed."

"And I figure he's offered extra pay, since sounds like he's looking for someone to take a cutlass-blow for him."

"Cut's one fifteenth of the take."

She raised her eyebrows. "Generous offer, that." She studied him, and he fought the urge to lean away. There was something dangerous and hard and ruthless about her, even well into her cups and smiling lazily.

"Who's your captain?" she asked after a moment.

"Captain Vin, of the *Bloody Hand*," he said.

"Shipped with him for a while, have you?"

Again, he hesitated. "Been with him this last twelve-month," he said at last. "Got another three years on my contract."

She nodded slowly, not taking her eyes from him. "And he's a fair one, is he? Ain't one to stiff his crew their take?"

Toothpick forced his expression not to turn bitter and ugly.

Three more damn years on his contract, if he survived them.

The fact that Vin wanted this woman specifically, the fact he was offering her a contract for one run only, rather than the years he usually insisted on—everything about this stank. But he'd been given a job, and that was to get Mad Dog on the crew. He wasn't being paid to moralize about it.

"Ain't never stiffed me my share," he said, measuring his words.

She nodded, still studying him. Then she turned away and tapped her knuckles on the bar. "Abigail! I'll have one more, put it on my tab. Looks like I got places to be."

The barkeep poured a generous measure into Mad Dog's glass and Mad Dog tipped it back, then pushed herself to her feet, swaying a little before she caught her balance. "What's your name?"

"Toothpick," he said, pushing back his own stool.

She gave him another dangerous grin. "Well, Tooth-pick. You aiming to take me to meet this captain of yours?"

There was something under her drunken grin, some-thing weary and desperate and haunted. Something he recognized, because it was how he must have looked when he took the four-year contract on the *Bloody Hand*, because there was no other option open except death.

And now that he knew better—perhaps he'd have taken that over this.

He hesitated, then leaned forward, using the excuse of fixing his jacket. "Don't want to say too much, and don't want to get in your business," he said in a low voice. "But figure you ought to know. This ain't a clean contract. Don't know what it is, but I figure it ain't clean."

She might be too drunk to put any stock in his words. But he couldn't quite clear it with his conscience to let this woman, whoever she was, bargain away her life like he'd bargained away his without at least trying to warn her.

She raised her eyebrows. Then she shook her head. "Ain't one for patience, I reckon, your Captain Vin. Leastways, not what I've heard. We'd best get going, you'n me, no?"

He sighed. He'd tried, he could tell himself that. "You're right, best we get going. Shipping off before four bells tonight."

He swallowed down the bitterness of it as he turned away for her to follow.

He recognized Mad Dog's anger, because he'd felt it himself, every damn day of the last twelvemonth. He knew very well he'd not likely survive the next three years. And the thought of Vin winning again—devouring Mad Dog the way he devoured the rest of the crew, only because he wanted to and he could—made a sick helplessness rise in Toothpick's throat like bile.

THE STREETS OUTSIDE were lit with the perpetual twilight of Blackrock, the guttering torches lining walls damp and glittering with moisture, the fans that pulled the oxygen up from the algae vats in the deep caverns clanking and groaning in their inset housings in the rough cave ceilings. Toothpick watched Mad Dog from the corner of his eye, but despite the slight stagger in her walk she seemed able to keep her feet.

There was a tight unease in his gut, but he shoved it down. If Mad Dog was incautious enough or unlucky enough to sign on to a bad bargain while she was too deep in her cups to think straight, that was her own lookout.

They were passing an empty alley when Toothpick felt the hint of icy air on his face. He whirled, yanking out his sparker, the blue haze of the ghost a dim glow in the dark of the alley.

The ghost was of a young man, the corners of his eyes and mouth lined with good humour. Not that it mattered —ghosts were a mindless echo of trauma, given form by the cellular damage that accompanied faster-than-light travel. Anyone who'd travelled faster than light could turn ghost when they died, and if they'd suffered sufficiently horrifying trauma during life, they would.

That described most of the population of Blackrock.

Any sparkle that would have been in the young man's eyes in life was absent in the ghost—its eyes burning black pits, fingers lengthened to claws, its jaw unhinging to show long spikes of teeth as vicious and burning as the cold of deep space.

Toothpick scrambled backwards, thrusting his sparker into the thing, hunting for the tiny spot that would dissolve it. Terror climbed his spine, freezing his muscles, making his fingers clumsy. His back hit the damp rock of the corridor and he cursed, his mouth filling with the acrid taste of fear.

Beside him, there was a flicker of motion.

The ghostly hand reaching to tear out his throat dissolved into a blue pool of mist that settled around his feet a moment before drifting away in the eddying air, leaving behind nothing but the flickering blue tip of a sparker.

Toothpick slumped against the wall.

Beside him, Mad Dog replaced her sparker in its holster on her belt. "Blackrock ain't a place to lose focus, I hear." Her words were amused, crisper than they'd been in the tavern, and the drunken slouch of her posture had straightened.

He frowned, despite the hammering in his chest.

She'd been drinking—he'd seen it himself, and he could smell the rum on her from here. But she wasn't nearly as drunk as she'd led him to believe.

"Thank you," he said.

She shrugged, but her gaze was still far too perceptive. "Don't forget it when someone tries to do me a good turn," she said. "Even if I'm a mite too drunk to listen."

She turned back towards the docks, her movements now with the characteristic over-exaggeration of someone who'd had too much rum. "Come on now, ain't no call to waste time."

THE FIRST FEW days of the voyage were uneventful enough. Mad Dog performed her duties without making any effort to interact with the rest of the crew, and retired to her hammock to drink her grog ration alone. Despite her reputation back on Blackrock, she seemed content to keep her own business and allow the rest of the crew to keep theirs.

Toothpick watched her carefully.

The *Bloody Hand* needed a crew of eight to work her. With Mad Dog, there were nine—Vin; Choker, the first mate; and Fly and Theo, who both had enough years of seniority and a big enough share of the take that they were like to stand by Vin if it came to it.

On his side, there was Vee, a slight, no-nonsense woman who'd signed on only a little before he had; Mirage, a laconic non-binary sailor whose vocabulary consisted mostly of grunts; and Rietta, a young woman who'd signed on a couple months past. He knew what the captain had on Vee—the man knew her wife's name and business. He didn't know what Vin had on Mirage and Reitta, but he guessed it was something similar.

They'd been talking, the four of them. But Vin had the weapons and the leverage, and if they tried this and failed, it was more than their own lives on the line.

But Toothpick had barely survived the first year of his contract. He wouldn't survive many months more. And his brother in the Stacks had a new baby, and she'd been poorly—that combination of bad air and bad food and water that plagued the health of any child born in the slums, but had hit his niece especially hard—and she'd not survive long if Toothpick wasn't there to send part of his take to help with the medicine.

Up until now, he'd advised caution. But there was something about Mad Dog, the quiet, deadly intensity of her, the easy, casual way she handled her weapons. She was as dangerous as rumour had it. If they could get her on their side, they might stand a chance. But she didn't seem eager to make friends with him and Vee any more than she did with any of the others.

✺

On the third day out, Toothpick was in the mess when Mad Dog ducked in. Her shirt was stained with sweat, the creases in her hands dark with engine grease.

Choker stepped in front of her, barring her way. "Mad Dog, is it?" The words were polite enough, but there was a sneer on the first mate's face.

"Figure there's a crew register if you ain't sure," Mad Dog said, with a half-smile that showed the tips of her teeth. She moved to step past Choker, but the woman grabbed her by the arm.

"You'll watch your damn mouth when you talk to me, sailor," she snapped. "Think you're something, I've been told, because you have some sort of a history." She yanked up the sleeve on Mad Dog's shirt.

Toothpick sucked in his breath. He recognized the ugly raised scar on Mad Dog's forearm instantly—the brand that marked a traitor against the government on the Level.

Mad Dog glanced down at Choker's hand on her arm, still with that half-smile on her lips.

Toothpick hardly saw her move. He blinked, and the first mate was pressed up against the table, her arm twisted behind her back, Mad Dog's knife pressed against her throat.

Choker made a strangled sound, and Fly and Theo leapt to their feet, yanking out their energy pistols.

"Don't figure as you'd better do that," Mad Dog said, still smiling. "Won't get me before I have time to slit her throat. And maybe one of you'll hit me before I can get to you. But do you really want to find out?"

The mess hall went completely still, except for Theo, who was muttering frantically into his comm.

Vin burst into the room a moment later, his face dark

with anger. "Mad Dog," he snapped. "Let her go before I damn well throw you out the airlock."

Mad Dog turned a little, the motion twisting Choker's arm higher behind her back and pressing the edge of the knife into her skin. A few drops of blood welled up and beaded on the silver of it before rolling down to drip onto the floor.

"Mad Dog," Vin growled, warning in his voice.

Mad Dog raised an eyebrow. "You signed me onto your ship to fight for you, what you told me," she said. "Didn't bring me on board so your crew could do as they pleased. That weren't part of the bargain. I'll follow orders, Captain. But you and your crew will keep your hands off me, or I'll take their hands myself. That understood?"

The words hung in the air for a long, fraught moment. Toothpick had seen the captain kill for less. But Mad Dog was holding a knife to the throat of his first mate, and there was nothing he could do to save her if Mad Dog decided to drive it home.

"Let her go, Mad Dog," Vin said at last, grudgingly. "And I'll see that no one on this ship touches you without your permission."

Mad Dog's smile widened, an edge to it sharper than her knife. "That's fine by me, Captain," she said. She lowered her blade and let go of Choker's wrist, shoving her forward so that she stumbled. Choker turned with an incoherent growl, reaching for a weapon, but the captain grabbed her by the arm. "Enough," he snapped.

When Choker relaxed, Mad Dog lowered her arm and turned to the captain. "I ain't going to forgive this twice," she said, her voice quiet. "Ain't one for giving second chances, me. Don't forget them as make themselves my friends, and I don't forget those as make themselves my enemies, neither." She turned away, but for just a moment, her eyes caught on Toothpick. He raised his eyebrows at her, and he thought she gave him a quick wink.

THAT NIGHT HE, Vee, Mirage, and Reitta huddled together in the small engine room. The noise of it should serve to cover their voices, and Vee was perched by the door to give warning if someone passed by.

"This is our best chance," Toothpick said in a low voice. "You saw Mad Dog today. She ain't one to make a threat she ain't willing to follow through with, and she ain't afraid."

"Maybe she'd be right to be." Rietta's voice was low. "Don't know what's coming up, but the captain was telling Choker that Mad Dog wouldn't be on board much longer."

"You think he's planning to space her?" Vee whispered.

Mirage looked up shook their head. "Don't know. Don't figure it, though—sent Toothpick out to find her special, didn't he?"

Toothpick nodded. "Aye. He wants her for something."

"Whatever it is, don't figure he means her to survive it," Mirage said in a sour voice.

Vee shook her head. "It don't pay to chart your jump course less'n you know it's clear on the other end. I say we wait, and if she survives it, we'll bring her in. I ain't risking my wife's life for something less certain than that."

Toothpick glanced around the group. He could see the wisdom in Vee's words. But he pictured Mad Dog as he'd first seen her in the tavern, the desperate, gasping relief of the sight of the blue tip of her sparker around the fading ghost that had been poised to rip his throat out.

"I'll wait for now," he said, turning to Vee. "But I ain't going to let her face the captain alone if it comes to it. You heard her—she'll remember a favour as well as she'll remember an offence. And if I have to choose, I know which I'd rather she remember me for."

Vee watched him a moment. "Didn't see you for someone who'd risk your neck for kindness' sake."

Toothpick gave a short laugh. "Ain't kindness. Figure if I'm going to gamble my life, I'll choose the one as shoved her sparker through a ghost before it could gut me, rather than the one as would have gut me himself if he'd seen profit in it."

On FIFTH DAY, the clanging of the ship's alarm jerked Toothpick awake.

"Ship we're going after is in view on the screens," Choker said once they'd gathered on deck. There was a tight excitement in her voice. "Get your weapons and get to the airlock."

Toothpick frowned. Vin never sent out a boarding party without at least softening the enemy with guns first. Something about this stank.

"Where's Mad Dog?" Vee whispered from beside him.

He glanced around quickly, his stomach tightening with anxiety.

Mad Dog wasn't there.

"Come on, quick-time," Choker snapped.

Back in the crew quarters, Toothpick scooped up his weapons, strapping on his cutlass and energy pistol and shoving a spare sparker in his pocket.

The dark lump of Mad Dog's body still lay in her hammock, and the knot of worry in his stomach twisted tighter.

He hesitated, then started over to her. The others had already left, and it was still possible he'd reach her unobserved, warn her about whatever was coming.

"Toothpick."

He spun. Choker had stepped through the door, a lazy smile on her face and her energy weapon in her hand. "What the hell you think you're doing?"

Toothpick jerked his chin towards the hammock, hoping the dimness of the cabin would hide the sweat beading on his forehead. "Thought I'd best wake her, seeing as this was what the captain signed her up for."

Choker's smiled turned cruel. "Figure the captain and I can deal with crew as drank a bit too much grog last night." She stepped closer to him, lowering her voice. "And I figure you'd best remember who's orders you're under. Because I figure there's a family back in the Stacks as might regret it if you don't." She shoved a bundle of rope into his hands. "Put yourself to use."

His feet heavy, Toothpick followed her to the hammock.

Mad Dog stirred as they got closer, trying to shove herself upright, but her movements were sluggish and uncoordinated. Choker dragged her out of the hammock, and Mad Dog stumbled, trying to get her feet under her.

Choker struck her hard across the face. "You're to come with me, Captain's orders."

Mad Dog moved as if to grab for a weapon, but Choker caught her wrist. Mad Dog cursed, her words slurred. "You drugged my drink, damn your eyes."

Choker pulled her around, dragging her hands behind her back. "Tie her," she snapped at Toothpick.

Mad Dog caught his eye as he stepped forward. Her pupils were too large, her gaze unfocused, but he saw the sharp, helpless anger in her.

Suddenly, the pieces slipped into place, and he had to bite back a curse.

How Vin had wanted no one on the guns. How he'd asked for Mad Dog specifically. The way Choker had pulled Mad Dog's sleeve up earlier in the mess hall, the tattoo that had been visible for just a moment.

"That ain't a merchant ship, is it?" Toothpick said in a low voice as he looped the ropes around Mad Dog's unresisting wrists. "That's a Level government ship. You're selling her out."

"Do as you're told," Choker spat. "You want a payout? Whatever the hell this Mad Dog did, government's willing to pay a pretty penny for her."

Toothpick snugged the ropes tighter.

Figure if I'm going to gamble my life, I'll choose the one as shoved her sparker through a ghost before it could gut me, rather than the one as would have gut me himself if he'd seen profit in it.

He hesitated the briefest moment. Then he reached down, as if to double-check his knots, and slipped the small shiv he carried in his sleeve between Mad Dog's bound hands before stepping back to let Choker check his knots.

The sweat that had been beading on his forehead trickled down the side of his face, but he didn't dare reach up to wipe it away. If Choker noticed the shiv, if Mad Dog gave him away without meaning to...

"Good," Choker said at last. "Help me bring her up, I don't trust her not to fight."

Mad Dog didn't fight as they dragged her to the airlock, just stumbled forward as if it was taking all her concentration to stay on her feet. Toothpick felt sick to his stomach.

He knew damn well what it was like to be desperate enough to contemplate selling someone out for money or favours. But this wasn't desperation. This was simple calculation on Vin's part. And shiv or no, Toothpick was part of it now. For the rest of his life, he'd be a man who'd sell out a crewmate to the Level government.

By the time they reached the airlock, a skiff from the Level ship had hooked on and a man in a Level naval uniform was standing in front of Vin in the airlock. He had a box with the stamped seal of the Level Banking Union on it and a disgusted expression on his face. When he saw Mad Dog, though, his look turned to one of cold triumph.

"Grace Madox," he said, his voice curt. "I see you've been outwitted at last. Don't worry, there are plenty of your old friends back on the Level who will be happy to see you pay for what you've done."

Choker jerked Mad Dog to a halt, and Mad Dog—Grace Madox—looked up at the Level officer. Her expression was weary, but there was still a spark of that burning fury Toothpick had noted when he first met her.

She turned and spat disdainfully at his feet.

"There. You see? Alive and as defiant as she ever were," Vin said.

"Does she have any kit with her? I'll want that as evidence."

"Aye," Vin said. "She's got her coat and weapons. I'll have them fetched." He turned to Toothpick. "Go on."

Mad Dog stumbled a little as Toothpick let go of her arm, and the movement put her mouth near his ear for a moment. "Get your friends, find yourself somewhere else to be," she whispered, then Choker yanked her upright again.

Toothpick didn't dare glance at her. "Captain," he said. "Permission to bring a few with me? Don't know where Mad Dog's stored her gear, and don't want you to wait for it."

The captain nodded impatiently, and Toothpick jerked his chin at where Vee was standing by Mirage and Reitta.

They followed him out of the airlock.

"What the hell you playing at?" Vee hissed the moment they were in the corridor.

"Something's going to happen," he said shortly. "We'll get the gear, hand it in, and then we'll get ourselves into the nearest ghost-lock."

Rietta's expression was skeptical.

"Ain't got time to argue," Toothpick hissed. "You pick your bet. But I figure I've picked mine, good or ill."

"I ain't going against the captain." Rietta's voice was sharp with fear. "You going to listen to some Level traitor, or the captain as holds our contracts? You do this, Toothpick, you ain't going to survive it."

Vee glanced between them. "If Toothpick trusts Mad Dog, that's good enough for me," she said at last.

Mirage nodded. "I'll take Vee's judgement on this one," they grunted.

They were in the crew's quarters now. Reitta took the bundle of Mad Dog's belongings. "I won't turn you in, but don't expect me to speak for you when he catches you." She looked around at them one last time, then started back for the airlock.

Toothpick turned and strode quickly back towards the galley. There was a porthole that looked through to the airlock, and with the lights off, they could watch through it without fear of being seen. They'd just have to hope the captain would be distracted enough by the credit chits that he'd put off hunting them down until after Mad Dog had done whatever she was planning.

"Mirage, Vee, take up places by the door," he said. "I'll watch, see if he sends someone after us." He glanced around grimly. "I figure we can hold our own here for a bit if this don't pan out."

From the look on Vee's face, she knew as well as he did that if Mad Dog's plan, whatever it was, didn't go through, they were as good as ghosts already. But she didn't say anything, just drew her cutlass and moved to stand by the door as Mirage sealed it behind them.

Through the porthole, Toothpick could see Reitta step through into the airlock. She handed the kit to the captain, who snapped a question that Toothpick could guess at easily enough.

A voice from above him made him jerk in surprise, and when he glanced over, he saw Vee had flipped on the internal comm.

"...don't get back here quick-time, they'll get a flogging they'll have cause to remember," Vin was growling.

"Aye, Captain," Rietta murmured.

"Go ahead, open it," Vin demanded, and Rietta unwrapped the ship's-cloth bundle that served as Mad Dog's trunk.

The rest seemed to happen all at once, and at the same time so slowly that Toothpick could take in every detail.

Rietta's look of surprise. The way it had just begun to turn to horror when the explosive hidden in Mad Dog's kit went off.

The scream, cut off instantly as the blast shattered the woman's face, the shrapnel that ripped across the cabin.

Mad Dog, already twisting out of the way before Rietta's hands had finished pulling the cloth open, using her momentum to bring Choker down, the shiv glittering between her fingers as she plunged it deep into the side of the first mate's throat.

The screams from pirates and Level sailors both as the shrapnel tore into heads and eyes and throats and chests. Bodies hitting the floor.

Mad Dog was on her feet again, blood soaking her clothing. She took two stumbling steps out of the airlock, then hit the controller with her bound hands and, grimacing at the effort, shoved her shiv deep into the mechanism to jam it.

It was only when another sharp scream echoed through the comm line that Toothpick noticed the blue haze forming over three of the bodies, one already a fully formed ghost.

The Level sailors were scrambling back to their skiff, but Mad Dog jammed her shoulder against the mag-lock. The seal-breaker inside the ship slammed down, impaling one sailor gruesomely against the now-shattered airlock of the skiff.

Toothpick turned away, not quite able to make himself watch as the ghosts tore into their victims, their ghostly claws and teeth shredding flesh and breaking bone.

"Unlock the door, damn you!" Vin screamed. His face was twisted in terror, eyes locked on Mad Dog's. "The credits are yours, ship's yours too if you want it! Open the seal and you can kill us yourself, but don't feed us to the ghosts!"

Toothpick was watching Mad Dog to keep from watching the slaughter inside the airlock. But the small smile on her face now was something that would haunt his nightmares.

"Told you," she said. "I ain't one for second chances."

She turned away. "Toothpick," she called over the comm, her voice still a little slurred. "Figure I could use a hand here, if you got a moment."

When they reached her, the screams from inside the airlock had faded. She gestured with a tip of her head. "Release the seal, but only enough to let the ghosts out. Don't want to lose the credit chits if we don't have to." She gave them a wry smile. "And I'd appreciate it if one of you'd cut my ropes. Toothpick's a hand with knots."

Vee stepped forward silently, pulling out her knife.

"The Level ship?" Mirage asked.

Mad Dog gave a one-shouldered shrug, cold anger glinting in her smile. "I'll be damned before I let any person try to take me and live through it. We'll shoot them down. Be easy enough, seeing as they won't be expecting it. A quick death is better'n they deserve, but I ain't got time to wait around."

Mirage saluted and turned away quickly, but Toothpick saw the fear in their face.

Mad Dog glanced at Toothpick, and there was a rueful amusement in her eyes that told him she'd seen it too. "Told you," she said, her voice low. "Don't forget an offence, but I don't forget a favour, neither. I'll split the take half and half with you. You want to split your share with the others, ain't my job to stop you."

Toothpick glanced through the small porthole and into the bloody airlock.

The pressure loss from the breaking of the seal had sucked the ghosts out into space along with the airlock's oxygen. The bodies had been dragged a little way across the floor as well, tangled together in a gruesome heap.

He recognized Vin's body, throat ripped open, face half torn off, and Choker, a crumpled heap in the corner.

He smiled a little, despite himself. "Aye, Captain," he said, turning back to her and saluting sharply. "Figure I can do that."

THEY MANAGED to limp the *Bloody Hand* back to Blackrock, even half-crewed as they were. Toothpick had split his share of the take with the other two—a one-sixth share of Mad Dog's blood price was still a bigger take than he'd dared dream of.

"You're a fair captain, looks of it," said Vee as she turned to go, meeting Mad Dog's eyes. "I'm fixing to sign onto my wife's ship if I can work it, but you'll find a crew quick enough."

Mad Dog smiled a little. "Ain't planning on signing anyone on for more'n a voyage at a time. But you can put the word out, I'd appreciate it."

Mirage nodded as well. "You going to captain the *Bloody Hand* then, rather'n sell her?"

Mad Dog shrugged. "Figure I will. But she'll need a new name." She paused. "*Sweet Jenny*'ll do, I think."

Mirage nodded. "*Sweet Jenny* it is, then. I'll spread the word." They grinned a little as they turned away. "And I'll spread the word that it don't pay to try to sell out Captain Mad Dog."

Then it was just Mad Dog and Toothpick standing on the gangplank.

"Know you said you weren't looking for long-term crew," he said at last. "But I figure even a ship like the *Sweet Jenny*'d do better with a first mate as knows her well."

Mad Dog raised her eyebrows. "Don't rightly want someone for more'n one voyage."

"Don't mean to sign on for more'n one voyage," Toothpick returned. "But that voyage goes well, I'd consider signing on for another."

Mad Dog paused. At last she gave him that small, sharp smile. "Well," she said. "Figure I could do worse than a first mate as would slip me a shiv if I needed one. Ain't going to make any promises, but we'll see how this voyage goes."

Toothpick found himself smiling as well. "Figure I can live with that," he said.

Pirate captain Gracie Madox has made a name for herself as the only pirate the Admiral herself is personally hunting. So when she shows up in the Stacks, her ship

damaged from a skirmish in deep space, to ask for a dry-dock, Recoil, the unofficial leader of the hardscrabble, ghost-haunted lower levels of the planetary settlement, knows better than to give it to her. But he can't afford to get into the middle of a pirate battle, either. So when Gracie proposes a solution—a game of supernatural Russian Roulette, where the winner walks away and the loser is devoured by hungry ghosts—Recoil can't afford to say no.

He can't afford to lose, either.

And with stakes like that, he's going to have to do more than send up a prayer to Our Lady of the Ghosts if he wants to walk out of this alive.

Download your free copy of Our Lady of Chance at:
dl.bookfunnel.com/a6sb7ufr49

Pick Your Poison

1. Gimme more of those twisted alliances! Head to "Rogue Negotiator" by Audrey Sharpe

2. Yeah. I know it's a trap. Go read "The Doubledealer" by Eric Warren in CROOKED V.1

3. Jobs gone wrong is so my jam. Turn the page to read "The Old Ship Job" by Arthur Mayor

THE OLD SHIP JOB

A SPACE STATION NOIR STORY

BY ARTHUR MAYOR

The room was tense. The six of us were all jammed into one of those cheap hotels in the Grays. You know the ones. Cater to all the Network runners that want to get off their ships for a couple of days while docked at the Station.

This one was chosen for its proximity to our target, not amenities. Thin, sluggish, cold-to-the-touch floor sand barely kept my claws from clicking on the underfloor. One of the chromatic walls had stopped working back before the Huns cut the Station off from the Prime world, the food prep area was small and barely usable for one person, and I have closets in my own apartment larger than the two bedrooms.

The main room, combination dining room, sitting room, and kitchen space, was crowded with foldable sitting baskets and all of the crew's gear.

I say crew and not team.

Sometimes it works. A dux gets the green light from their Boss and assembles a group from their Book, hires mercenaries, and the magic happens. A crew becomes a team. But mostly... not.

My partner Gunny is a monster, not a person, but he and I *are* a team. We've worked together for a year and half now. But the rest... not so much.

And the crew was tense. All our work might be for nothing.

"That's what I saw." Gunny finished his report and leaned against the wall, folding his arms. He towered over the rest of us sitting in baskets.

He towers a lot. Like all the time. Monsters are tall. Even the short ones are super tall. Five feet, for a monster, is short! And Gunny, even for a monster, is not short. He is very very not short. Why do monsters have to be so tall? Maybe if they spent less time growing and more time thinking about stuff, they could've figured out space travel, built their own wormhole network, and not been completely conquered and enslaved by a heretic break-away faction.

Kind of makes you wonder. What if there's a third sentient species out there? Will they be shorter than people? Have better technology? Conquer us? Scary thought.

"What if the treewalker is right?" Rufus didn't look at Gunny as he made his casual speciesist slur. Rufus did that a lot, not just to Gunny. With his aristocratic accent, all of his yellow and dark orange plumage in place, I don't even think he thought of it as insulting. He assumed we all knew he was better than the rest of us. He had a fancy education and his daddy came from money.

I think the joke's on him. His family lost all their money when the Huns took their home planet, and if his fancy engineering education meant anything on the

Station he wouldn't be tech support for a crew of criminals.

The next guy to speak was the exact opposite of Rufus. His accent was pure low living Space Station Noir. His brown and light blue plumage was anything but in place. He looked like he just woke up after a hard night of drinking. "We have to s-stop the j-job," Dim Wit stammered, his crest feather slamming flat on his head.

Now, at this point it's important to acknowledge the limits of the medium we're choosing to practice the art of the narrative.

Monster writing is great at capturing the sound of Monster words. Well, fine. But it's crap at copying real language. Gunny says we make chirps, whistles, and hisses. That's not how I would characterize it. So when monsters use their writing they have taken to swapping out names for things with Monster words.

All the monsters on the Station have an agreed upon lexicon for big things. For example, the Emperor is Fredrick, the space station we are on is Noir, the group of savages currently invading and collapsing Fredrick's empire are the Huns, and each of the factions that have broken off from the Empire in the last twenty years have their own names, that kind of thing.

But Gunny and I also do the same for people we know. It isn't like my dad called me Clive on my naming day. Most of the time our names are swapped out with Monster names—Rufus, for example—but sometimes they're descriptive.

"Shut up, Dim Wit," Gordon barked. But he used Dim Wit's real name so Dim Wit wasn't insulted. I mean, he was. He was just told to shut up, but not because he was called a dimwit. You get the idea.

Gordon was a little taller than me and bigger. His plumage was white and gray. A really bright white. If his plumage was all white we would look like brothers. A comparison that ended there. Gordon was not a mercenary, he was in Fernando's Book. He dressed like he was in a Book, too, and never let the mercenaries in the crew forget it.

"You're hired help," Gordon said. See what I mean? "It's not your call." He twitched his crest feather at me. "You took the job, you do the job. The most you can do is change *how* to *do* the job!"

"Gordon," Darla admonished. Darla ran the job, and was a beauty, with light brown plumage with splashes of vibrant orange. I really liked the contrast. Also, she knew how to dress. Wraps just draped on her. I don't know what vat the fabric came from but it was like spun starlight and rainbows. Plus, I always go for defined head ridges and you could cut glass with hers. And if you wanted me to talk about her tail... Well, it was like magic and desire given shape in a taut whip. Wow!

Darla looked at Gordon, then at the rest of us. "If a competing crew is in the area." She tried to sound regal, but her accent was pure low Station with a thin aristocratic candy coating. "Then we need more information."

"They were mercenaries," Gunny said. "Scouting out the docking ring. The target we're going to use." Gunny was sure.

So I was sure.

Rufus's plumage ruffled in annoyance. "So a tree-walker says." With a flick of his crest feather he showed how little that should count.

"Can't you go up the chain?" I asked. In the history of the Station Noir underworld, this wasn't the first time something like this happened. The Station is big, one of the biggest in the Network, but the different criminal elements still could trip over each other. Bosses developed systems to prevent gang war inducing misunderstandings.

Darla's crest feather twitched in the negative, but I think unconsciously. She cleared her throat and tried to look more regal.

"Ah, hell." Gunny caught the gesture, too. Also, he actually said, "Ah, hell." I'm not translating from normal speech on that one. Of the millions and millions of people who live or are just passing through Station Noir, I'm the only one I know of who ever bothered to learn Monster. So it wasn't like anyone else in the crew understood him. "This isn't a sanctioned job," he continued in Monster.

My plumage deflated. I couldn't unsee it. All the pieces fit: the low budget, the understaffing. This job was literally just the six of us, and Dim Wit wasn't even a member of the 147. He was a low-level dock worker taking a bribe.

Darla's teeth clicked together for a long minute as she thought. "If we do cross paths with another crew, I'm responsible. You're mercenaries. If you fulfill the contract, you have nothing to worry about."

That was the code, and sometimes the code mattered. More often it felt very lonely as those with connections started covering their tail feathers.

We could quit, of course. Then we would never get a job again. And best case would be poverty. Worst case would be a sudden trip to my ancestors. Not happening.

I inhaled to lay out the obvious plan. "Let me and Gordon scout it out." Then I lied. "We still have time—"

And everything got flipped.

The door to the apartment opened and two guys walked in.

That's right, the door just opened. No chime, no nothing. Only someone with the door codes should be able to do that. And these guys shouldn't have had door codes.

"Don't get up." They were both dressed like Gordon. Not a uniform but a uniform, if you get my meaning. The 147 has its own fashion.

The other one leveled his slender rod at Gunny, and twitched his crest feather for him to sit.

Gunny slowly showed his hands and raised them, then slid down the wall to sit on his butt.

Darla's fangs flashed and her crest feather went flat back in anger at the intrusion. "What is the meaning of this?"

I didn't know these guys from the First Emperor, but Darla did.

"I should ask you." A third person walked in behind the other two. He didn't have a stagger stick out. He was way too in charge to need a weapon.

And let me just say, stagger sticks look like slender little tubes until they're pointed at you. Then that small hole in front could be the Noir wormhole. They probably had non-lethal flechettes loaded, but you were never sure.

"Ricky." Darla showed her fangs again.

"So let's be quick," Ricky said. "I know what you're up to."

I looked at Gunny. Gunny was not looking at me. He was looking at Gordon.

Fun fact, Gordon was *not* sitting down. He wasn't before they entered, and he wasn't sitting now. He was standing behind Darla, casually putting his portal back in his pocket.

You know, I would have picked Rufus for the sellout. Just goes to show, sometimes the horrible aristocratic trash aren't the worst people in the room. I've learned a little lesson about making assumptions today, and I've become a better person. Dare I say, we all have.

"You're trying to... impress," Ricky said with derision, "Fernando with your ambition."

Darla looked mad, her crest feather flat back and quivering. The lack of a denial was pretty evident, too.

Ricky looked around in judgment. "You think that if you present the boss with enough credits and twitch your slender little tail at him, he'd make you the sub boss for the open territory." Ricky seemed to find the idea comical. "That you could steal MY promotion!" Ricky's fake geniality cracked and his crest feather flashed back level like a razor.

Dim Wit gave a squeak and tried to burrow into his basket.

"You deserve NOTHING!" Darla snapped back.

And Gordon smacked her on the back of the head. "Shut up, whore."

Ricky forced his crest feather into a neutral position and fluffed up his facial feathers.

"You--" Darla craned her head back, one hand with claws splayed resting where she'd been struck. If looks could kill, Gordon would be spread all over the broken chromatic wall.

"I've been monitoring your little enterprise from the start," Ricky said. "I think it was wise of you to call me in, since you're so over your head."

She didn't take that well. Gordon smacked her again. Not like someone trying to get someone to shut up. Like someone with a lot of issues coming out. "Stupid whore, ordering real members of Fernando's Book around." And there was the issue!

Confident that things had been resolved, Ricky turned to the hired help in the room. "Nothing has changed for you. Your contract was with the Fernando organization."

We could argue that point, and quit. We would have plenty of free time to argue whatever point we wanted between starving and not eating.

"And it's Go time." He clapped his claws together. "You know what you're supposed to do." He motioned with his portal and projected a countdown clock. "You need to get to your positions."

"But... what about..." Dim Wit stammered. "What... the monster said..."

Ricky looked at Gordon.

Gordon tossed off the concern with a casual flick of his crest feather. "The monster is jumping at shadows."

Ricky made an acknowledging shake of his crest feather. He knew how excitable monsters could be. Then, "DO YOUR JOBS!"

So, the thing about being a human in a hisser world is you don't expect to be believed. I raised that point when they sent me to do the final scouting. I doubt Darla would have pulled the plug on my word alone anyway, but it wasn't her call now. And Ricky didn't think humans could speak.

So here we are.

When you're a mercenary you don't get what you want, you get a job.

The next steps were straightforward. Dim Wit led us to a cargo crawler that was tasked with servicing the target ship. He got paid, and if Clive hadn't talked me into telling my side of this story, that would be the last time I thought of him.

Hisser crawlers come in all different shapes and sizes, but they're all automated. The ones they use like cars are big cylinders with hundreds of little legs, like a Coke can the size of a minivan that squashed an equally large centipede. The cargo ones had retractable loading arms.

The inside of this model was stripped down, empty space. So, like riding in a Coke can.

Me and three little hissers—Clive, Rufus, and Gordon —and all of Rufus's gear crowded in with some crates and rode the crawler right into the ship.

"Now we find out if you're worth the money." Gordon puffed up his facial feathers at Rufus in a menacing way and casually put his hand on the stagger stick in his holster.

"It will work," Rufus stated with confidence, but his plumage gave the lie. "This ship's sensors are old. My scrambler will run rings around it."

This was the first time I'd heard the ship was old. What I understand about hisser tech would fit on a three by five card with room to doodle. But what I did know was, the older the ship, the more experienced and mature the ship's Core. The Station's Core was over eight hundred years old, and Clive was always talking about how hard it was to outsmart the Old Lady.

Rufus looked at some projection fed into his eye. "We're being scanned." He did not say it with confidence. Then he started breathing. "And my scrambler worked." His facial feathers puffed up in relief. "It thinks we're the first load of..." Then he said something technical. See my note above about the three by five card.

A heartbeat later the crawler was moving again. If you've never been on a hisser umbilical, I would keep that streak going. The weird change from Station gravity to nothing to ship gravity always flips my stomach. Some people say they don't notice it, but they're lying. I also get a mild feeling of claustrophobia aboard a ship. Spent too much time with a slave collar around my neck on ships like this.

And the crawler stopped.

"Go!" Gordon activated the door, pulling his stagger stick as he leapt out the back.

Rufus grabbed a bag of stuff and followed him.

Clive gave me a look, a look I always interpret as "things are going to go sideways fast, I can't wait—so fun!"

Clive's the best partner I've ever had, but he's not okay.

And now I made my money. Hissers like Rufus may hate working with humans, but we're the best pack mules. I pulled the duffel of Rufus' gear, maybe sixty pounds of assorted hisser tech crap, on my shoulder and followed.

GUNNY WASN'T FEELING it yet, but this was going to be awesome!

I could just feel it in the ship's processed air. The plan was going to go right out the airlock and we would need to IMPROVISE! It's when you're improvising where the skills of crime meet the art. That's where the magic happens.

On the downside, the cargo bay stunk. It was kind of

the smell I associate with crash dens. Unwashed people jammed into a small area.

The space was empty, chromatic walls giving off harsh light, with no signs of life. The ceiling was high enough that I doubt Gunny could touch it, and about seven more cargo crawlers could fit in and still have room to maneuver.

The friction matting was covered with random trash, mostly prepackaged food wrappers but also other assorted crap.

Behind us, other crawlers with actual cargo and supplies were filing in through the umbilical waiting for ship crawlers to start unloading.

Gunny came out behind me with a pack strapped to his back. It was heavier than two and a half people, but it barely slowed him down. He also had his pistol out. It shot the same flechettes as my stagger stick, but fit into a big clawless monster hand.

We were off the Station, so my portal couldn't connect with the Old Lady. I could try and connect with the ship's Core, but that would announce our presence to all it may concern. Before we left the Station, I did load a ship map. I projected that for Gunny's benefit.

Gordon, leading from the rear, gestured us forward.

I'm the slicer, so I get to go first with Gunny at my back.

We got to the first door and it was locked. Kind of surprised me. I didn't think security would be that tight. I dropped to my knees and pulled out my slicer kit. My visualization paddles had the light knot hovering at eye level in less than a second.

My refractory hook spun through the light threads, and I had a lattice up in two hearts beat. It was like this

core had never even tried to lock a door before. A far cry
from going head-to-head with the Old Lady.

The door opened and the chatter of people talking
came down the hall.

"All our certifications are current." Someone was
trying to walk the edge of obsequiousness and reasonably
assertive. "I don't know why this inspection is necessary."
His accent was not from the Station. Could have been
from the other end of the Network. Starmaker's tools, it
could have been all the way from the Prime World for all
I knew.

"Surprise inspections don't need to be necessary."
That voice was pure Station Noir.

The ship outside the cargo chamber was more of the
same. Well-lit surfaces. Old but kept up friction matting.
The halls were narrower on the ship than the Station, of
course, but wouldn't stop Gunny from getting around.
The hall went straight or to the right. The voices came
from straight. Unfortunately, the same direction we
wanted to go.

Gunny pointed right.

Maybe Gordon would want something else, but he
could start leading from the front. I scooped up my kit,
pulled my stagger stick, and moved to the right.

What did I envision I'd find? Well, ship hallway and
friction matting. And it's not *not* what was there, but it
was also lined with... piles of fabric and small piping. And
the smell was worse.

I looked at everyone else, but their crest feathers were
bowed in confusion just like mine.

I shut the door behind Gordon. Did I think about
locking him in the cargo hold? Yes, I did. But I'm a
professional.

We moved down the corridor to where it turned left. It was like this main path was overflow storage for... I don't know, some kind of theater set?

The voices were moving toward the cargo area. We got around the corner without seconds to spare.

I peeked back the way we'd come.

At the cargo bay door were a few people. One guy was in a faded and wrinkled pair of overalls, like he had been too busy not sleeping to do laundry.

One of the other guys asked, "This the cargo bay?" That guy was in Sector whites, and if you weren't familiar with the Station's police force, you might believe they were legitimate.

Also, I knew the guy in the fake uniform. Bill was a mercenary in the 147. Not like we were close or anything. I worked on his side and on the other from time to time, but he always stood his ground. And if you can get him to tell you about the Blue 72 job, do it. That's all I'll say, do it! I was laughing so hard my facial feathers hurt.

Bill was not alone. Two other guys in B+ Sector looka-like uniforms were with him.

"That's cargo we bought from *your* station." The Network runner seemed on his last nerve, but also exhausted. "It hasn't even finished unloading. How could WE have smuggled anything with it?"

I pulled back around the corner. With a quick look at my portal, I made sure my work on the cargo bay door lock wouldn't be detected and the lock would work as it should.

"It's Bill." My crest feather almost folded up as I whispered to the rest of the team.

"Bill?" Gunny said. "That guy who backflowed the sanitation pipe into his crawler?"

Oh, and that doesn't even spoil the story. So good. Comedy gold.

"That's the guy." I gave a meaningful look to Gordon. "Looks like there *is* another crew in the field. Wish we knew that before."

Gordon's crest feather flicked at me in annoyance. He couldn't check in with Ricky. We were cut off from the Station's Core, so it was his call.

And he didn't make the right one. "Lock them in the cargo hold and let's go."

"If they're locked in the cargo hold, how do we get out?" Gunny asked. He must be getting frustrated because he didn't pretend to be a big dumb monster.

"Fine," Gordon snapped. "Tell us when the door is shut and we can get around them." Gordon twitched his eyes to look at a clock projection fed directly into his eyes.

I was feeling the time pressure, too. So exciting. Nothing better than a ticking clock to get all seven hearts going. Well, six right now, but I bet number seven is going to click on any second.

"They're mobile sleeping baskets." Rufus' crest feather twitched straight up in surprise at his own realization.

And once he said it, it was obvious. The fabric and the small poles that were kind of kicked to the walls were indeed mobile sleeping baskets. Hastily disassembled and moved, probably out of the cargo bay to make room for the supplies. There were enough baskets for maybe a hundred people.

Gunny leaned down and picked up a small hatchling doll, a few bald patches on the fake green feathers, one eye missing and its muzzle bent. "What is this ship?"

"You care?" Gordon challenged.

Gunny's nostrils flared and he dropped the doll. "I don't."

Once Bill's group were in the hold, we snuck back out and down the hall.

We made it to another locked door, and if anything, it was easier to open. It was almost like this Core wanted me to open the doors.

"What's wrong?" Gunny asked in Monster.

"This is too easy." I didn't know I was letting my concern show on my plumage.

"Trap?" Gunny asked in Monster.

I whirled my crest feather inconclusively.

"Move," Gordon ordered.

We moved.

Two more doors, each easier to slice than the last. I was beginning to feel I wasn't really needed for this job. A mottled feather with a decent visualization paddle and luminosity gauge could untie these knots.

I sliced another door. The intense musky smell hit me, then sounds from up the corridor and around a corner. Sounds of yelling and complaining. And "Move!" from someone with authority.

And that kind of authority came from a weapon. It's subtle, but if you've been in the 147 as long as I have you get an ear for it.

A shocked female voice said, "Station Noir does not have authority to—" And somebody got hit. Hit hard.

"I got all the authority I need." You also get an ear for those who love using that power. "All you get in there under your own power or after I stitch you up!"

Shocked complaints and frightened grumbling.

I got to the corner and peeked around to see what all the drama was.

Again, more fake Sector, bullying a really bedraggled and worn-out looking group of Network runners. I mean, these guys were of the shower optional, preen every month whether you need to or not kind of crowd. They were angry, scared, and had the numbers on the six fake Sector agents, but just didn't seem to have the energy or the will to resist.

And not all of them had the overalls I'd seen on the guy Bill was bossing around. Some did, sure, but the rest looked like a collection of civilian tunics. Tunics were popular on the Station like three hundred years ago, but still a fashion statement in some clusters.

I didn't recognize any of these fake Sector. They shut the door.

The Bully barked at one of the not-Sector standing next to him. "Make sure you get all of them. We're heading to the bridge."

Let's take a second. Bridge can't be the right word. I know what a bridge is and it's not where they were going. Why would there be a bridge on a ship? But Gunny insists. He's all, "This is my native language." I'm just saying, I did what I could, but got overridden.

Bully and his right hand bully moved off purposefully to the thing that is definitely in no way a bridge.

The other four walked purposefully toward us.

I held up all my claws and thumb on one hand alerting them to how many were coming.

The four of them didn't know what hit them as Gordon, Gunny, and I stitched them up, a soft electrical discharge sending them to a zap nap.

"Starmaker's whores," Gordon swore. His crest feather dipped down as he looked at one of the stunned fake Sector.

"What?" I asked.

"Nothing," Gordon lied and lied badly.

"You recognize him. You know who the other crew is working for." Gunny didn't ask.

Gordon looked at Gunny and twitched his crest feather. "Doesn't matter. We have a job to do."

"You look like it might matter," Gunny contradicted him.

Gordon snorted. "Stop wasting time!" He gestured for us to move.

Every door we came to was locked, but I might as well have had the key code at this point. And we came to the corridor that led to the ship's Core.

Without a map, you might walk by it. It looked like every other corridor, but this one was twenty feet long, ending in a dead end with a large security hatch.

"Who goes there?" someone demanded. The accent was Station Noir.

"We couldn't reach you," I called back, hoping my accent would make him think we were on the same team. "Any problems on your end?"

"No..." Then, "Who are you—"

Gunny stepped out and opened fire.

I leaned around the corner and did the same.

Two guys, fake Sector, guarding the core chamber door. They twitched as flechettes stitched them up, and face planted.

The core door was still shut. It looked large and imposing with "Do not enter" written all over it.

"Get the door." Gordon came around the corner.

"We're running out of time. I might not be able to—" Rufus protested.

And yes, we were out of time. The time display was blinking blue.

"Won't be a second." I flicked off the concern and pulled my slicer kit. Was that a little pump from heart number seven? I love my job.

CLIVE GOT to work on the door. He looked like he was enjoying himself.

"So whose crew are we messing with?" I asked Gordon.

"None of your concern," Gordon snapped.

"We still want to do this? The risk this high?" I asked. "Call off the job. We'll back your call."

He looked up at me, half his fang showing, then at Clive. "How much time?"

"What is time?" Clive asked philosophically.

"He'll be faster if you don't bother him." At least that's what Clive always whines when I ask how long it will take.

Gordon flashed his fangs but turned back to the corridor entrance.

I felt as exposed as the two guards we just dealt with. There was no place to hide.

"This ship," I said. "It looks like six shades of crap." I was thinking of all the garbage everywhere. I wouldn't know if the ship itself looked good or not. "And there are crash addicts in the low Reds who dress better than the crew and passengers."

"So?" Gordon said.

"What's on this ship that's worth *two* crews' time?"

"It's not your job to know." I think even if Gordon wanted to tell me, he wouldn't on principle.

And, "You're right. Nothing I need to know."

"Done!" Clive said with triumph, stepping away as the door slowly opened.

We had rehearsed this part. Rufus went in as soon as the door was cracked enough to wriggle through. I had to wait a couple seconds longer for the thick door to open enough for me and Rufus' gear to fit through. Once in I put the pack where he pointed and pulled the straps so he could access his weird box made of crystal and dull gray blocks.

The core chamber was kind of a letdown. We couldn't actually see the Core. There was a blast shield concealing the crystal. I'd never seen one the size of a ship's core before, just the apple-sized ones that powered illegal vats.

If I remember apples right. It's been decades since I've seen an apple.

The controls, and again I'm no expert, looked different than other hisser tech I've seen. Was the difference stylistic or functional... I got nothing. But it did have an old and worn feel to it. Some scrapes to the housing and a part of the panel had been ripped up and covered with some kind of epoxy, like instrumentation once useful had been removed.

Rufus wasn't concerned by the difference. If anything, he was the calmest I'd seen him since... well, ever. He slapped two cup disk things on the blast screen. The second the last cup was attached the wires from the gear and cup both lit up in swirling rainbow colors.

Rufus tentatively tapped a control, though until he tapped it I would have called it a yellow patch, and dozens of projections sprang to life. "We are in! Full access!" he called to Gordon.

"Good!" Gordon sounded happy for once. We were making up time.

Rufus attacked the projections floating in the air, tapping on some and tossing some out of the way like pieces of glowing floating paper.

"That seems easy," I said.

"It was," Rufus mumbled distractedly. "That's why this ship was chosen. It's so old."

"I thought an old core made for a better core." That's about a quarter of my three by five card I was talking about earlier.

"It is." Rufus was in his element now and had the bandwidth to be all professorial as he worked. "But it depends what you have used it for. This core is probably excellent at caring for its crew, cargo, and navigating the real-wormhole space transition. But it obviously has little experience with security." His facial feathers puffed up and more projections appeared. "There you are."

The new projections were floating cubes of video feeds. He found one he cared about. It looked like the inside of a vault. Stacks and stacks of hard credits in boxes.

With a twitch of his fingers, we could see loading crawlers jump to life and start loading the credit boxes for delivery.

It didn't seem that fast, but he wasn't freaking out about the time, so we were ahead of schedule for once. Bully and his crew made our schedule meaningless, but why point that out?

Still, there was a strangeness. "Why isn't the other crew already in the vault?"

Rufus bent his crest feather. "I don't know." He made some more selections. "We might not be able to use the internal monitors to find them if they have a scrambler like we do, but I'll do a search for movement."

More images appeared. These were of three or four different rooms. I don't know what the rooms' original purposes were, but they were too small for what they were being used for now. Wall to wall, standing room only, blocks of hissers.

Some were clutching small duffels, some clutched green feathered children, and some clutched each other. Their crest feathers were down flat, but not in new fear. It was more like the muscles used to flatten the crest feather were exhausted and doing a half-assed job, but the fear was still there.

Different species, but I recognized it. I recognized it to my bones. I'd lived it. Twenty plus years ago, I was in a school gymnasium, not a spaceship, but everything else was the same. The dry terror, everything you thought was true and safe was a lie, your powerlessness poisoning your blood. "They're refugees." In my example I was a prisoner waiting on a slave auction, but there was overlap.

"Maybe..." Rufus said.

"Why would refugees have money worth stealing?" I asked.

Rufus tapped in the air and found a projection. "It's everything they were able to get off their gravity well as the Huns invaded... but most of it is aid from a cluster they passed through."

Rufus found another entry. "They found a world to take them in..." His plumage deflated.

"If they show up with buckets of credits," I finished.

"They will need to pay for life support systems, gravity webbing, and new production vats," Rufus agreed.

The other side of my metaphorical three by five card said all that stuff was expensive. Depending on how big of an area they needed to make livable, what we were stealing might only be a down payment.

So now the big question. Did I care?

Did I care?

Did I care?

If you lined up those quivering hissers and asked everyone to step forward who did a damn thing to help Earth, no one would move. Hell, how many of them had human slaves, slaves they abandoned to the Huns?

I had bills to pay and a contract that meant my life would be over if I broke it. I was a mercenary. I don't get what I want, I get a job.

Screw 'em.

"How much longer on the loading?" I asked.

"Fifteen minutes. It's going faster than my estimate." Rufus didn't sound as happy as he did a second ago.

"Great, give me a yell when you need this stuff carted up." According to our rehearsal I was supposed to stay in the core chamber until Rufus told me otherwise, but... there were all those projections... faces... and... I don't have to explain a damn thing.

I stepped out into the hall, breathed deeply, and wiped a gleam of sweat off my forehead.

Clive gave me a look. He had heard my conversation with Rufus.

So had Gordon. Gordon puffed out his facial feathers, but in a sadistic way. "Know what this ship is now, monster?" He dismissed me with a twitch of his crest feather and looked back up the corridor.

"No." Clive coughed so if you didn't know English it might have sounded like a sneeze.

I realized my pistol was in my hand and lifting toward Gordon's back.

And I'm usually the calm one.

I got control of myself without shooting anyone. Totally a moot point because a second later Gordon arched and dropped to the floor in an electric crackle.

For a half a second I thought maybe I did shoot him, but then I saw the guy at the end of the corridor.

"Back!" I sprayed a stream of flechettes at the corner our attacker came from.

"I don't know!" the shooter yelled. "They're in the core chamber."

So, I know I just said *back*, but I reconsidered. Or at least, I wasn't sure. How safe would we be in the core chamber? My three by five card was mute on the subject, and there was no time for a consult.

I ran up the hall as fast as I could.

A lot of the stereotypes hissers have about humans are dumb and annoying. But for some reason they think we're slow. Our legs are literally longer than they are, but we're supposed to be slow. They're never ready when I sprint.

"At least four of them," the guy said from behind the corner. "Get Bill and his guys down here now—" At least I'm sure he would have said now if I gave him the chance.

I did not.

I bellowed and dove out into the hall spraying flechettes at the corner like water from a hose.

Reporter was not alone. Another fake Sector was shoulder to shoulder. Easy pickings.

I landed hard on the friction matting, knocking the air

out of me for a second, but I rolled on my back to the right to make sure no one was on the other corner.

Clive ran after me and made sure the hall was clear on his own. "So when you say *back* is it like *bridge*?" He knelt down and picked up something that Reporter had dropped. It had the disk shape of a portal, but it was red.

"What's going on!" came from the disk as soon as Clive touched it.

"We got it under control." Clive tried to copy Reporter's voice, but how could he?

There was a pause, then, "Void Eater's teeth, who are you?" Maybe I was just hearing what I expected, but it sounded like Bully.

Clive bent his crest feather in question to me, then twitched it like it didn't matter and I shouldn't worry about it. "We represent a small but aggressive conglomeration of fin fruit producers." Then in a sing-songy jingle, "You can have it fresh, you can have it fast, you CAN have it ALL!" He tapped the non-portal portal. "How do I come up with this stuff? I just pluck it out of the air."

"Do you know who you're crossing?" Bully demanded.

"Crossing?" Clive said after unmuting. "We were invited. Not that fin fruit this fresh and tasty needs an invitation." Muted it. "I'm going to keep going with the produce thing until his head explodes. Oh, I love my job." Clive's facial feathers puffed up.

Right. Whatever.

I had gotten my feet under me and went back down the hall to Rufus.

"You think this is a joke! What puny sub boss do you work for!" I could hear Bully demand.

Clive was spending his time collecting stagger sticks

from the guys I just stunned. "Produce is never a joke. What is a joke is our competitor's prices!"

"Rufus," I said in a stage whisper. Hopefully Bully couldn't hear me over Clive's sales pitch.

Rufus' attention was split between his gear pack and peeking down the hall at me. His crest feather was bobbing straight up in surprise then back flat on his head in fear then back up to surprise. "They're preparing to disengage the ship." He said it like he'd just realized what was happening when I walked into the core chamber.

"You're messing with Isaac!" Bully screamed.

Isaac, I knew. He was one of the more powerful, bloodthirsty and violent bosses.

"Why would they disengage?" Rufus' crest feather stopped in its continual up and down to bow in confusion. "They won't be able to get the credits off the ship. *They* won't even be able to get off the ship." Then as if he was talking to himself, "Ship to ship cargo transports maybe?"

"Who has more control of the ship's systems? You?" I waved my hand at the Core behind the blast shield. "Or them?"

"Them." Then Rufus hedged. "I mean, I have more control over the things I built. With this." He pointed a claw at all the gear laid out in front of him. "I can control all the ship's service crawlers and loading and unloading protocols."

"Great. Park a loading crawler half in and half out of the ship's docking gate," I told him. "That might slow them down."

Rufus flicked his crest feather in agreement, tapping on his machinery and floating projections. "If I do that we won't be able to get the credits off the ship, either."

"Won't matter if they unhook the umbilical."

Another flick of agreement.

"Let me sweeten the deal," Clive said with customer service cheer. "We'll throw in twelve gift trays of rolled greens and our dried meat platter. Perfect Cycle Six gifts around the office. Or to impress that special someone's family."

"NO ONE WILL PROTECT YOU. ISAAC WILL DEMAND YOUR SUB BOSS' HEAD OR THERE WILL BE WAR!" Bully was getting very close to "head explosion."

"What else can you control?" I asked Rufus.

His plumage deflated a little. "I scrambled all the internal sensors. That was a contingency if we got discovered." He patted his device. Not sure if that was affection or he was activating something. "And I convinced the Core not to use life support against us... so far, at least. The people from the other crew on the bridge were trying to squish us with gravity."

Swallow. Hadn't thought about that.

"But the Core objected. For almost two hundred years its been caring for its passengers. It's not going to start killing people now"

Okay, good? And to summarize, "To get off this ship with our score we need to take control of the bridge?"

That deflated all of Rufus' plumage. "Yes, or come to an arrangement with our competitors."

"We need to leave!" Clive called.

Long story short, now that everything was hooked up, Rufus could control his stuff from his portal until he got out of range of his equipment. And Clive could use a device he called a "door stopper," something he claimed was his own design. And when I say claimed, I mean always and often. Maybe it was as cool as he said. I don't know.

But the door stopper scrambled the lock so it was harder to open a door, even if you had the original door code. He gave the treatment to the core chamber.

Another moral quandary, but against my better judgment, I picked up Gordon and tossed him over my shoulder. Maybe I could use him as a meat shield or level a table.

"Can they track us with that thing?" I nodded at the red disk in Clive's hand.

"Yes," Rufus said.

But at the same time Clive said, "Only if we let them." He started to pull out his slicer kit.

I shook my head. "We can make that work."

Gᴜɴɴʏ ꜱᴇᴇꜱ ᴛʜᴇꜱᴇ ᴍᴏᴍᴇɴᴛꜱ ᴅɪꜰꜰᴇʀᴇɴᴛʟʏ.

But I love them.

These are the moments that make the work worth it. When you can toss out the plan, look the Void in the eye, and say, "What you got? We can take it!"

There were two ways onto the *bridge*.

Nope, still can't get past it. Not what a bridge is.

One way is the elevator and the other is the crawler entrance. The crawler entrance wasn't for loader crawlers, of course. Monsters should really come up with better names than *crawler* for all automatons, but not a problem I'm going to solve now. Starmakers' whores. I'm talking about a platform to connect two spaces separated by a gulf for the control center. There are problems with the naming system.

The crawler entrance was for smaller cleaner and food service crawlers. The tallest of those stood two feet, so the path was low.

I had to bend over and could still feel my crest feather rub against the ceiling.

Gunny was on his hands and knees and it was a little tight. I know this because...

"This is so damn tight!" Gunny grunted, again.

Making it more awkward, Gunny had to move Gordon's unconscious body by shoving him forward.

"We're there," I told Gunny.

He made a noise that I associate with half relief and half "I'm still Gunny so everything annoys me."

The access to the "bridge" wasn't locked, exactly, but there wasn't a hand access so I still had to slice it open.

And I thought the corridor doors were easy. There wasn't even a knot. I just selected the threads already laid out. The light threads practically jumped onto my lattice.

"What's wrong?" Gunny asked.

He must have seen my plumage deflate a little. "Nothing." My shoulders slumped. "It's fine." Would be nice to get a really good knot in on this job. Especially at the final moment of our quest. A kind of do or die thing, you know? I mean at this rate my skills are going to atrophy. Or I might fall asleep. "Quiet," I warned everyone, and broke the sound proofing by opening the crawler entrance a crack, not even enough to slip a chin feather through.

"Where are they!" Bully demanded from someone.

"They could be in the core chamber," another voice answered. "We still can't get that open."

And they wouldn't be able to, either. I allowed myself

a little laugh. I am so good at this. I mean, really impressive.

"We almost have the loading door free." If I had to guess, I would say that was a projection of Bill. "But as soon as we get one crawler out of the way another one takes its place. We're running out of room to stack them in here," Bill said with the unshakable voice of experience. That guy backfilled his escape vehicle with excrement once, and lived to tell the tale. He knows things do not always go to plan. "I need help."

"My team is close." Another voice from a different projection. "We found the communication disk on a cleaning crawler." That guy was annoyed. "It was a distraction."

Gunny's plan worked. Drew more of Bully's guys off the—in no way actually a—bridge.

Bully screamed and pounded his fists into something hard, probably a control console. "Get the internal sensors back up!"

"I'm trying," a terrified and not Station-accented voice said. "They've done something at the Core. I can't get around it."

"Bill!" Bully yelled. "As soon as you get it cleared we are disengaging and doing a floor by floor sweep."

"It will just be a few more minutes. They're running out of crawlers." Bill didn't sound too confident.

"Station control is asking about the delay," a very Station accent said.

"Explain we're having technical issues. It will be resolved soon," Bully said in a growl. "This ship is so old they'll believe that."

My guess? At least four hostiles on the bridge. Bully, the guy talking with Station Control, and at a minimum two guys to watch the press-ganged ship personnel at the controls.

Now it would all come down to luck. Was anyone looking at the crawler door?

I just felt heart number seven start pumping!

This is amazing!

I opened the door full and looked for a target.

The ship's *whatever you want to call it but it is certainly not a bridge* layout was old-fashioned. Everything was set up for there to be a "front". It was still a circular room with the domed walls projecting the image of the exterior of the ship like we were standing on a disk in space. That was still how the bridge was set up on the new ships.

The half of the ship that faced the dome of the Station looked like it was pressed against a wall. On the other half you could see the domes and cylinders of the bottom of dozens and dozens of other ships.

The wormhole, the platform to open the wormhole, and the lines of ships getting ready to use it were on the other side of the Station and not visible.

Which is too bad. It's quite a sight.

On the bridge, instead of everything being a circle with the captain's basket in the center, it was more like stadium seating with the floor at a slight angle and a command basket on the topmost elevated row.

The Starmakers *love* me. The captain's basket was empty or someone would have been looking right at me.

All the controls had polished stone veneer instead of a more modern look. As a rule, I'm all about the current fashion, but the vintage thing this ship had was working for me.

The crawler door came out in the center of the downward floor angle and there was a row of control panels with corresponding baskets, but no one was at those controls.

A quick look to the right and left. The coast was clear. I darted across and kept low.

I motioned for Rufus to do the same.

Still no, "Hey, what's that!" Or a "Hey, what's that!" equivalent. So, good.

Gunny looked both ways, and then scampered over on one hand and knees. With the other hand he dragged Gordon with him.

So, I think I called it. From my hiding place I only saw four crest feathers dipping and bobbing. There could be four or five members of the original crew, but I wasn't going to see their crest feathers. They must be terrified. Their crest feathers would be flat on their scalps.

Rufus found a control panel, tucked under it, and started taking things apart.

Not sure what Rufus was doing, but let the Star-makers guide him.

Gunny got his feet under him, but stayed low. He pointed for me to go around the far end and he would go around the other.

I twitched my crest feather in assent and moved out.

There was one guy by the main door. He was in the fake Sector uniform, and judging by how deflated his plumage looked he was not having fun.

Door guard duty does suck. I get it. But if you're not enjoying crime, what are we doing here?

"Bill!" Bully yelled.

"Starmaker's whore," Bill said in exasperation. "We got a loader now trying to right the ones we already tipped over. This will be another minute."

I would like to know how they were tipping the crawlers over in the first place, but go Rufus.

Gunny bellowed like the very Void Eater had been unleashed on our souls and then the thrum of stagger sticks and the electric discharge of zappers filled the air.

Followed very closely with screams of fear and return fire.

Door Guard didn't have a chance, and I'm okay with that. I moved up the next row of control panels.

"What are you idiots doing here!" Technically a question, but he was giving off a lot of exclamation point energy, so I made an artistic choice.

I shot at him, but my flechettes discharged harmlessly on a control console a few inches from his shoulder.

Bully and the guy who was talking with the Station Control—and I might feel dumb when I actually get a good look at him, but he sounds like a Randy, so I'm making the call. Bully and Randy were the two guys still standing.

"Get back to the bridge!" Bully screamed.

"We're on the bridge!" I called back, then realization. "Oh, you weren't talking to us." Awkward.

"Bill!" Bully screamed, and a few other names but they aren't important so no need to list them. And no one replied. "What did you do!"

Was he talking to us now? I can't tell with this guy.

I saw movement and aimed to fire, but held as I realized it was a person in the ship's overall uniform. We made eye contact and he froze.

I waved him on.

He kept crawling.

"I don't get it," Gunny called from the far right of the room. "How are you going to get the credits off the ship?"

But at the same time, Bully demanded, "How are you going to take the ship with four guys?"

Then again, at the same time, Bully said "Credits?"

And Gunny said, "Ship?" Gunny was the first to hit him with a follow up. "Why would a Station Noir crime boss want a beat-up old ship?"

"To sell it to the New Empire's fleet." Bully was still giving us "you're an idiot" tone.

Randy ducked his head out. I took a shot and he took a shot. We both missed and took cover.

"Okay," Gunny allowed, taking a shot of his own. I didn't hear a body drop and he cursed in Monster so I'm prepared to call that a miss. "Why THIS ship?"

"It's registered to a cluster that has fallen to the Huns. No one will miss it," Randy piped in like it was obviously why we were all here.

And now that I hear a little more, I was wrong. Not a Randy. More like a Daniel.

I crawled on my hands and knees to a small space between control consoles. I saw movement, but it wasn't Randy—sorry, Daniel—or Bully, but another ship crew member balled up on the floor.

"And you think the New Empire is going to want an old cargo ship?" Gunny was tossing the idiot vibe right back at him.

"Not the ship, the ship's Core. The New Empire is making the largest armada the Network has ever seen." Bully was tipping his pro New Empire position.

Just some quick coordinates. The New Empire is one of those breakaway groups that I mentioned before. They're a big deal in this end of the Network.

"This Core is going to be a battleship?" Gunny laughed.

I moved up a little more. I was getting a good bead on everyone's location as they yelled at each other. Which was Gunny's plan.

"Not a battleship. A scout ship." And Bully and Daniel were doing the same thing to Gunny. They jumped out of cover right behind Gunny.

Gunny spun, catching their volley of zappers with Gordon.

And I stitched them up from behind, exactly like Gunny planned it.

Gunny dropped Gordon and vigorously shook feeling back into his hand from the zapper nimbus. "That was close."

And now that I saw Daniel, all stunned and peaceful... I have to go back to Randy.

"Why couldn't he reach his people?" Gunny asked.

"I jammed their communicators." Rufus stood up.

"Rufus for the win!" I was impressed. I thought he was just curled up in a ball praying to his ancestors.

Rufus weakly puffed up his crest feathers at the praise.

Two people in overalls stood up and Gunny almost shot them.

"It's okay," I said. "You're safe."

Gunny gave me a look.

"You're here to steal all our money," one of the crew accused. "You're taking our one chance for a new home."

"That's true," I allowed. "You're *safer*." And to pad our stats a little, "We aren't going to send you to a New Empire labor camp."

"Please." The other guy gave us possibly the most pathetic beg I've ever heard. "We've lost everything, everyone." And only the thinnest of hope. "I've tried so hard... but." All his plumage was quivering. "Please."

Gunny sniffed, and his eyes went cold. "Yeah, I know how that goes."

"I was on a ship like this," Rufus' voice was low. "I made it to the Station. My family—"

"We are mercenaries." Gunny cut off the discussion. "We decide how to do the job, not *IF*."

The crew member twitched like Gunny screamed in his face.

The room that wasn't a bridge was silent for a long minute.

"Now lower the jamming," Gunny ordered. "We need to explain things to Bill and whoever else."

Rufus' shoulders slumped, but his crest feather slowly wobbled in the affirmative. But then, "We could—"

"We could do our job," I cut him off, but without heat.

Whatever was keeping the ship's people's plumage aloft finally gave out and it all compressed like they were wet.

I don't mind being a criminal, but I don't like being the bad guy. I looked at Gunny.

He looked away.

"I think we could—" Rufus started again.

"You're not a rich school kid anymore," I countered, the heat in my voice not really directed at him. "You sold your right to think anything when you became a mercenary for the 147!"

The ship's crew both took a sitting basket like they just couldn't stand anymore.

"Yep," Gunny finally looked up. "We are mercenaries. We do the job we are hired for. The only thing we can change is the method." Then to Rufus. "Open a connection to Bill."

"You think he'll work with us?" I asked.

"We have control of life support," Gunny said. "What's he going to do?"

"You're late," Ricky said to Clive, like I wasn't there as we walked into the small private warehouse.

Ricky sat on a folded basket, flanked by his goons. Darla was standing at the far wall, also flanked by a goon. Her plumage was deflated, her muzzle pointed down.

There was nothing else in this empty room. If I remember right, it was smaller than a two-car garage.

"Where is the rest of your crew?" Ricky asked.

"Rufus said you intimidate him." Clive bowed his crest feather like he couldn't imagine why.

I readjusted the bag I had over my shoulder and pulled Gordon out far enough to be identified. "Still zap napping. Where should I put him?" I asked in my "I'm just a big dumb human, no reason to worry about me" voice.

Ricky's crest feather twitched in annoyance. He dismissed Gordon and me with a look, his attention back on Clive. "Where are MY credits?"

I put on an act of being lost, stumbling to the back of the warehouse by Darla and setting the bag down gently. Intelligent people can disagree how gently.

"We ran into a bit of an issue on that end," Clive said. "Turns out another crew *was* working the same job."

That sent all the crest feathers straight up.

"Let's talk about the job." I pitched my voice for only Darla.

The goon on the other side of her knew I was talking, but I was just a big dumb monster so whatever I said wasn't important. What Clive was saying was the main event. Guard Goon took a couple steps forward so he could hear better.

"What about it?" Darla didn't want to talk with the monster, either.

"As far as everyone is concerned, the contract we took was with you," I said. "So you decide if we fulfilled it or not."

She snorted. "After today, no one is going to care about my lunch order, never mind a contract."

"Who did the other crew work for!" Ricky's false bravado cracked like an egg.

"Turns out," Clive said nonchalantly, "Isaac. In fact, it was directly his operation."

Ricky's crest feather dropped to his scalp. "Did they identify you!"

For the first time since Ricky entered our story, Darla's crest feather perked up. "Fernando would sacrifice us all to keep Isaac happy," she murmured.

"No, no," Clive said, like the notion was insane. "They didn't know what hit them." He looked at his portal. "Oh, and here is your delivery."

The loading gate opened and two cargo crawlers approached.

Clive got out of the way as the goons came forward.

Darla's crest feather deflated. "The job was to steal the credits. You did it."

"No," I countered. "That wasn't the job."

I pulled her to the side door Clive was already at.

"The *Job* was to improve your chances of promotion. The credits were just the How. As mercenaries, we can change the how."

We got out the side door the second the cargo crawlers opened.

"Who in all the Void do you think you are playing with!" Bully screamed from inside the cargo crawler.

I could hear Bully and all his armed men stomping out of the crawler.

"I... I..." Ricky stammered.

The side door shut and we kept walking.

LATER, Gunny and I were on a stakeout job. Not important to the story, but someone spending a lot of money. Was it his or his boss'? I'm sure it was innocent, but our employer was not.

"A ship just docked and gave me a data drop from Rufus." I looked over the information displaying on my portal.

"Rufus?" Gunny was surprised. "He's still alive?"

"I guess, at least a week ago when he posted this," I reflected. "I was surprised he stayed with the refugees."

"He wasn't cut out for the 147," Gunny said.

Had to agree. "He says with his tech skills he was able to stretch those aid credits further and they are on their way to a functioning colony." I showed Gunny a projection of green feathers chasing each other, laughing on some beach.

"Great," he said, but like something sticky was on his foot. "Happy ending."

I pocketed my portal. "Happy ending for Darla, too. She got the promotion."

"Yep." His foot was really sticky.

"So we helped someone willing to steal from refugees." Just calling it like I saw it.

Gunny inhaled and exhaled. "We're mercenaries. We don't get what we want, we get a job."

Thanks for reading. Gunny and Clive's story continues in the complete series, <u>Space Station Noir</u>.

Pick Your Poison

1. *Let's make this heist extra heisty.* Head to "The Alshaita Uplift Job" by Mark Teppo

2. *Let's make this heist extra weird.* Go read Narrow EscApe by Maddi Davidson in CROOKED V.2

3. *Let's make this heist extra techy.* Keep going to read "Proof of Life" by MJ Blehart

PROOF OF LIFE

A FORGOTTEN FODDER STORY

BY MJ BLEHART

THE REQUEST FOR CONTACT HAD ARRIVED VIA THE usual channels.

Feroz could be reached by a very limited few. Requests for contact were via a whole lot of different blinds, diverted channels, encryptions, and algorithms. These served two purposes. First, keeping Feroz relatively off the grid; and second, protecting the people who might seek him for his services.

The encryptions and algorithms he created to maintain his anonymity, in addition to spoofing any network he was on, were some of the best you could have. Feroz was sure of this. That was because he'd created them.

Before the prior plans he'd been part of had all come crashing down, Feroz had taken great care in cultivating all sorts of useful relationships with people both high and low. He had associates who could get him burner data-pads and datacards for single-use, as well as connections to get top-of-the-line infodrives and communications gear.

Feroz saw the value in redundancies and variable

contacts at different ends of society. He was, first and foremost, a survivor. He may have been among the most wanted criminals in the AECC, but that wouldn't stop him from remaining part of the game.

He paused a moment before opening the contact request, stress sharpening the ache in the center of his chest. Months later, even with plasma-proof gear, short of an armored shell or full armor, getting shot by a laser hurt.

Feroz had been shot twice in the chest, and the impact had stopped his heart. It had restarted almost immediately after, but the pain and trauma had kept him unconscious. Fortunately, his associates had gotten him clear.

Still, Feroz remained bitter. He'd made a mistake, his overconfidence getting the better of him. He'd fallen for the most perfect forgery he'd even seen, a clever deputy marshal, and underestimated a clone.

Four months since the failed operation, Feroz had been laying low. The whole plan had collapsed, and the people he and his companions had been working to bring down remained in power. Some had even gotten stronger. Then, most of his companions were found out and arrested. The trials had begun, and Feroz caught video of them from time to time.

Feroz didn't intend to share their fate.

At first, he'd used extra precautions. He'd been the best cryptanalyst in the Confederation Bureau of Investigation, so he knew exactly what he was up against and knew that anything he left behind could be traced. Apart from the CBI agents that he'd trained, a select few were his equal.

Fortunately.

Initially, Feroz had stayed relatively underground and used burner coms, datapads, and datacards. He remained in the suburbs and around colleges in the cities, as well as other atypical locales a man on the run might hide out. He made almost no use of the accounts and other things he'd set up in case his plans had gone sideways. To all intents and purposes, Feroz Jones had vanished into thin air.

Cautiously, at the end of the second month, he started to make his way to the places where he'd stashed things. He stalked them, staked them out, but never visited them. He remained constantly on guard, wary that they would not have given up the search for him. He let one or two of his most trusted contacts know he was still out there but shared nothing of value with them.

In the middle of the third month, he collected some of his stashed things. He'd placed himself back in the network after setting up numerous new blinds, encryptions, and algorithms. Feroz remained as off the grid and out of sight as he possibly could.

The contact request had been from a channel Feroz trusted implicitly. Only someone very powerful and very important could have reached him that way. This would be an opportunity to potentially stop hiding and start participating in new plans and operation.

Unless he could adequately fake his death—which he knew was impossible given who he was up against—Feroz had to be extra cautious. He'd removed his goatee and wore a wig when he was out and about.

Facial recognition software and AI wouldn't be fooled, but he had some tricks up his sleeve to deal with them, and could avoid them at least semi-regularly. The real concern was getting spotted on a camera or in person by CBI agents, informants, and others who would be on the lookout.

He paused at the front door and checked to make sure that the wig was settled, his contacts were in, and that his hood didn't look too obvious. At least there was a light drizzle out there.

Feroz left his dwelling. He checked his surroundings as he started down the street, making his way to the vehicle rental lot. He'd already reserved a car for the trip from his suburban hideout to the spaceport.

He passed a few people out in the rain, largely walking dogs or heading to their homes from the carshare. Between the weather and the tendency of people in the local area to keep to themselves and seldom acknowledge anyone else, nobody paid Feroz any mind.

He reached the carshare. This was where the most risk would be until he got to the spaceport. He took his time, knowing where the cameras were and doing his best to make certain that he angled to keep his face from appearing clearly. Even with the glasses and contacts, his eyes might still give him away to facial recognition AI systems.

He got into the car quickly and closed the door. He made a show of looking over the dashboard and instrument panel, striving to keep his face from being clearly visible through the windscreen. He started the car up, fed power to the lifts, and glided out of the lot.

Once Feroz was on the road, he relaxed some. He set the car on road-guidance, allowing the autopilot to take him from the suburbs to the spaceport. Though he couldn't completely avoid surveillance systems, so long as he was just another commuter using a car on the road, he should have no trouble maintaining his anonymity.

This was another advantage of the car's autopilot. It made the chances of getting into any sort of accident or traffic jam practically zero. Avoiding being seen in plain sight was frequently a matter of acting normal as much as practical.

Feroz checked his datapad. The flight arrangements were all set. The challenge would be getting to his destination and doing what he needed to get on the necessary starship. He was still avoiding travel that included any form of public transport, like a passenger liner.

The last few times he'd moved from world to world, he'd once gotten packed as cargo, once joined as a part of the shipboard crew for a corporate transport, and another time acted as a uniformed employee for a different company on someone's private yacht.

This time he'd be boarding a private yacht as an invited guest. Fortunately, he trusted his contact enough that he was certain they would not be setting him up. They had similar interests, after all.

Those who had already paid for being part of the conspiracy were not alone. Others were still out there. Feroz had known there were enough moving parts and people involved that, no matter how good the CBI was, many would stay under the radar. They'd bide their time for another opportunity. That was, he suspected, part of why Feroz was being asked to make contact now.

Just outside the spaceport, Feroz disengaged the autopilot. He wasn't going to the main terminal, but instead the private landing pads and bays east of the main port.

Feroz drove around in a wide arc, avoiding where he

knew the cameras were. He made his way to an appropriate lot and left the car there. The rain had sped up some, so the hood made him even more inconspicuous.

There were several ways into the private landing bays, but none were on foot. Feroz, however, knew that multiple automated transports passed the way he was going. He awaited one of the small trucks, hovering less than a meter above the pavement. He grabbed ahold of a bar on the back and rode it in, turning on a personal suppressor as he did.

The device was good for short-term use. The "hole" it created, however, made it impractical for long-term usage. There were very few places, and none that Feroz knew, where you could be entirely absent from the grid. At least, if you cared to be anywhere other than nowhere.

The automated vehicles passed through an equally automated checkpoint. Once on the other side, Feroz jumped off.

When he was able to leave the main thoroughfare he turned off the suppressor. Given all the signal traffic within the spaceport, being a virtual "hole" would draw far too much attention.

Feroz had committed to memory which landing pad he needed to go to. Doing his best to avoid cameras and sensors, he made his way there.

The yacht was similar to many Feroz had seen. It was considerably larger than one of the CBI's bigger troop shuttles. Given the status of the owner and possible passengers, he knew there was a significant disconnect between them and the crew. This meant there were fewer people who might see him and potentially identify him.

The crew on a yacht of this nature might be employees of the Office of Confederation Defense. He didn't think his contact or any associates would make use of them. Still, you could never be too careful.

Doing a final check for cameras, using a small datacard, he took a deep breath and approached the person standing at the base of the boarding ramp into the yacht.

"Can I help you?" they asked. Feroz could identify no gender for them.

"Yeah," Feroz replied. "Is it just me, or is this rain too wet?"

The person guarding the ramp snickered. "Degrees of wetness, or some such. You care?"

"Not at all," replied Feroz.

The person at the base of the ramp gestured, and Feroz ascended.

Another reason Feroz appreciated his associates was the caution they all took. Feroz didn't need to give his name or a false one. The person from the bottom of the ramp might have gotten a partial look at Feroz's face and heard his voice, but that was little to go on. This allowed for plausible deniability for his contact as well as his own added safety.

There was an open area where Feroz deposited his coat and hood. He kept his pack and wig, then moved towards the main compartment on this level of the yacht.

Because they were on the ground, the hatches were all open. Feroz made his way into a compartment that did not appear like what you'd expect on a starship. It looked like it had sheetrock walls, painted a calming sandstone color. There was art on them, and a faux fireplace along one. There were three viewports that could be turned into displays or left tinted but transparent, providing a view of whatever was outside the starship.

Feroz noticed a small dining table on a raised area

across the room, and what looked like hardwood floors beneath. The rest of the space featured a soft-looking carpet and a trio of half-circle couches, tables between each, and a larger table in front of them. It was tastefully designed and well-decorated without being too loudly opulent.

Seated on one of the couches was a very large, dark-skinned, impeccably dressed man. His suit spoke of wealth, his bearing of confidence, and his casual nonchalance of control.

"You must be Mister Jones," he said, arising. Feroz went towards him, stepping down onto the carpet and extending his hand. "I didn't expect you to be blonde"

They shook hands and Feroz chuckled. "Sometimes it's fashionable to be uniquely coiffed."

"Good to know you have a sense of humor," his host stated. "You can speak freely. I'm Doroga Usman."

Feroz didn't let his face show anything, but he knew now who his host was. Doroga Usman was not just some middle-manager or bit player. He was a powerhouse. As president of Interplanetary Business Infomatics, Usman had a great deal of power, sway, and ESCA.

Feroz reached up and removed his wig. He placed it on a table as Usman gestured for him to take a seat on one of the couches. "Would you care for a drink, Mister Jones?"

"Sure," Feroz agreed. "I'd love a gin and tonic. Haven't had a good one in ages."

Usman grinned, sitting back down on the couch and taking up a datapad. "I gather you've been in less-than-savory places of late?"

"Fewer than you'd think," Feroz replied. "Mostly, I prefer not to risk letting down my guard."

"Of course," Usman agreed. "Tell me something, Mister Jones. Where do your loyalties lie?"

"That depends," Feroz replied. "Sometimes the highest bidder. Other times, wherever I can stay safe and sufficiently comfortable. Mostly with myself."

A drone buzzed into the compartment. It glided in, hovering above the table, before descending vertically. It delivered a pair of drinks, then rose vertically again before departing the way it had come.

Feroz knew that independent drones of that nature could be more costly than paid staff. Certainly more than you could pay clones to do that kind of menial work.

Usman gestured the way the drone had departed. "I value my privacy. Apart from Mx. Laurent, who you met upon your arrival, there's nobody else with access to my compartments. The crew of the yacht are all in my employ."

"Smart," said Feroz, taking his glass.

Usman took up his own glass. "What about the Confederation?"

Feroz chuckled. "The AECC? I mean, they probably are more stable having survived the plan. For now. But they're imperfect in ways they just don't get. It's only a matter of time 'til something internal or external collapses the whole thing."

"And the Coalition? The Alliance?" asked Usman.

"Dead and buried," Feroz stated. "Certain short-sighted individuals I previously worked with had notions of restoring one or the other. But neither could have filled the vacuum a collapsed AECC would create."

"So you couldn't care less about who governs?" pressed Usman.

Feroz took a drink, considering how to answer. "Overall, no. That's because, really, are any governments in control? Maybe they set laws and give you order and a modicum of safety. But really, it's their bureaucracies that run the show on a day-to-day basis. Those are seldom political, and the people working them who fail to rise in the often *bhakvass* meritocracy get bought and paid for. So really, who governs? Not who, what. ESCA."

Usman grinned. "You're a cynic."

"No, sir," Feroz stated. "I'm a realist. Money talks. Even with UBI, to truly get ahead you need to either earn your ESCA or find an angle to otherwise bring it in. For example, you only get a vessel like this that way."

"You know who I am?"

"Of course," replied Feroz. "If I didn't, I wouldn't even be having this conversation with you, would I?"

Usman took a drink. He looked at Feroz for a moment, sizing him up. He set his glass back onto the table and said, "I imagine you'd like nothing better than to come in out of the cold?"

"Sure," Feroz replied. "But there's an entire bureau of people looking for me. My skills tend to make me noticeable. But yeah, I'd love to be able to be me and operate on my terms again."

"My associates and I figured as much," Usman said. "We'd like to offer you an opportunity to be part of something similar to your prior engagement, but with a broader concept and more varied approach."

"You and your 'associates' trying to take down the Confederation?" asked Feroz.

Usman shrugged. "Perhaps. That's not the primary goal, however. The specifics aren't important, at least, not at this time. But we could use a man with your skills to help us reach our various goals. As you know the CBI and how they operate, and worked with a few former acquaintances, we feel bringing you into our fold would be in our best interest."

"Not trying to take down the AECC has me intrigued," remarked Feroz. He took a drink. "If that was your main goal, I don't think I'd be interested. ESCA?"

"Among other things," stated Usman coyly. "Let's just say that the way certain entities function leaves a lot to be desired. My associates and I think that might be a better asteroid field to navigate."

Feroz chuckled. "No specifics yet, huh? You got a job for me as a test?"

"I do," Usman replied. He tapped a control on his datapad and a holographic screen appeared above the central table. "Recognize this?"

Feroz looked at what appeared on the display. It was some kind of infodrive, but beyond that, it wasn't familiar. "I know what that is, of course. But I don't see anything special or specific about it."

"So you're not aware of the R&D on this infodrive?" asked Usman.

Feroz looked more closely, but it wasn't ringing any bells. "No."

"Doesn't matter," Usman stated. "This is under active development by Gray and Chuang. At least, it was. Certain circumstances have placed its R&D on hold for the time being. That this has stalled is good for my interests, directly. However, an employee of Infomatics recently poached from Gray and Chuang let us know it was not simply speculative, but actively being assembled. Or at least, it was."

Feroz looked once more at the device on the display, and a memory struck him. "If that's what I think it is, it would be a major game changer in data storage, access, and processing."

"Exactly," agreed Usman. "Knowing that Gray and Chuang is closer to realizing this than Infomatics is, my interest has increased. Knowing that development is stalled, but a prototype was created, I'd very much like to get a closer look at it."

Feroz chuckled. "And you know that I've successfully hacked Gray and Chuang before. It'll be behind some pretty serious security, but that won't do more than make it take longer."

"You have part of what I want to hire you for," admitted Usman. "But there's more. See, my researchers have lots of theoretical ideas, but aren't sure how to move past that. The logistics aren't something I fully under-stand, as this is some next-level stuff. But I do recognize that reverse-engineering from prototype would accelerate things more than adequately."

"You want me to help someone break into a secure Gray and Chuang R&D department?" asked Feroz.

"No," Usman said. "That adds an unknown to an already chancy operation. I want *you* to break into a secure Gray and Chuang R&D department."

As a special agent in the Confederation Bureau of Investigation, Feroz had received a wide range of training.

Although he'd been accepted into the CBI, rather than prison, for his cryptanalytical skills, he'd still become a fully trained special agent. That meant he'd gone through coursework that included behavioral science, legal fundamentals, forensic science, counterintelligence, operations planning, undercover operations, and weapons training. While he'd not overly excelled in anything unrelated to cryptanalysis and all things computer and network-related, he'd proven himself adequate in the rest.

Hence, he approached his current gig like one part CBI stakeout and one part special operations infiltration. He'd partaken in one or two of those in the past.

The building where the Gray and Chuang research and development department was located was like most other offices in the city: a tall tower, an open plaza with sculptures, trees, a fountain, or some combination therein before it. Apart from the main public entrance, there would be a delivery bay, one or two private employee entrances, service and maintenance crew entrance, and a landing pad for shuttles and small craft on or just below the roof.

Feroz had multiple options for entry. The trouble was that each came with pitfalls. The employee entrance required identification and was well-secured. Scaling the building to reach the landing pad was idiotic. There was next to no way to do so without being noticed. He had no way to land on the landing pad above, and security there would be as tight if not tighter than employee security.

Service and maintenance was always an option. It was not hard to either buy your way into those crews, pay off security at the bay, or get a uniform and blend in quietly. However, the level of security was still unpredictable, and the risk of exposing himself and being noticed was too high.

It was also frequently a major clone employment source. Feroz felt his ire rising. One damned clone had been the reason that the previous plans had collapsed and why Feroz was in hiding. If that one clone hadn't been an unexpected witness to a clean-up operation, by the time the CBI would have otherwise gotten wind of things it would have been too late.

Feroz shook it off. That was not a helpful direction to take. He had a job to do, and it would not be an easy one.

The front door might well be his best option. While that came with a number of pitfalls, it was also one of the best ways to sneak in without sneaking.

While you still had to pass through security to get into the offices via the front door, it was more generalized. Most of the mid-level employees passed through the main entrance lobby since it was the most direct entrance accessible via public transit.

Visitors needed to sign in and were tracked. Employees passed through security via badges and biometrics but once in the building were free to move around within certain areas. A business like Gray and Chuang had different levels of security throughout the building.

Executive offices were more secure than other offices. Storage spaces had variable degrees of security. Research and development would be among the most secure, to keep away the curious, prevent theft, and deter corporate espionage.

Feroz had means to trick biometrics, though these were limited and wouldn't stand up to close scrutiny. When you were dealing with offices that held thousands of employees, there were limitations to low and mid-level security.

The other downside to this plan, however, was that Feroz needed to enter the building during the rush. What's more, that meant he'd be constantly having to look out for and dodge people at work. Arguably the best time for stealing something was in front of the masses, while that was also the worst time to steal something.

Fortunately, the lab Feroz needed to infiltrate was currently locked down and not in use. That would make the actual theft somewhat less challenging.

Feroz was nothing if not methodical. He'd spent the day before observing the comings and goings of Gray and Chuang's employees, visitors, and the like. He'd also hacked into their security and had learned the best ways to avoid notice. All the while, he'd been working out how, once inside, to get to the R&D lab and steal the prototype infodrive.

When you had the degree of skill that Feroz did, forging an ID badge was easy. There were only so many types of ID devices, even across all the colonies of the AECC. Getting the physical badge, in this case a tiny card fob, was a matter of "bumping" into a Gray and Chuang employee and lifting it off them. CBI training again coming in handy.

Doing so at the end of the day meant the employee wouldn't likely notice its absence until the next day. That meant Feroz could hack the contents of the badge and forge a new identity to it. When the hapless employee reported it lost the next morning, even though it would be deactivated Feroz would already have changed it to prevent its shutdown.

Dressing in business casual attire—a shirt, blazer, and khaki pants— Feroz joined the large crowd of Gray and Chuang employees entering the lobby. He activated his faux biometrics, which would scramble his eye and facial features in a way that the system wouldn't see as hacked but as a valid employee with a proper ID badge. Unless someone was looking at the system directly at the exact moment Feroz passed through security, he'd go unnoticed.

Gray and Chaung had offices in multiple cities on multiple worlds across the Confederation. They had millions of employees. Thus, an unfamiliar face in the lift would not draw much attention, since transfers, visitors from other branches and offices were regular, and new hires frequent.

The only danger was that someone might recognize Feroz Jones. Fortunately, he was wearing stylish AR/VR-enhanced glasses, a form-fitting wig, and a false nose. He was doing his best not to make eye contact with anyone. What's more, he didn't think he knew anyone working at Gray and Chaung presently, and the CBI had no reason to have anyone there.

Feroz made it through the lobby and onto the lift. He rode it up fifty stories to what he'd identified as central corporate administration. That meant a lot of employees dealing with customer service, sales, support, bookkeeping, legal integrity, and numerous other busywork a corporation the size of Gray and Chuang always had going on.

It never ceased to amaze Feroz that jobs long expected to be handled by AI and machine intelligence still needed human interaction and guidance. On the one hand it created added failsafes and security, while on the other hand creating potential points of human error and breaches of security.

That was why Feroz loved data, cryptanalysis, and hacking. There was a predictability in the machines and tech that humans and clones lacked.

Feroz exited the lift with the other employees. He

made a point of staying with the flow as long as he could, until he wound up at a restroom and went into it.

Feroz took a few minutes to let the masses settle into their routines, claiming a stall in the restroom. Unsurprisingly, several employees came and went. After fifteen minutes had passed, he left the restroom to get his plan underway.

Feroz made his way to the nearest stairwell. It would be locked as a matter of security. Systems were in place to unlock the doors in case of emergency, fire, or some other need to utilize the stairs. Otherwise, only maintenance and security had coded ID badges to access and unlock them.

Because of that, more advanced biometrics were not employed. What's more, while the system might note one of the stairwell doors being unlocked and opened, so long as an expected ID badge did so it escaped further notice.

There were cameras looking at the door and in the stairwell itself. However, Feroz had a dampener that would prevent them from taking notice of him. Unless he made a mistake and was otherwise detected, nobody would be checking the camera feeds.

Feroz had, of course, coded his forged ID to access the stairwells. Making sure nobody was in the hallway when he reached the door, Feroz used his stolen ID fob to unlock it. He made his way into the stairwell.

This Gray and Chuang office building was a hundred and ten stories tall. The executive offices, suites, and conference rooms began at the eighteenth floor, and went the rest of the way up. Central corporate administration occupied the forty-fifth through seventy-fifth floors.

Research and development ranged from the twenty-fifth to the fortieth floor. This was not wholly accurate, given that some of the labs were five stories or more tall. But the R&D lab Feroz needed was on the thirtieth floor. Fortunately, the stairwell accessed every floor, even if it only reached an escape catwalk or scaffold.

Quickly, but not too quickly, Feroz descended the stairwell. He took off his blazer, turned it inside out, then pulled down the panels that had been secured on the inner lining. He pulled the lab coat it had been transformed into over his shoulders.

Feroz reached the thirtieth floor. Before leaving the stairwell, he activated his AR/VR glasses. Connecting with his internal augments and tech implants, he was able to check the camera on the other side without security knowing he was there, to make sure it was clear before he entered the hallway.

The hallway was unoccupied. Feroz left the stairwell and entered the corridor. Effecting an air of nonchalance, Feroz strode confidently toward the lab he needed to access.

"Hey!" someone called out. Feroz did his best not to start, and turned to face the person who'd called to him.

A middle-aged woman in a lab coat approached. Hiding his nerves, but checking that he could easily access his pistol, Feroz said, "Hello?"

"What are you doing here?" she asked, sounding positively sure of herself. "I know everyone who works on this floor. You're not one of them."

"Oh," Feroz said, sounding relieved and equally uncertain. "I, uh, thought this was where the navigation systems research lab was?"

"You're part of Doctor Cruz's team?" she asked haughtily.

"No," Feroz admitted. "I was sent here by Doctor Baek to compare notes."

She looked at him skeptically, taking in his coat and his distressed manner. She sighed and said, "Well you're two floors up from where you should be. Can you find the elevator without help?"

"Oh, yes ma'am. And thank you!" Feroz said genially.

The scientist gave him one last look, shook her head, and then left him to go back on her way.

Feroz kept moving, taking no time to breathe a sigh of relief. He'd done his homework just in case something like that might happen. Doctor Kira Baek was the head of navigation systems R&D in a different Gray and Chuang office.

He reached the abandoned lab where the infodrive research had been carried out. Checking first visually that nobody was near, then once more using his AR/VR glasses to check the security feeds, Feroz went to work on the security lock to the door of the lab.

This would take a bit more finesse. First, the lab had been closed and sealed. Nobody had accessed it in some time. According to the data Feroz had pulled up, this had involved a former Gray and Chuang board director named Amelia Khatri. When she'd been indicted and convicted a month or so earlier, the project had been halted and those working on it reassigned or let go.

Had the new board known how far along the project had been, according to Usman, they'd not have shut it down so unceremoniously. Feroz wasn't concerned of that, save what he needed to know when he accessed the lab.

Laboratory security was among the best in the Gray and

Chuang offices. Between additional forms of ID and biometrics, regulating access was a high priority. While Feroz might have been able to get into an active lab, the odds of him being discovered where he shouldn't be were far higher.

When it came to a closed R&D lab, security was still impressive. However, once accessed, the biometrics would be offline. Getting access was the challenge.

Gray and Chuang employed top-notch cryptographers and specialists to set up, maintain, and run their security. Only a careful, patient, and skilled hacker stood a chance of bypassing them. Feroz had hacked into Gray and Chuang security before. That made this hack into their security to access the lab possible.

Fortunately, Feroz was the best. The mistake he'd made as a teen had been entirely due to his youth and impatience. Apart from that, he'd been told by the CBI deputy marshal that had caught him that he was the finest hacker he'd ever encountered.

Feroz was getting nervous. Nobody had entered the hallway for a while, and he didn't think he'd have long before someone did. He'd known this hack would take time and he could only stay relatively invisible to the cameras for so long. Anyone who found him messing with the lock system of the sealed lab would be a problem.

Despite being armed, Feroz knew that if he used his gun he'd set off all sorts of alarms and draw unwanted attention. It was a last resort, even as a deterrent.

Feroz's chest began to ache where the laser blast had hit him, ignited by the stress. He did what he could to shunt the feeling away, focusing on the work at hand.

The lab had been locked in such a way that only a few specific codes would be able to open it. This was typical when you were dealing with potentially volatile materials or ideas for something that you might not be actively manufacturing but didn't want someone stumbling upon. Locking and sealing a lab tended to be a post-accident, post-mistake move, or done because of the loss of a researcher, funding, or reaching a dead-end on a project that still had potential.

Feroz knew he wasn't preparing to enter a lab sealed due to an accident. With his knowledge of how Gray and Chuang operated he'd eliminated several code and encryption permutations from being possibilities. That both made it easier to work out what he needed, but harder due to fewer options.

This hack was a two-fold measure. First, he needed to work out what kind of code the encryption sought to release the lock. Then, he needed to spoof the code and feed that to the lock. Many hackers had small devices or datacards they used when performing a complex hack. Feroz, fortunately, had implants and cybernetics that, coupled with his AR/VR glasses, removed the need for such a tool.

He found what kind of code he needed to open the locked lab. Switching gears, he began the methodical process of spoofing the encryption code. Rushing this would produce an incomplete and possibly inaccurate code, which would trigger alarms and alert Gray and Chuang security. Even as good as Feroz was, if that happened, he'd be trapped. Security would know instantly exactly where he was and lock the area down in every way while dispatching people to him.

Just when he felt like he couldn't take the ache in his chest anymore, he saw that he had it. He gave the lock the code. After several seconds it chimed and then clicked.

Feroz withdrew a datacard and placed it on the door

jamb next to the lock. While releasing the lock on the sealed lab would not trigger any security measures, the door opening would. This was not about any concern that someone who shouldn't have disengaged the lock to unseal the lab but was part of the overall building system security.

Before knowing who might be accessing the lab, the system noted when laboratory doors were opened and closed. This was a part of every lab door, no matter the level of security overall. The datacard would spoof the system. It would not register the door opening or closing.

Confirming that he was still alone in the hallway, Feroz entered the lab. The lights turned on automatically. He found himself inside a relatively small lab. There were no windows. One wall was all shelves with various circuit boards, raw polycarbonates, aluminum, ceramic bits, crystal, quartz, chips of various shapes and sizes, microtransmitters, and other components and parts.

Two walls featured work benches with displays mounted to them. They were all powered off. The workbenches had been cleared off before the lab had been sealed.

On one of those workbenches, however, there was a transparent aluminum box about fifteen centimeters long and wide, and six centimeters tall with a coded lock. Inside the box was an encased infodrive.

This didn't require hacking, because Feroz had been given the code to open that box. He disabled the security on it, then lifted the box off the workbench. Carefully, he settled it into the sealed pocket of his coat.

Feroz had a vague idea of what it was he'd been sent to acquire. He knew that the infodrive prototype had the potential to revolutionize data storage. While he had some idea of how it worked, it didn't matter to his current situation.

Checking with his AR/VR glasses, Feroz made certain that nobody was in the hallway outside. He departed from the lab, pausing to re-engage the lock and reseal the lab.

Once again, unless someone checked in it, nobody would note that the lab had been unsealed. Especially as it had only been unlocked for less than five minutes. The passive systems of Gray and Chuang security should not have been alerted by any of what Feroz had done, and unless someone was currently checking something specific to lab security, this would remain unnoticed.

Of course, Gray and Chaung would perform active checks from time to time. Hence, they'd eventually learn that the lab had been unsealed. With all the encryption and algorithms he'd employed along the way, Feroz would have left no trace of himself and his involvement in that.

Careful to avoid notice, Feroz made his way to the stairwell door. He had his dampener set, and again checked that nobody was in the hallway when he reached the door. He used his stolen ID fob to unlock it and made his way into the stairwell.

Feroz paused. He checked the time and saw that he should be able to avoid any security moving through the stairwells. He began to ascend, pausing a few flights up to remove the lab coat, flip it inside out, reattach the longer white coat into the lining of the other, and then re-settled the blazer onto his shoulders once again.

Feroz checked in with Gray and Chuang's security system via his implants and AR/VR glasses as he took his time ascending the stairs. Thus far, nothing he'd done appeared to have set anything off.

At the fifty-sixth floor, Feroz checked the door out of the stairwell for anyone nearby. Seeing nobody, he entered the corridor. Calmly, he walked to the nearest restroom and occupied one of the stalls.

Over the next few hours, Feroz kept an eye on the Gray and Chuang building security systems, performing a form of oversight that would alert nobody to his presence in their system. He was on the lookout for any alerts, any warnings, and any signs he might have been detected. None presented themselves.

Feroz otherwise entertained himself by looking through cameras around the office building, never seeing anything more interesting than a brief argument between a trio of employees, a couple thinking they were sneaking away undetected for a quick snog, and general office happenings.

Just before noon, Feroz made his way from the restroom to the lift. When he entered it, there was already a crowd of employees heading to the cafeteria on the ground level or to leave the building for their lunch break. Like his entrance into Gray and Chuang, Feroz's departure was in the middle of a crowd, another corporate drone doing their daily routine.

A WEEK and two separate planetary hops later, Feroz was in a closed-up storefront on a space station. This was a shop owned by one of his trusted contacts. It was eternally either "for sale" or "under contract" but never opened as a new store.

Through Usman and his network, Feroz had felt almost secure between leaving his Gray and Chuang heist and finally arriving at this store. He'd still taken a great many precautions, but true to his word, after Usman had given Feroz "an opportunity to be part of something similar to your prior engagement" and he'd reported back his success, several useful tools that would allow him to move more freely had been delivered.

It was a first step into returning to a life where he wasn't always in hiding.

The job done, Usman needed the pilfered infodrive delivered. To do that, however, he would not be a direct party to it. Usman wanted to keep a degree of distance from the theft. Feroz respected that, as he knew Usman's company was a competitor of Gray and Chuang's in infodrive manufacturing. Though the drive would end up in the hands of Infomatics, Usman would be able to claim ignorance about how it had done so.

Thus, Feroz awaited the person who was going to get it to Usman. Or at least to the lower-level person or designated recipient who'd make sure it found its way to the appropriate R&D lab. That was one part of this delivery. The other was that Feroz would learn what his contacts had been cooking up and become a more intricate part of that.

After a short while longer, a trio entered the store from the back. Feroz had known they were there immediately upon their arrival via his ever-present AR/VR glasses and security he had access to and control over. He was still being careful.

The leader of the party had the bearing of a politician in the cut of his suit, the way he carried himself, the way his hair was styled. Another boon of Feroz's CBI training was recognizing a legitimate businessperson from a gang leader from an illicit businessperson to a politician.

What's more, the man looked vaguely familiar to Feroz. He'd not been a direct part of the previous foiled plot but still had some sort of connection.

"Mister Jones?" the politician queried.

"That was my grandfather. Feroz." He extended his hand.

The politician took it. "The sins of the father, eh?"

"Something like that," Feroz replied.

The politician smiled that fake, camera-ready smile only politicians wore. "It's good to meet you. If you'll join my companions and I, we have a number of things to discuss. From those in the know, I believe you're the man who can help us get this new arrangement underway."

Feroz grinned. "Sounds like fun. What's this conspiracy going to look like?"

"Proof of Life" is part of MJ Blehart's Forgotten Fodder series—a sci-fi series about clones, conspiracies, and murder.

Infantry Clone Jace Rojas witnessed an execution-style murder. He and CBI Marshal Onima Gwok uncovered a sinister conspiracy that could topple the government. The first four novels of the series are available across multiple platforms in multiple formats. Four more books and a new conspiracy (a year after the first) are coming soon!

Read more at:
mjblehart.com/forgotten-fodder

Pick Your Poison

1. Time to blow some shit up. Head to "Love of Mine" by K. Gorman

2. Hey, can you dial up the noir to 11? Go read "Case City Cowboy" by Greg Dragon in CROOKED V.2

3. Let's stick it to the man. Keep going to read "Fool's Gold" by Jessie Kwak

FOOL'S GOLD

A NANSHE CHRONICLES STORY

BY JESSIE KWAK

"This one would go well with chocolate," Jay says. The *Nanshe*'s mechanic rolls golden liquid in his glass, eyes half-closed in appreciation. "It's the cinnamon."

"Nutmeg," Ruby corrects with a hacker's certainty. "And vanilla."

"I'm tasting coffee," says Ruby's little brother Alex, lifting his glass in nimble fingers.

Raj turns to him in surprise. "Look who's got a sophisticated palate."

"Is he even legal age to drink?" asks Jay.

"You aren't worried about the law when you need a thief," retorts Alex.

"Love," says Ruby patiently. "We're trying to channel your criminal tendencies for good, only."

Jay lifts a dark eyebrow. "By teaching him to enjoy whiskey?"

"Among the other finer things in life," Ruby says.

Raj turns to Lasadi, who hasn't joined in her crew's

banter. The five of them are ensconced at Segafredo's, each in what Raj has come to think of as their usual spots: Ruby settled like a queen in the well-worn armchair, Alex and Jay on the couch to her left, Raj and Lasadi to her right, where they have a clear view of the door and the bar —not that Segafredo's is the sort of place you have to watch your back.

It's a dive near the dock levels of Artemis City, lovingly done up in decommissioned mining vessel chic. Tourists pop in from time to time looking for a taste of "real Artemis City," and drifters in port—like the *Nanshe* is currently—tend to congregate here for the reasonable prices, decent food, and earfuls of gossip doled out by Stacia, the proprietor. The dinner rush hasn't hit yet today, so the crew of the *Nanshe* has the place practically to themselves.

"How about you, Las?" Raj asks, slipping a hand onto her knee; her thigh is warm against his. "What do you think it tastes like?"

"Trouble," Lasadi answers.

"Agreed." Ruby takes another drink. "This goes down way too easy."

"I'm not talking about the whiskey," Lasadi says, and Raj shifts to follow her gaze. Two men have cornered Stacia at the bar.

He'd clocked them when they entered: they had the costume and cocky strides of local toughs. Now, the taller one is looming over Stacia while the shorter one massages one thick fist into the palm of his opposite hand. Looks like a move he learned in bad guy school.

Lasadi drums her fingers on the rim of her glass in a quick, decisive tattoo. Raj knows that gesture all too well.

"Be right back," she says, standing.

Ruby glances at the bar. "Captain . . ."

"Stay here, it's fine." Lasadi throws back her whiskey and heads to the bar, empty glass in her fist; Raj exchanges a glance with Jay and gets a "your turn" shrug. He sets his own glass down and follows. Their captain can hold her own in a barfight, he's not worried about that. But he'd rather be on hand if someone needs a head cracked.

Lasadi sets her elbow on the bar close enough that Stacia can't help but notice her. The toughs don't look over.

"You have until tomorrow night," the taller one growls to Stacia. When she spits back an angry response, his hand snakes across the bar to grab her wrist. She catches her breath in pain. The glass she was polishing clatters to the floor. "*Tomorrow night.*"

"'Scuse me." Lasadi raps her empty glass on the bartop. When the toughs finally turn, she shifts to face them. "Sorry to interrupt."

Stacia's eyes hold pure fear, but the toughs only seem confused. The taller one studies them, evaluating. Asking himself: Is the slim woman in drifter's gear and long blond braid a threat? How about the man beside her with the black ponytail and hands in his pockets? Raj gives a well-practiced "don't worry about me" grin. Lasadi flashes a smile.

"Looking for another round," she says to Stacia, tilting the glass so it catches the light of the bar. "When you get a minute."

"Of course." Stacia snatches her hand back from her assailant, rubbing her wrist surreptitiously as she turns to the shelves of liquor. Raj can see her fear in the tightness of her shoulders, the way her hand shakes as she reaches for bottle of Mishavin 14 they'd been drinking.

"Actually, we wanted to try something different," Las says. "Any local distilleries you'd recommend?"

Stacia glances back at the toughs. "Sure," she says slowly. "If you liked that fourteen, I've got a bottle from Fujita with a lot of those same notes." She pulls down one bottle, then reaches for another. "Or you might like the twelve year from Dusters." She uncorks both bottles for Lasadi to smell.

The toughs shift, uncertain what to do about the woman who is completely ignoring their pheromones of violent intention in order to casually compare whiskies.

"That Fujita is good." Lasadi turns, calls back across the room. "Jay—you said you liked more spice? Tell me what you think of this one."

Jay had said nothing of the sort, but whiskey's not the reason Lasadi's calling him over. Jay's not big, but he's more dedicated to training than anyone Raj has met since leaving the Arquellian Navy. Between that and his work in the *Nanshe*'s engine room, his compact, wiry strength and muscled shoulders are a nice addition to the party.

Jay lifts his chin in greeting to the two toughs, then leans to take a whiff from the bottle Stacia proffers like their presence doesn't bother him in the slightest.

The taller one's nostrils flare. "Tomorrow night, Stace," he snarls, then stalks back out the door.

The shorter one deliberately hits Lasadi's shoulder as he muscles by—she ignores him—then meets Raj's gaze with smug challenge. Raj just tilts him a nod and leans elbows behind him on the bar to watch them leave.

Stacia lets out a shaky breath.

"Who're they, then?" Ruby and her little brother Alex have joined them at the bar; Ruby hikes herself up on one of the stools and reaches to squeeze Stacia's hand.

"Than's boys," Stacia says; Raj doesn't recognize the name. She slumps back and wraps her arms around herself. "Thanks for coming over, but I was handling them."

Raj's attention flicks to Stacia's wrist, which is still ringed in red from where the tall one grabbed her. "What did they want?"

Stacia's lips flatten, and for a minute Raj thinks she won't answer. It's none of their business, of course, but Raj would like to think of Stacia as a friend. The crew of the *Nanshe* has become regulars whenever they're docked in Artemis City, mostly because of her. She and Ruby have bonded over a shared questionable taste in dramas. She and Jay over both being trans. She and Raj over teasing Alex for probably not being old enough to drink in her establishment.

And Las—well, Captain Lasadi Cazinho doesn't bond much with anyone, but she also doesn't stand by and watch someone get taken advantage of. Even if Lasadi hadn't known Stacia from a house plant, she would have stepped in.

And maybe Stacia wouldn't have answered any other friendly regulars, but her resolve seems to break when she meets that banked, smoky anger in Lasadi's gaze.

"It's my fault," Stacia says; a muscle jumps in Lasadi's cheek. "Six months ago I needed some cash to repair the recyclers when they crashed, and I went to Than. He used to come in all the time, and seemed like he'd treat me fair. But now he wants money, and I don't have it. He'll take the bar if I don't pay."

"How much?" Raj asks.

"I borrowed ten thousand credits." Stacia waves an angry hand. "But I already paid that back. Along with an extra two last month, and three the month before. Now he wants five more—for interest, he says, but that's obviously bullshit. He wants the bar, and he'll keep bleeding me dry until he gets it."

"We can help," Alex says. When Lasadi shoots him a look, he shrugs his lanky teen shoulders. "I mean."

"Of course we can help," Lasadi says, then turns back to Stacia. "Start at the beginning."

"Stephen Than's your basic scum, only." Ruby flicks a hologram ident card into the center of the table to show a man with sneering lips, a chiseled jaw, and thick eyebrows that disappear into his unruly hairline. Raj can't remember seeing him around, but that doesn't mean much. It's been a while since Raj was working solo, scrounging for jobs in Artemis City.

And good riddance to those days.

The crew of the *Nanshe* has settled at the dining table in the *Nanshe*'s galley, nursing mugs of tea. It's grassy with a hint of ginger, something Ruby picked up in Ironfall.

"Than mostly makes his money through floater loans," Ruby says.

"Sanctioned?" Raj asks.

"No, all off the books. But he's not quiet about his

services, is he—authorities know him. He hasn't dusted up enough to get picked up, only."

Hardly unusual. Plenty of people in Artemis City offer floater loans, providing drifter crews with the capital to gear up for a job in exchange for a percentage of the anticipated payday. And in Artemis City—in every part of the Pearls—where there's a legal way there's also a half dozen people skirting regs.

Ruby flicks through her notes, frowning. "Than's not with any of the local crews, that I could tell. No real criminal record—he got picked up a while ago as part of a counterfeiting scheme, but only spent a couple of months in work release before they cut him loose. He's pretty good at staying out of trouble."

"So, he's a solo runner," muses Lasadi. "Riskier for Stacia than a legit lender, but better than getting caught owing one of the crews."

"Why doesn't she just go to the AC police?" Alex asks. "She'd have to pay a fine or whatever, right? For taking an illegal loan? But it's gotta be easier than deal with this asshole."

"Same reason she didn't go to a legit lender in the first place," Ruby says. "Her recyclers were years out of date before they went static. If she reports this, they'll start digging and she'll be in even bigger trouble."

Raj leans back in his chair, frowning at Than's hologram in the center of the table. "Here's what I don't get. Ruby, you said he's stayed under the radar for years. Why take a risk like this now?"

"Meaning?"

"You can make good money floating credits, especially if you're not paying the Federation their cut. And he knows Stacia's situation. She's tolerated a little light extortion without complaint." Raj pushes his fingers through his hair in thought. "Why such a heavy hand now? It risks drawing attention."

Ruby cracks a knuckle, then turns to her little brother. "Alex. One of the guys was wearing a hat with a business logo on the side. Can you draw it?"

"I was all the way across the room," he protests.

"But tell me you saw it, boy genius."

"Hold, please." Alex squeezes his eyes shut a moment, knee bouncing as he thinks. "Yeah, okay," he finally says. "Gimme a sec."

He pulls out his comm and plucks Ruby's stylus out of her fingers, then sketches out a quick collection of half circles and lines. He turns his comm to Ruby.

"That was it," she confirms. She frowns down at her own tablet, namesake-red nails clattering against the screen as she types. On her collarbones, gold tattoos featuring the stylized planets of the Pearls glimmer against her dark skin.

"Saints in hell," she finally says, sitting back. "It's Jude Alberola's logo."

"Who?" ask Raj and Lasadi in unison.

But it's Jay who answers: "The restaurant guy." It's the first thing he's said since they all sat down. "He owns Kalabi Street in this sector, and a couple spots down in the Bell." At Lasadi's surprised look, he shrugs. "Chiara," he says in explanation.

Chiara, Jay's ex-girlfriend, the one who'd given him an ultimatum to settle down in Ironfall with her, or continue to ship with Lasadi on the *Nanshe*. Her name doesn't often pass Jay's lips, these days.

"Exactly," says Ruby. "And I ran a search through security footage outside Kalabi Street—

Than's short bruiser works there. He's one of Alberola's bouncers."

"Good job he's got all that muscle, then," says Lasadi. "Since he doesn't have enough brains to not wear his work logo when doing off the book jobs."

"Alberola puts his logo on everything," Jay says. "He's a hound for attention—he was always being interviewed on those entertainment news feeds Chiara watched. And his sister-in-law is on the city council, so he's pretty good at sweeping away scandals."

"He's acquired three new restaurants just this year," Ruby adds, flicking a news story about Alberola into the center of the table.

"And now he's trying to buy out Segafredos." Raj leans forward, elbows on the table, studying the smug face of the restaurant owner in front of them. "He's looking for a goldmine, huh? Let's give him one."

THE CAVERNOUS RING corridor surrounding Artemis City's dockyards never sleeps. Pedestrians and mototaxis bustle through at all hours of the day, while driverless cargo trains spirit incoming goods deeper into the city, injecting raw materials and spendy imported goods from far beyond Durga's Belt into its veins.

The far side of the ring—where the *Nanshe* is currently docked in one of the long-term berths—is studded with warehouses, shipping offices, inspections centers, and cheap body lockers that rent by the hour. This side of the ring connects to the passenger terminal, and is a hub for those leaving or entering Artemis City.

The sign for Kalabi Street glows prominently in the

midst of the chaos, a beacon advertising the perfect place for a farewell dinner before soaring into the unforgiving black, or to grab a trendy bite to eat before descending into Artemis City's Bell.

Segafredo's couldn't possibly be a competitor, not in a serious sense. But if Alberola wants to expand his operations and get more of the locals market, it would be a good addition to his portfolio.

The man himself has been waiting for them at the bar with one eye on the door; he launches himself from his stool as soon as Raj and Ruby walk in, hand outstretched.

"Jude Alberola," he says, closing his hand around Raj's. "A pleasure to meet you."

"I'm Richard." Raj gives Alberola his most sparkling smile. "Richard Cason Smith."

"Of course, of course." Alberola returns Raj's smile a touch too brightly, greed glimmering in his gaze. "I'm a huge fan of your work."

"You're too kind," Raj says. *And you're lying.* Richard Cason Smith may have a reasonably impressive list of credits in minor drama serials—the most famous being *Jewel in the Palace*—but no one can say they're a fan. The entire persona is one of Ruby's creations, fabricated out of doctored vid clips and fake profiles in celebrity sighting magazines.

She'd whipped it up a few months back when they'd needed to infiltrate the inner sanctum of a predatory cult leader in order to save a friend, and it had been no bother to dust off the profile for this job and refresh it with a few new articles. These, spoofed in well-known restaurateur magazines, waxed poetic about the wealthy Arquellian actor's transition from stage to entrepreneurship, and his newfound success as a celebrity investor in exclusive restaurants.

It wouldn't have taken Alberola long to figure out that any restaurant owner who gets a call from Richard Cason Smith's manager—played by Ruby Quiñones in her smart maroon dress and heels—is on the road to riches.

Alberola shakes Ruby's hand as an afterthought, then waves an arm to welcome them in. "Let me give you the grand tour."

The grand tour doesn't take long. Kalabi Street is two levels: a bustling main floor and mezzanine bar featuring floor-to-ceiling windows that overlook Artemis City's passenger terminal. The restaurant is all bright colors and faux elegance and two-for-one drinks deals. The food is supposed to be excellent, Jay had told them, but otherwise the main thing Kalabi Street has going for it is its location.

Which is all a celebrity investor like Richard Cason Smith needs.

Raj plays his enthusiastic actor's persona to perfection, complimenting Alberola's restaurant (and business acumen) at every turn. Ruby, on the other hand, hands out nothing but noncommittal grunts and skeptical twitches of her eyebrow. When she responds to yet another of Raj's declarations of perfection with a sniff—a sniff Raj acknowledges with chagrin—Alberola finally looks at her.

"And what is it *you're* looking for in an investment, Ms. . . ?" His cheeks color slightly as he realizes he never asked Ruby her name.

"More than flash and glitter." Ruby examines a smudge on her manicure with a frown. "It's about whether or not a restaurant has good bones."

She's dropped her Artemisian gutter trash accent for

this gig, opting instead for a passable Arquellian drawl similar to Raj's. He can spot the influence of Ruby's ex-girlfriend, Kitty, in her posh performance.

"Good bones?" asks Alberola.

"Operationally." Ruby turns to Raj. "I know vibe is important, Richard—and it's great here. But if Kalabi Street isn't being operated efficiently, your vibe's foundations will wash out to sea in a heartbeat."

Look at her, Raj thinks, using a sea metaphor correctly. Pretty good for someone who's never seen an ocean, even from orbit.

"Tossed out an airlock, I think they say here." Raj grins at Alberola. "She's right, though. I don't just invest in any business. I'm a hands-off kind of guy—I don't like to come in and start changing things around."

"Which I appreciate," says Alberola.

"But that means things have to be running well ahead of time. No outstanding debts, no out-of-date licenses, no health regulation fines, no pending lawsuits from disgruntled employees, no personal scandals in the owner's life." Raj waves a hand like he can't imagine Alberola having any of those problems. "That sort of thing."

"Absolutely nothing to worry about," says Alberola. "We get top marks from the health inspectors, every time. Absolutely top marks. I can show you the paperwork."

Raj exchanges a quick glance with Ruby to confirm she caught that, too. From the laundry list of potential problems, Alberola seems a bit too quick to reassure them about health inspections in particular. Ruby taps a quick message on her comm, flagging that for the rest of the team.

"Here," Alberola says. "Let me call up that health inspection paperwork."

"No need!" Raj claps Alberola on the shoulder. "We trust you."

"No need *yet*," Ruby says with an indulgent look at Raj. "We'll check everything out if we decide to make an offer."

"*When*," Raj corrects. He turns back to Alberola. "We've seen a lot of businesses on this rock, and yours is the first one I've really gotten excited about." He holds out his hand; Alberola can't keep the greed out of his expression as he shakes. "We'll be in touch."

LASADI'S GOOD AT WAITING. Good at filling long, lonely moments with tasks to keep her mind occupied; she'd turned it into an art form during the three excruciating years she spent in near isolation after waking up in pieces here in the Pearls.

She'd always had Jay, of course, their friendship forged in the furnace of the Coruscan resistance movement. But even he hadn't been able to pull her out of the dark cocoon of solitude she'd wrapped herself in during their exile, after the disastrous final battle to save their homeland from the Alliance.

Raj had been the one to do that.

Even though the *Nanshe* is now home to a lively crew —and even though she'd never go back to how things were before—Lasadi still appreciates these quiet moments. Jay and Alex have gone off to dig deeper into Alberola's health inspections, Ruby's ensconced in her room, and Raj ran out to pick up dinner.

Lasadi is doing inventory for their next trip. She's elbow deep in the pantry when she hears footsteps behind her, smells the spicy heat of curry. She turns to find Raj with bags of takeaway in his hands.

"You know Ruby's got a program that does all this." Raj sets the bags on a crate and holds out his arms to receive the tub of dried pasta Lasadi is looking to set down. "It puts a shopping list together and everything."

"Yeah, but can it tell what I'll want to eat for dinner next week?"

"Sure it can. A dehydrated ration box, whatever flavor is nearest to the front of the shelf." He laughs when she scowls at him. "Jay told me all about the horrible things you'd call food back when it was just the two of you."

"I can cook just fine."

"Like pasta? You *do* know you have to boil it, Las. You can't just eat it raw."

"It was one time!" But she laughs; he's not wrong. "And it was fine once you put some hot sauce on it."

"The Lasadi Cazinho way: everything's better with hot sauce." Raj sets the box down and catches her wrist, tugging her closer to him. "C'mon. Once we've got this sorted out with Stacia, I'll take you to a nice restaurant down in the Bell and teach you to appreciate food."

"I appreciate food." But she's not thinking about food; she's still marveling at the way her body lights up at his proximity. Still marveling at the way this Arquellian charmer—the enemy—had slid straight through her defenses.

"You appreciate nutrition," says Raj. "I blame your Coruscan rebel fanatic years. You have no appreciation for culture."

"Says the Alliance bastard who was trying to eradicate our culture."

"Only the parts that gave you a taste for rehydrated trash."

Lasadi traces fingers down his abdomen, smiling as Raj shivers. "And what gave me a taste for deserter trash?"

"Ouch." He leans in, lips tantalizing close. "Is seducing the enemy one of the CLA's standard plays?"

"I'm writing my own rule book now," Lasadi murmurs.

"Well, your reeducation tactics are working, rebel queen."

Voices at the cargo hold door reach her ears just as Raj's lips touch hers, and she stiffens, one hand firm on his chest to hold him back. He must hear them, too—or he feels her discomfort; the heat dissolves out of his kiss and he leaves her with a chaste, sweet brush of the lips before creating space between them.

If he's blushing, she can't tell through his tawny complexion. But she knows her own pale cheeks have flamed red with heat.

The others know about them, of course. Raj has been sharing her cabin for some time now. But she's the captain. It still feels wrong to be caught showing affection to him in front of the rest of the crew.

Jay and Alex climb the ramp to the cargo bay, arguing as they come. Jay catches the moment, of course—he knows her better than she knows herself—but he just flashes her a knowing smile. Alex, as always, only has eyes for food.

"Dibs on the seven-spice tofu," he says, reaching for the takeaway.

Raj swats his hand. "There's enough for everyone."

"And dinner can wait until we've debriefed," Jay

adds. He elbows Alex. "We've got news. Go grab your sister."

"Sure, sure." Alex saunters over to the ladder that leads up to the crew level and cups his hands around his mouth. "*FAMILY MEETING, SIS*," he hollers.

Jay winces. "Effective, I guess." He leans against a crate, arms folded over his chest while he waits for Ruby. "Turns out that Kalabi Street's supposed clean bill of health is totally moxed," he says once she's joined them. "But Alberola's money and connections let him sweep some major issues under the rug."

"He's literally gotten away with murder," says Alex, eyes bright. "An employee made a complaint about health violations last year, but Alberola paid them off and his sister-in-law on city council buried the negative report."

"Just a complaint?" Ruby asks. "No one died?"

Alex turns teenaged scorn on her. "Are you defending him?"

"Of course not. I'm saying it's literally *not* murder if no one died."

"The point being,"—Jay holds his hands between the Quiñones siblings—"the report would have shut anyone else down, but his sister-in-law kept him open and dusted any further inspections."

"Good work," says Raj. "We can use this. Right now, we have two goals. We need Alberola to believe that the deal with a celebrity investor is for real, while also putting pressure on him to cover his tracks. We need him to do something juicy. On camera."

Lasadi can't help but think how oddly similar these little planning sessions sound to those she had with her Mercury Squadron fighters before a mission: *feint, misdirect, put on the pressure, force the Alliance to make mistakes*. She nods slowly. "We want him worried this deal will be snatched away if the problem he thought was buried comes to light. Which will make him double down in a way that exposes him for who he really is."

Raj grins at her. "Exactly."

"We send in a reporter," says Ruby. "Makes 'Richard' seem more legit while ratcheting up the stakes." She catches her lower lip between her teeth, thinking. "He's already seen Raj and I."

Alex's hand shoots up. "I'll do it!"

"No," says Raj, as Lasadi says, "That won't work." She continues, at Alex's wounded expression: "You look way too much like Ruby."

"Ew, I don't."

"It's the freckles," points out Jay.

"Besides," Raj says. "You're our thief. We need you to break into Kalabi Street and document how many of these health code violations are still happening."

Jay lifts his chin. "I can do it. I've watched enough of those gossip shows with Chiara."

Ruby's eyebrow tilts skeptical. "Introduce yourself like a gossip show host, then, love."

"Okay." Jay clears his throat, shifting his lean against the crates. "Hi, I'm Nick Mondal," he says; he sounds exactly like Jay Kamiya the Coruscan mechanic, and no one else. "I'm with Pearls 889 Today, and I'm talking with Jude Alberola from Kalabi Street."

Jay glances around the little group for feedback.

Alex is first to speak. "That was terrible, man."

"It wasn't—" Ruby flicks a pinky nail against thumb, a sure sign she's about to hedge the truth. "It wasn't bad."

Jay gives them both a hurt look. "I can practice."

Lasadi sighs, holding out a hand before anyone else

can respond. One benefit of being the captain is that's all it takes to keep them quiet.

"I can do it," she says. She doesn't miss the dubious shifting around her. "Remember how I charmed all those investors in Bulari?"

"No offense, Cap," Alex says. "But Raj was with you."

"I held my own." Lasadi lifts her chin and shakes out her shoulders. She takes a deep breath, channeling every ounce of her chatty younger sister.

"Heya!" Lasadi says it with her sister's bubbly tone, though she shifts her accent to match Ruby and Alex's Artemesian lilt. "I'm Nicki Mondal with Pearls 889 Today, and I'm *sooo* excited to be talking with Jude Alberola of the famous Kalabi Street restaurant!"

Raj and Alex are staring at her with a level of surprise she finds frankly insulting. Jay nods thoughtfully. "That actually wasn't bad."

"I think you got the job," Ruby says. "But you know what that means, don't you."

Olds. She hadn't thought this part through.

"Hair and makeup," Lasadi says, shoulders slumping.

Ruby grins at her. "Hair and makeup! C'mon, Cap."

LASADI BARELY RECOGNIZES herself by the time Ruby is done, which is probably for the best. Her usual uniform is trousers and a button-up to hide her scars, dark blond hair pulled back in a severe braid. But Ruby's teased and curled her hair into a bouncy ponytail, done her makeup in garish colors, and dressed her in a flouncy, high-necked silk dress that she pairs with leggings and smartly heeled boots.

Jay has joined her as the camera guy and interview coach, because even if Lasadi can shine it on just fine, no one on the crew trusts her to know an apéritif from an appetizer.

Lasadi checks her reflection once more as they head in, then thrusts her hand confidently at the host. Her newly painted nails gleam like they belong to someone else. "Nicki Mondal with Pearls 889 Today. I was hoping to speak with Alberola? I'm on a deadline?"

That upward lilt to her tone, the batting of her false eyelashes, and the host glances up at the office. "Um? One second."

If Alberola had been busy with something else when she arrives, he doesn't show it. True to their intel, he's not one to pass up publicity—even a made-up gossip channel catches his attention.

He gives Lasadi an appraising look that makes her want to whip the knife out of her boot and drive it deep into the meat of his thigh, but she contents herself with enjoying the fantasy and instead settles into the chair he offers. Jay's camera drones whir to life around them.

"Mr. Alberola? Is it true that Richard Cason Smith visited you earlier today?"

"Oh, ah." The battle between discretion and an opportunity to brag wars behind his eyes. "Where might you have heard that?"

"I saw it. He's been in town all week, keeping a low profile. But I've been following him—it's just too thrilling that he might be expanding to the Pearls!" Lasadi's aiming for breathlessly conspiratorial. Jay gives her a nod of encouragement. "Mr. Alberola. Believe me. I've been watching him visit restaurants all through Artemis City, and this is the first one he left looking excited about. You have to be only delighted."

Alberola purses his lips, but it doesn't take long for pride to win out over caution. "Mr. Cason Smith and I did have a very productive meeting this afternoon," he concedes.

And with that, it's a simple matter of flirty coaxing to goad him into an exclusive interview—not to be shared until after the deal's inked, of course. She keeps her questions light and fluffy, consulting the notes Jay keeps sending to her comm. After a few minutes, she finds herself relaxing into the play. Turns out pulling cons is no different than the missions she and Jay flew. They're still fighting for the underdog, she's just using charm instead of piloting a CLA fighter.

Finally, Lasadi tosses Alberola a final question and wraps up the "interview."

"Like I said, we won't publish any of this until you give us the go-ahead," she says. "I know these deals take time, there's just so much to fact check."

A flicker of uncertainty crosses Alberola's face. "Fact check?"

She waves a hand. "You know investors, tightening the bolts, only. A poke at past reviews, a chat with other restaurant owners in the area. That sort of thing."

"I wouldn't worry about it," Jay chimes in. He's moving about the office, collecting his camera drones. His faux Artemisian accent wouldn't hold up under scrutiny, but Alberola doesn't seem to notice. "A place like this must be an investor's dream."

"Absolutely! And you've got plenty of time to make sure your reputation's shining." Lasadi lets her smile dim. "Unless . . ."

Alberola straightens, his attention entirely on Lasadi. Jay leans casually against the cabinet behind Alberola's desk. "Unless what?"

"You're not already under contract, are you?"

"Of course not."

"Oh good!" She gives him a winning smile. "Just make sure all your loose ends are tied up before you sign any offers and you'll be fine."

Lasadi gives him a final wave on her way out the door, keeping the airy bounce in her step until she and Jay are out of sight. They slip through the door of a nearby cafe, where Raj, Ruby, and Alex are sipping coffees in a booth.

Alex is wearing a pair of gray coveralls that are smudged and grubby, a smear of gray dust bright against his dark forehead. He's been hard at work, too.

"Did you get the evidence of health violations?" Lasadi asks him.

"It's so bad," Alex says with glee. "You're gonna love it."

"Good job, both of you," Raj says. "Las, you definitely rattled him." He nods to Ruby. "Time to set the final trap."

Ruby squares her shoulders and smooths her hair, slipping effortlessly into character even though she's only making a voice call. Lasadi watches her, impressed.

"Mr. Alberola?" Ruby says in an Arquellian drawl when the restaurateur answers. "After touring some of the other restaurants in Artemis City, it's clear that yours is the only real option. We'd love to offer an exclusivity contract with the intention to go forward with the investment—but there's a catch. Mr. Cason Smith is leaving tomorrow, and would like to have things in motion before he goes. Is that too soon to return the contract? Oh? Yes, of course you can see the offer first. Let me send it over right now."

She taps a red lacquered fingernail against her screen. "Did that come through?" Ruby smiles. "Glad to hear it. And, yes, that *is* a lot of money. Mr. Cason Smith doesn't do small-time deals. Now, about that contract . . . you can return it by tomorrow? Excellent! Now, of course, I want to be clear the deal is contingent on anything we find during due diligence, but don't worry. Our team has never turned up anything so scandalous we couldn't make it work. Mr. Cason Smith has unerring judgment. Fantastic. We look forward to working with you."

Her pleasant smile vanishes as soon as she ends the call. She pulls up a new screen on her tablet, sifting through the health code violation images Alex took on his excursion. She sweeps them all into a message along with a nearby address and a simple headline:

I need 5k credits or I send these to the press. Meet me here at midnight.

She hits Send and sits back with a grin. "Time to make our final call."

SEGAFREDO'S IS CLOSED when Raj knocks on the door. It's almost midnight, but that shouldn't matter. Bar time isn't the same as normal time—especially near the dock-yards where transports are arriving and leaving at all hours of the day. Segafredo's should be open, but the storefront's normal neon buzz is a dark, empty slash in the wall of businesses lining this part of the corridor.

Raj lifts his hand to knock again, but before his knuckles hit metal the door slides open to reveal Stacia.

She looks ill with stress, her nails chewed to the quick, her makeup doing nothing to conceal the worried bags under her eyes.

She waves them inside with a furtive glance behind them, but no one in the corridor is paying them any mind. She triple-locks the door, then sags into a nearby booth.

"I can't get the funds," she says. "I might just need to sell the business to Than and move on."

"Than's actually not your problem," says Raj. "But we figured out who is—and we brought you a present."

Ruby steps forward, her tablet in hand. "Scootch."

Stacia makes room in the booth beside her, frowning in confusion as Ruby calls up a feed on her tablet. "What's this?"

"Poetic justice," says Ruby with a grin. "Give us a look."

Raj, Lasadi, Jay, and Alex all crowd around to watch over Ruby and Stacia's shoulders. Raj slips his hand into Lasadi's; she squeezes back and doesn't let go.

The location that appears on the screen may not be the most iconic view in Artemis City—Raj would say that distinction belongs to the observation ring a few levels below this one, a fully transparent circuit at the top of the Bell where you can stare past your feet into the neon-and-latticework heart of Artemis City, or stare up through the Bell's clear dome to watch ships maneuver through the dockyard ring and into the stars beyond.

But the location displayed in the feed on Ruby's tablet is one that nearly everyone who visits Artemis City knows well: the grubby, well-worn station for the transit loop that spirals travelers down into the Bell. This time of night it's nearly deserted. Which makes it especially noticeable when Alberola strolls in, flanked by the two toughs who'd been bothering Stacia earlier today.

"Than's guys," Stacia says bitterly, then leans into the screen. "Wait. They work for Alberola? That bastard. I should have known—he made me an offer last year and I laughed him out the door."

"Hey!"

The tinny shout comes from Ruby's tablet. She strokes a finger up the side to raise the volume.

"You can get audio from a security feed?" Stacia asks.

"It's my equipment," Ruby says primly. "We set it up earlier."

"*I* set it up," grumbles Alex.

"Yes, love. You do everything. Now quiet."

"Hey!" shouts Alberola again. His target is a shadowy figure wearing a drifter's jacket and visor, but awkwardly, as though trying to keep their identity hidden. "You the asshole who's trying to blackmail me?"

"Excuse me?"

Alberola reaches for the figure's collar. "Are you the asshole who's blackmailing me."

"Oh, for fuck's sake," says the figure, whipping off the visor. "What are you talking about?"

Alberola catches just short from grabbing the figure, flinching back in surprise. "Veronica?"

Stacia's nose wrinkles. "Who?"

"His sister-in-law," says Raj. "She's on the city council."

On the screen, Alberola has stepped back, hands raised to his sister-in-law. She plants her fists on her hips.

"Blackmail you?" Veronica asks, throwing his words back at him. "Why are you blackmail-able? You told me you were going to clean things up."

"And I did."

"Then what's all this?" She thrusts a screen in his face. From the view of Ruby's cameras, it's impossible to see what's on it, but Raj knows. Ruby'd sent the council-woman the same set of photos she'd sent to Alberola. "These photos are all time-stamped today, and they're the exact same problems as the ones on last year's health report."

"That's not true."

"Then why are you here trying to pay someone off to keep it quiet?"

"I'm not paying anyone off!"

"Then what's in the briefcase?"

"None of your business."

"No?" Veronica flicks through her tablet, then shows Alberola another file. "How about *this*? Is *this* my business?"

Again, it's impossible to see what's on the screen, but the audio comes through faintly. "We need to tie up loose ends by tonight, Than," Alberola is saying in the record-ing. "We'll deal with Segafredo's after we've finished with this blackmailer. Once Stacia sells, we'll make sure all the paperwork is tidy and she's too afraid to talk, just like the others. What do you mean, how will I handle the paper-work? Veronica, obviously." He laughs. "She's never both-ered looking at anything I've had her sign before."

Even in the feed on Ruby's tablet Raj can tell Alberola has lost all his coloring.

"Where did you get that?" he asks, hoarsely.

"An anonymous tip," Veronica says.

An anonymous tip from Ruby, of course. Once Alberola had been rattled by Lasadi's visit and put under enough pressure by the time-sensitive offer, he'd started making calls. Calls which were recorded by the camera drone Jay had left running surreptitiously in the cabinet behind his desk.

The councilwoman shakes her head at Alberola. "You complete and utter jackass."

"Veronica."

"Fuck you, Jude." She glares at the two toughs, who look to Alberola uncertainly. "I literally caught you in the act of intimidating a blackmailer like some wannabe crime boss, with these two muscle meats prancing after you. I love my sister. I can cover up a bad health inspection—even if it ended up with people in the hospital. But bribery? And extortion?"

"It's not what it sounded like."

"I don't care if you drag your own name through the mud, but you're threatening mine. Get your shit together. And believe me. I'll be taking a long hard look at every piece of paperwork I've ever helped you file."

Alberola tenses, almost like he'll strike her, but when the councilwoman snaps her fingers a pair of burly Federation agents step out of an alcove to flank her. The toughs beside Alberola both melt back, clearly uninterested in tangling with well-armed law enforcement.

"Good night, Jude," Veronica calls over her shoulder as she walks away.

Alberola growls something at his toughs and follows after, calling for her to calm down and talk to him. The toughs share a look and a shrug, then leave through the other exit.

"I don't think he'll be pushing his weight around anymore," says Ruby. "And if he gives you any more trouble, I'm sure the councilwoman would be interested in the security footage of Alberola's men threatening you."

Stacia sits back, stunned. "Thank you," she finally says. "I can't believe this nightmare is over. I had no idea where I was going to get the rest of Than's—Alberola's —money."

"Oh!" Alex grins, then pulls off his backpack. "Speaking of Alberola's money."

Stacia's eyes go wide as he dumps bundles of credit chips onto the table in front of her.

"It's the five thousand Alberola was about to pay in bribes," says Raj. "Which is what you overpaid on your loan. We figured you should have that back."

Stacia shakes her head. "I can't take it. You all are the ones who earned it."

"We don't need payment," Lasadi says. "We just wanted our favorite bar to stay open."

"Well, you're never paying for drinks again, at least." Stacia stands and heads to the bar. "Speaking of which, I think you were wanting a round of the Fujita? I have a bottle of their twenty-five year in the safe, I've been saving it for something special."

"We'd love to try it," says Lasadi.

Stacia pours six glasses, and they all raise them in a toast.

"To the *Nanshe*," says Raj. Whiskey gleams gold in the barlight. "And to friends."

"Fool's Gold" is a side story in Jessie Kwak's Nanshe Chronicles series.

*Download the Nanshe Chronicles prequel novella,
Artemis City Shuffle, for free and start the adventure at
jessiekwak.com/nanshe.*

Pick Your Poison

*1. Hell yeah! That's what happens when you try to pick on
the little guy!* Head to "On Ignition" by Heather Texle

2. Psst! Do you have any robots? Go read "Full Core" by
Wade Peterson in CROOKED V.1

3. You're not going to get away with this! Keep going to
read "Ransomware" by Robin Jeffrey

RANSOMWARE

A CADENCE TURING MYSTERY

BY ROBIN JEFFREY

A PULSAR, I KNEW, WAS A HANDGUN-SHAPED WEAPON. A weapon that could fire a pulse of energy with enough force to tear a hole through muscle and bone in less than a second. I knew this because my company, Halcyon Enterprises, used to make them. Before I shut down the Defensive Technology Division, pulsars had been what one might call a "best seller" for us. But I had never seen one in person before tonight.

As I stuttered to a halt outside the abandoned Halcyon Enterprises warehouse, I wondered if the pulsar currently kissing the back of my neck was one of ours. At this point, I wouldn't be surprised if karma had decided to balance itself out that way.

Several feet in front of me, Lewis Galt stood frozen, fresh blood trickling down his cheek from a cut below his left eye. His clothes had seen better days, given that he'd been kept hostage for the past several nights—it was clear his captors had not been kind.

"Get back here, kid," said Hunter Davis from behind

me. There was a faint, high pitched whir as the pulsar safety was switched off. "Now."

"Lewis," I said, keeping my voice calm and steady. "Your dad is waiting for you at home. You need to go."

The sixteen-year-old boy looked between Hunter and me, his eyes wide with panic. He took a hesitant step towards me across the cracked concrete ground. "But—"

I smiled. "I'll be fine."

"Fine?" Hunter dug the pulsar into the back of my head, grunting his next words from between gritted teeth. "I swear by the moons above, kid, I'm going to blow this asshole's brains out the front of his skull—now get back here."

Lewis took another shuffling step towards us. Then, his eyes met mine. He froze.

"Is he mad?" Lewis asked.

"I'm fucking furious—" started Davis, but Lewis spoke over him, shaking his head.

"My dad." Lewis swallowed hard, his Adam's apple bobbing. "Is he mad at me?"

"He just wants you home, Lewis." I gave the smallest of nods towards the empty public walkway behind him. "So go."

The boy nodded, his bottom lip trembling. With one last look at Hunter, Lewis turned and ran into the night as fast as he could, keeping low and zigzagging as he went.

"Shit." The word came out from between Davis' lips like a glob of spit. I couldn't help but smile at his displeasure.

A scuffling of shoes against stone, and I felt the pulsar pull away from my scalp. "Do you have any idea how many credits you just cost me, Mr. Money? How much business?"

"Honestly? I don't care," I said, turning around, my arms crossed high over my chest. Sneering at Hunter in open disgust, the barrel of his pulsar now inches from my chest, I scoffed. "You're a thug who would rather hide behind children than do his business out in the open like a real man."

Hunter Davis, all six foot six of him, gave a mirthless laugh, the pulsar falling to his side. "Why did you even come here tonight?" he asked, almost conversationally, a small, tight smile on his cracked lips. Without warning, he lunged for me, grabbing me by the front of my shirt, the pulsar still in his right hand. I instinctively reached up and pulled at his hands, trying to free myself, but his grip was too strong. He tugged me towards him, and I caught the full brunt of his pheromone-spray-soaked odor. He shook me to and fro like a sack of apples. He breathed heavily, grinding his teeth. "You have a death wish, Mr. Money? Huh? Because let me tell you: there are quicker ways to die than what I'm going to do to you."

As he manhandled me, my gaze fell over his shoulder. My smile returned. "That's the second time you've threatened me, Mr. Davis," I managed, shaking my head. "There won't be a third."

Enraged, he widened his bloodshot eyes, the vein on his forehead distended to the point of bursting. He let go of me with his right hand, drawing back to strike me with the butt of the pulsar across the face. "You son of a—!"

Instinctively closing my eyes, I couldn't help but think of how differently my evening had started.

※

THE ENTERTAINMENT MARKET in District 49 was a chaotic hodgepodge of sounds and bodies, all flowing in and out and around each other. Screens of every shape and size flashed out into the crowd. Discordant tunes fought for dominance above my head—one moment a sweet melody, the next, a raging backbeat.

At the end of the dizzying maze of streets, story cubes glittered on stall shelves. Sometimes these were placed out of reach, like precious jewels, while other times sellers had jumbled them together in multi-colored bins, as if begging for them to be nicked. Several cubes were plugged into modified audio devices, spewing their secreted words into the atmosphere, filling the air with the sound of stories.

Half of the stalls sold everything, every genre, every era, every author. The rest, the less-trafficked stalls, were the specialty sellers. These merchants didn't bother coming up with catchy names for their stalls, less interested in grabbing your attention than in giving you information. 'Existentialism' was written above one, 'Fantastical Romance' over another. Tucked in its own little corner was a stall with a simple, hand-printed sign that read: 'Mystery'.

I stood outside this stall, somewhat at a loss for what to do next. Cadence and I had agreed to enjoy an early dinner together after our mutual workdays concluded. But there was no sign of my friend at her shop when I went to greet her, and a growing sense of unease began to creep over me. Ignoring the 'Closed' sign resting on the counter, I stepped into the seemingly abandoned stall.

"Cadence?" I peered into the darkness and took a tentative step towards the curtains that separated the front of the store from the storage area. "Cay, where are you?"

"Back here, Chance." Her voice floated out from behind the curtains.

I felt a thrill go through me at the sound of her voice. Like a sailor drawn in by a siren, I moved quickly towards the storage area, suddenly desperate to see my darling again.

Cadence had come to Arrhidaeus as a refugee. She had fled from the war on her home moon of Whiston but had found herself to be an unwelcome guest on my home planet. Animanecrons had been barred from Arrhidaeus for some hundreds of years, shortly after their creation by my family's company, and shortly after humanity realized that they had created an entirely new form of life. No longer just the means to preserve my species' lives after death, animanecrons were sentient, self-contained, and self-governing. Banished to the moon of Whiston by their creators, it had been almost a century since animanecrons had been on Arrhidaeus—until the planet had been flooded with those seeking asylum from the tyranny of Whiston's warmongering planetary neighbor, Char-cornac. Those like Cadence.

But to me, Cadence Turning would always be one of a kind. Not just because she had believed in me when no one else would. No... Because I was quite hopelessly in love with her.

I pushed aside the curtain and came to an abrupt halt. Cadence had her back to me as she leant against a low, plastic table. Sitting at the table was a bloody, beaten man —a stranger I had never seen before, but whose current appearance I would not soon forget. It'd been some time since I'd seen anyone looking so thoroughly thrashed. A large bruise was visible beneath the collar of his bowl-necked shirt, dried streaks of blood and dirt smeared across his face. One eye was purpling, and he held a thin, blue rag to his bald head, through which blood steadily seeped.

Cadence turned when I entered. She dropped a bottle of disinfectant into an open medkit as she waved to me, her hand bloody. "Hello, Chance."

"Uh, good evening," I said, frozen at the edge of the space, the stall curtain still lifted halfway above my head.

"Hello," said the older gentleman, looking over at me blankly. As I stared, blood continued to seep from the cut on his head into the rag.

Cadence got up from the table, indicating the injured man. "Chance, this is Mr. Galt. He runs the Magical Realism shop a few spaces down from me."

Galt waved, his face the very picture of misery. "Call me Andy."

I nodded, trying on a weak smile as I stepped forward into the room. "Pleasure to meet you, Andy." I looked from him to Cadence and back again. "Is everything alright? Was there some kind of accident?"

"Anta, it was no accident." She narrowed her blue eyes, curling her hands into fists at her sides. "People did this to him. On purpose. Rus, for money!"

My eyes widened. "You were robbed?"

Closing his eyes, Andy leaned back against a thick pile of story cubes, sighing loudly. "No. Not exactly."

When it became clear that Andy was not going to say anything more without prompting, Cadence stepped up beside me, nodding. "Sinc, It's okay, Mr. Galt. You can trust, Chance—he's a friend."

Andy stared at Cadence for a moment before

nodding. He swallowed hard. The words came out thick, half-choked by the man's fear and grief. "It's Lewis. My son. They've... got my son."

A sharp stab of dread tore through my heart. I looked at Cadence, who only stared grimly at the floor, her face contorted.

"Who?" I asked.

Anger flashed in Andy's powder-blue eyes. He straightened, wiping tears off the tip of his nose. "This group of punks. Call themselves the Pack—they sell drogan, mostly. Lewis started running with them a few months ago. I told him they were no good, I told him he could do better, but—he's sixteen, you know? They just stop listening at that age." He dropped his hand from his head, examining the bloodstained rag before tossing it away. "Turns out they just wanted to use him to get to me. Here, I have..." The man fumbled into his back pocket and produced a small, flexible optric. He held it out to me. "This is Lewis. My boy."

I took the optric and looked into the face of a smiling, teenage boy. I sat down in front of Andy on an upturned, empty crate. "Do you know what these people want?"

Andy nodded. "My shop does good business. The lease is coming up for renewal. They want me to cut them in as business partners."

I drew back, shaking my head. "Why?"

Andy shrugged, leaning forward over the table, his fleshy arms sliding against the plastic. "Easy way for them to make a buck. I do all the work, they get a place to clean their dirty cash when they need it." He closed his hand into a fist. "I told them no. So, they... they took Lewis. They say they're going to kill him if I don't do what they want."

Nodding, I licked my dry lips. "When did all this happen?" I asked, a sinking feeling in the pit of my stomach.

Andy hung his head low between his shoulders. "A few days ago." His shaved head glistened with sweat and flecks of blood as he shook it, lifting his hands to cover his pale face. "The lease renewal is due by midnight. If I don't cut them in, they're going to kill him. If I go to the EO, they kill him." Pulling himself together with a shudder, he sat back in the chair, gesturing to his injuries with one hand. "This was just a reminder of that. Miss Turing heard the ruckus and came down to check on me. Thankfully, they were gone by the time she arrived."

"Animals," spat Cadence, her arms crossed high over her chest.

Andy sighed deeply, gripping his own chest. "I just... I don't know what to do." He looked into my face, and I saw the tears in his eyes. "I don't even know where they're keeping him."

Cadence must have seen his anguish as well because she moved through the room towards him. She crouched down, placing one hand on his shoulder and the other on his knee. "Andy, please—don't worry." She shook her head emphatically. "I'm not going to let anything happen to your son."

"What?" chorused Andy and I, albeit with slightly different tenors—Andy sounded confused, but I sounded thoroughly alarmed.

Smiling, her space-black hair falling into her face, Cadence leaned back onto her heels. Her voice took on an edge of excitement. "I'm a detective. Just ask Chance."

I glared at her, leaning forward. I rested my elbow on my knee. "Well, an amateur detective, certainly."

If she heard the censure in my words, Cadence ignored it, focusing on Andy. "I've got thousands of literature's cleverest detectives and their cases in my memory banks—I can find your son, and I can bring him home."

Andy looked Cadence up and down, his mouth slightly agape. "Do you think...?" He swallowed, and for the first time since I entered the room, I saw a glimmer of hope in his eyes. "Could you really?"

Standing abruptly, I gestured towards the curtain. "Cadence, can I talk to you for a moment?"

Cadence looked over her shoulder at me. "Right now?"

"If you don't mind."

Patting Andy's knee one final time, she shrugged, following me out to the front of the store. I waited until the curtain closed behind us before I turned on her with a glare.

"He needs to go to the Enforcement Office," I said, doing my best to be stern.

Cadence gaped at me, scandalized. She threw up her hands. "Chance, he can't! Haven't you been listening?"

I crossed my arms over my chest and leaned forward. "Haven't you?" I chewed the inside of my cheek, letting out a sharp breath through my nose. "You are not some kind of masked vigilante or superhero, Cay. You can't take on a street gang by yourself!"

Cadence shook her head, shifting her weight onto her back foot. "I'm not going to take on a street gang by myself."

Some of the tension drained out of my shoulders, and I relaxed. "Good."

"We're going to do it together, obviously," she said, rolling her eyes.

"Like fun we are!" I sputtered.

"Are you going to pout the whole time?" asked Cadence, taking a long drink from her lemonade.

Glowering at her from over my mostly empty pint of beer, I grumbled, "I am a grown man—I do not pout."

Smacking her lips, she nodded, her eyes fixed on the other occupants of the bar. "You're pouting."

Killing time at a gang-ridden watering hole, even with my charming companion, was not my idea of pleasant evening. I was about to relate as much to Cadence when I saw her eyes widen. The corner of her mouth twitched as she leaned back in her seat, attempting to appear nonchalant even as she whispered, "Xio, there she is..."

"Who?" I said, pivoting back and forth as I searched the bar for the target of Cadence's rapt attention.

"Chance!" hissed Cadence, kicking me under the table.

"Ow!" I said, grabbing at my aching shin. "What the hell was that for?"

"Don't be so obvious," chided my friend. "Honestly, don't you know anything about detective work?"

I fixed her with a dubious, unamused stare. "Given that I am the CEO of a system-spanning tech conglomerate, and not a gumshoe, no. No, Cay, I don't know anything about detective work." I muttered, "Not all of us have a head full of crime fiction..."

Cadence ignored my snide remark and instead inclined her head towards someone at the bar. "Mr. Galt described a young lady with green hair and earlobe piercings, who comes into this bar every night to get drinks for the crew. That must be her."

Several silent moments passed as I sipped what was left of my beer. Curiosity got the best of me in the end, and I finally inquired. "Well, what is she doing?"

"Buying copious amounts of alcohol, just as Mr. Galt said she would." Cadence shook her head, frowning. "Tris, she's so young—sad to think that she'd be involved in something like a kidnapping."

I drained my drink. "Ah, the follies of youth."

Cadence furrowed her brow. "Yes, I suppose so." From behind me, I heard calls of farewell. Cadence shifted in her seat. "Let's go." She shot to her feet, grabbing her coat and shoving her arms through the sleeves as she hurried towards the door. I had little choice but to follow her.

The green-haired youth took us on a torturous route through some of the less than pleasant sections of the city of Römer. The buildings we passed were run down—in need of repair or in need of a wrecking ball—and the few people we passed on the streets were sullen and sour-looking.

Cadence and I were careful to keep some distance from our quarry, but I doubted we needed to be so cautious. Loaded down with her precious cargo of alcohol, the woman seemed keen to get where she was going as quickly as possible.

"Too easy," chuckled Cadence, grinning wickedly. "She's not even checking to see if she's being followed!"

"Because who would be stupid enough to do something like that?" I said, rolling my eyes. "Oh, wait..."

Cadence continued to ignore my sarcasm and focus on the task at hand. We followed the delinquent out of one district and into another, until we found ourselves surrounded by derelict warehouses, one of which the young lady entered, while we remained several hundred yards behind her.

With a jerk of her head, Cadence indicated the building opposite the warehouse into which our mark had vanished. With only dim streetlights to guide us, we concealed ourselves in the condemned building's recessed doorway, from which we had a clear view of the site.

Cadence was silent for several long minutes as she kept watch. I let her think, hopeful that she would come to some solution to this scenario that would allow us to abandon this madness and go home. After a quarter of an hour, she let out a sharp breath through her nose and said, "Well... I don't see any obvious way to get in undetected..."

I leaned away from the filthy glass portal, glancing to either side of the building to make sure that we were as alone as I hoped. "Even if there was a way, Cadence, it's a warehouse—there could be any number of places inside that they're keeping the boy." I gripped her wrist, drawing her attention to me fully. "Cay, we need to call the EO. They're equipped to handle this kind of situation."

Cadence shook her head. "If we do that, this will turn into a shootout. Lewis could get hurt."

I dropped my hand back to my side, letting out a huff. "Serves him right for not listening," I growled darkly.

"Chance!" exclaimed Cadence. "How can you say that? Didn't you make mistakes in your youth?"

Her question pricked at a sensitive spot in my soul. To call my youth 'misspent' was a kindness. I had been an ass, and if I hadn't met Cadence, I would in all likelihood still be one—and serving a life sentence in the penal district.

"Don't make it sound as if my youth was some far-flung era from the present-day," I sighed, attempting to hide how deeply her words had affected me. I jiggled the thin gold band on my wrist to life and observed the time. I licked my dry lips. "Cadence, we have three hours until the deadline, no way to sneak inside, and—" My eyes caught on the blocky building across the street, and I was struck with an inescapable sense of deja vu. The proverbial wheels in my head began turning. "Wait, hold on."

Staring at the structure, I was finally able to place the sense of familiarity that its shape and size engendered within me. I pointed to the building, turning my head over my shoulder to whisper at Cadence, "That's an old Halcyon property."

Her keen eyes strained against the dark. "What?"

"Look." One hand on her shoulder, I positioned her in front of me so she could look down the length of my arm to where I was pointing. "See? That's where the logo used to be."

"I see it," she said at length, looking askance at me with a quirked brow. "Does this fact help us?"

"All the Halcyon Enterprise shipping warehouses have the same basic layout. Father designed them that way—cheaper, you see? Better to train a workforce that can move seamlessly from building to building." I scanned the warehouse for signs of movement, signs of a lookout, and, seeing none, whispered: "Follow me."

Crouching, I led her across the darkened street, hoping we remained unobserved. I knew what I was looking for, but it'd been a long while since I'd seen one—

and it was possible the design had changed in the intervening ten or so years...

I felt, rather than saw, the emergency hatch to the overflow shipping tunnel for which I had been looking. The metal sang out under me as my foot clapped on top of it, and I bounced back with a triumphant, but quiet 'ha!'.

Kneeling down in the near total dark, my fingers searched for the hatch's outside lever. Finding it, I worked the rusted mechanical device up. The ground in front of me fell open with a creak.

"See?" I smiled, waving a hand down into the newly appeared hole. "This runs under the length of the street beneath the warehouses. There's your way in."

Without hesitation, Cadence peeled off her jacket, tossing the flapping fabric off to one side as she prepared to leap down into the opening. My arms jerked out to block her descent, as I stuttered out, "Woah, hold on, what are you doing?"

She lifted her brow. "Going in. Like you said, we only have three hours."

I shook my head. "The whole gang could be in there. They could have someone guarding the boy. What are you going to do? What's your plan for getting him out without getting hurt?"

"Hm." She leaned back on her haunches, twisting her lips into a thoughtful grimace. "You make a good point." Looking up at me, she smiled. It was a sweet summer smile that had no place in that dingy district. "What I need is a distraction."

I sat down hard on my backside, my heart tight in my chest. "Oh, good Lord," I groaned, squeezing my eyes shut.

❋

I walked towards the front of the abandoned warehouse. The deafening crunch of cracked concrete under my shoes grated on my frayed nerves. Part of me couldn't believe that Cadence had talked me into this, but in all actuality, this was par for the course in our relationship—she was always hurling me out of my comfort zone.

When I got within thirty feet of the main doors, they burst open, and a handful of rough looking men and women flooded out, guns and pulsars of various kinds pointed at me.

My comfort zone was now in another galaxy.

I stopped dead in my tracks and put on my best, winning smile. "Hello!" I waved, careful to keep both hands visible and high in the air. "Nice night, eh? Um, I'd like to speak with whoever's in charge, please. Andy Galt sent me."

The loading dock door rolled open with a teeth-rattling clatter, revealing several more unfriendly-looking personages. One of these figures gave a loud sniff and jumped down from the dock. He began walking in my direction, seemingly unarmed and unconcerned by my arrival. "What the hell are you supposed to be?" asked the man strolling towards me, a wide grin revealing two rows of painfully white teeth.

"I thought that would be fairly obvious," I said, doing my best to channel every corporate lawyer I'd ever met. I gave an oily smirk, lowering my hands to my sides as he approached. "I'm the money."

A snort of laughter was his response. He continued to amble forward, seemingly in no hurry to close the gap between us. "You say Galt sent you?" he asked at length, shaking his head. "Galt doesn't know where we are."

"No," I confirmed, gesturing to myself languidly. "That's why he hired me—to find you and negotiate. I get paid to do that sort of thing, you see."

Finally, the man reached the spot where I was standing. He cast a glance behind him, tossing his bangs out of his face with a jerk of his head. "Pay must be good."

I forced my smile wider, trying to hide my nerves behind my teeth. "Exorbitant." I reached out a hand, not entirely certain it would be accepted. "Are you in charge?"

"Hunter Davis," he offered, taking my hand in a firm grip. "This is my crew."

Without warning, he jerked me forward. I lost my footing just long enough for him to pull a pulsar from behind his back and press it into my torso. It was a fluid, practiced maneuver, and I would have admired it, had I not been so preoccupied with staying alive.

"Can you think of a single, good reason why I shouldn't shoot you right now, Mr. Money?" Davis asked, child-like curiosity dripping off every word, his smile never wavering.

I did my best not to look at the weapon digging into my stomach, keeping my gaze locked with Davis' bloodshot eyes. "I can think of several thousand, Mr. Davis."

"Credits?" Davis released me, and I bounced away from him as if I was on a spring. If he noticed me recoiling, he didn't show it, his gaze heavenward as he pondered aloud, "Galt don't have that kind of cash..."

Straightening out my ruffled clothes, I shook my head. "You'd be amazed at the lengths a man will go to when it means the life of his child." I clasped my hands in front of my hips. "Now, I've been instructed to transfer these credits to you, upon the release of Lewis Galt. So, if you'll just let the boy go—"

"Nothing doing, Mr. Money," cut in Davis, shaking his head from side to side with all the languidness of a snake.

I crooked my head to one side, lifting my brows. "You don't want to suddenly become a very wealthy man?"

Davis sniffed, rubbing at the patch of dark brown hair under his chin. "You know, it's not always about the money, Mr. Money." He stood akimbo, head drifting towards his left shoulder in a mirror image of mine. "Galt's got a sweet set-up down there at the Entertainment Market. Government doesn't look too close at his books—it's perfect for tidying up our investments."

"Plus," I said, sighing and doing my best to look nonchalant as I glanced at my watch, "if the government does get curious, I'm guessing that he'll go down for it, and not you, right?"

"Ha," exclaimed Davis without mirth. "Exactly. Got brains on you, Mr. Money."

Too long. It'd been too long. Cadence should have sent some kind of signal to me by now. Something had gone wrong. And I was running out of ideas. My jaw taut, I looked back up at Hunter Davis, shaking my head. "He won't do it, you know."

Davis shrugged. "Then he'll be watching his only child go up in smoke," he said. "Man's got to learn: actions have con—"

The windows on the left side of the warehouse exploded outward with a roar of fire that shook the ground. Before anyone had time to react to the first blast, a second followed, then a third, coming so quickly that they were almost indistinguishable from each other.

The shouts and screams started immediately, people scrambling over each other to get away from the destruction, but it was too late. Within seconds, the building was on fire, debris from the explosions raining down onto the street.

I did the only sensible thing I could do, of course. I sprinted away from the chaos and towards Cadence.

I hadn't gone more than a few steps when a lanky body pinballed into mine and knocked us both to the ground. Pushing myself up onto my elbows, I looked across and found myself staring at a beaten and bruised Lewis Galt.

"You must be Lewis!" I shouted over the cacophony of flames and falling debris.

"What the hell is going on?!" demanded the teenager, breathless and terrified.

Risking a quick glance around us, and seeing the path to the street clear, I grabbed hold of him by the shoulders and heaved him to his feet. "We're getting you out of here —now, come on!"

I shoved the lad in front of myself, sending him running away from the burning building and towards the dark, empty street. "Come on, we have to go before—"

"You bastard," growled Davis, leveling his pulsar at the back of my head.

As DAVIS DREW BACK his hand to strike me with the butt of the pulsar, I instinctively closed my eyes.

A fleshy crunch. A scream.

Davis released me from his grip, and I dropped onto the hard ground, my eyes jolting open. I looked up to see Cadence, who had appeared from out of the smoke and moved behind Hunter Davis without a sound. She gripped his hand so tightly that I was certain she had broken every bone inside the appendage, not to mention the pulsar he had been holding.

Davis dropped onto his knees, screaming loudly, but Cadence did not relent, twisting the appendage behind his back. "If you come after the Galts again," she said, seemingly heedless to the man's shouts of agony, "I won't be so gentle. Do you understand?"

Tears streaming down his face, Davis jerked his head up and down. Cadence waited a beat longer before releasing him with a flick of her wrist. The man collapsed, cradling his ruined hand close to his chest and writhing in agony.

Stepping over him, Cadence looked at me, smiling.

"Lewis made it out alright?"

"Er," I looked from the tortured man to Cadence and then back again.

"Well, did he?"

"Yes. Yes, he's on his way home."

"Good." Strolling past me, she gestured towards the street. "Shall we?"

Leaving the burning building and broken man behind us, I hurried to catch up with her. "What was that explosion?" I asked as casually as I possibly could, casting a final glance at the smoking wreckage.

"Open containers of biofuel and lit nixes do not mix well," Cadence said, tucking her hair behind her ear as we walked, the building ablaze behind us.

I fixed her with an incredulous stare. She adopted an expression of exaggerated innocence, raising her shoulders to brush the bottoms of her ears. "Sinc, it was an accident! Everyone was alright though—save for some scorching."

The sounds of sirens reached me, and I grabbed ahold of her hand, tugging Cadence forward as I broke out into a jog. "We better get out of here before the EO arrives to admire your handiwork."

"Gav, I told you that we could do it!" she said, smiling and laughing as she dropped my hand to run past me.

It must have been the adrenaline still coursing through my system—that, or there was something truly infectious about her smile. But I found myself laughing as I ran, shaking my head as I shouted after her, "Remind me never to doubt you!"

"Ransomware" is a story in Robin Jeffrey's Cadence Turing Mystery series.

Looking for more Cadence & Chance? Follow Robin's adventures and get more sci-fi crime goodness on her website, RobinJeffreyAuthor.com.

PICK YOUR POISON

1. *Whisk me away to Mars!* Head to "Second Breath" by Peter J. Foote

2. *Dammit. It's always something.* Go read "Sparrow" by G.J. Ogden in CROOKED V.2

3. *It's time for one last job.* Keep going to read "The Alshaita Uplift Job" by Mark Teppo

THE ALSHAITA UPLIFT JOB

BY MARK TEPPO

Editor's Note: While this story is perfectly delightful on its own, I highly recommend also checking out Mark Teppo's two previous Maisiverse stories. You can find those in CROOKED V.1 and CROOKED V.2.

SINCE THE LATEST EXTRAPOLATION FROM LONG-range scans said they were the only ship in this vector plane between Hallabow and the Venture Gate at Alshaita, Maisi took advantage of the vast emptiness of space to call her first team meeting.

She had sent the 'all-hands' from the common room of *Who's a Pretty Sparrow, All Aflutter in the Morning Sky?*, so Maisi was already there when the others arrived. Nome showed up first, strolling in from the forward viewing bay where he coded by starlight. He was a rangy fellow who appeared half asleep and thoroughly uninter-ested in anything going on around him, but anyone with a half-slice of sitware would scope his feigned indifference. Nome was wired—through and true—and any inattentiveness to his physical surroundings was due to an intense scrutiny of all the digital intelligence he was slurping in a thirty meter radius.

Sheets followed soon thereafter. If you were to pop a glimpse into the lower left quadrant of Nome's ocular field, you'd see Sheet's real name was Hadrax Thoolsenj and that he had once been a Fist. One of those testosterone-pinging rage-rounders whose understanding of diplomatic solutions was measured in RPC (Rounds per Cycle) and TDP (Total Destructive Power, usually expressed in megatons). Sheets carried a sanctioned data vault in his gut, and its quantum lattice processing core did the complicated math necessary to operate milspec assault hardware, everything from a Berolock AAA mobile assault rig to the latest and greatest in autonomous planetary assault units.

Speaking of which, shortly before life in the mercenary corps came to an abrupt end with the Maricolosa Insurrection, the ASL—the hot death family where Sheets did his breakout work, dusting and dooming small settlements on backwards planets—had contracted out for a next-gen build of their Fists' thunder thumpers. The dissolution of the corps left whoever had been burning R & D to upgrade these blunt-force pacification monstrosities with a couple million datasets of theoretical design specs and a suite of C-level executives whose only remaining value to the company was how quickly they could sell these scorched assets to a spotless conglomerate who could wash them clean.

It doesn't take much imagination to figure where all this abandoned and sanctioned tech disappeared to, does it?

Anyway, with the quantum entanglement box in his belly, Sheets could crunch numbers better than a flight of gold star graduates from the Czekekeka Institute of Theoretical Mathematics and Applied Numerologies, which meant he could both balance the ship's budget and keep it on course during these long transits.

And so then, we come to the latest addition to the crew. One Lallay Leotemorah, a quick-fingered fixer who had been doing a ten-year stint with the Kaplodonic Extraction Company on Gloassia IV. In her usual style, Maisi had negotiated Leo's release from his contract and offered him a no-fuss consideration ("ride with us or walk a thousand clicks to the nearest star port"). Leo, who had been counting the days left in his time on the rock, hadn't fussed, and since coming on-board the *Sparrow*, he had spent most of his time rearranging tools in the work bay and customizing the interfaces on the shopbots.

"You all know who I work for," Maisi said when they were gathered. "The Ministry of Accordance, Recompense, and Solidarity is tasked with ensuring that Anslaage's membership—the Great Houses, the HTF—don't go stomping all over the Interstellar Exploration and Commerce Accords. That job takes a lot of infrastructure—people, paperwork, and processors—but some of us are given license to roam. We're the ones who seek and cite, peep and pipe, and"—Nome made a noise in his throat, and she gave him a quick side-eye—"Well, you know, nothing ruins a party faster than a MARS agent flashing their seal."

"All kinds of names for folks like you," Sheets rumbled.

Maisi flashed him a smile. "Most of them won't raise a

flush in my cheeks, so don't feel like you need to try." She glanced at Leo, who showed her the palm of one hand—bunker talk for a variety of responses like "don't know," "don't care," and "not really paying attention."

"Right, and MARS knows what the rest of the galaxy knows, and that is the Houses don't play fair. And so, MARS has their own rulebreakers: the Special Circumstances Division. SCD is fully autonomous. Budget sealed. SCD doesn't file paperwork. CORE doesn't get to shove an auditor up our asses. Management can't shackle what they can't acknowledge. This is the freshest whiff of free air that all of you'll ever get. But, the flip of this freedom is MARS won't save or salvage. Local law enforcement takes a shine? House bangers and biters get a taste? We're on our own."

"No catchy, all snatchy," Nome said.

"Self-funding and self-managing," Sheets rumbled, translating Nome's oblique commentary.

"That we are." Maisi leaned forward. "There are, however, two wrinkles to taking this ride. One, the *Sparrow* is an independent equality orgo—ship-shares are straight split, as are responsibilities; and, secondly, I am Queen Bee around here. My law is the only law that matters. Clear?" She looked at each of them in turn.

Sheets made a noise like granite shifting; Leo made eye contact. "Aeyo, boss lady," he said.

Maisi waited a beat, in case anyone had further commentary to add, and when no one peeped, she produced a set of data cards from the pocket of her jacket and skipped one to each. "Passage Keys," she said. "Familiarize yourself with the Licensing Agreement and Terms of Service—or not, your call—but you need to make a choice, one way or another, before we reach port." She flashed a cutting smile. "If you don't want to sign and seal, I'll be happy to drop you off, but you will be billed at an egregious rate."

Leo picked up the plastform card. It sensed the warmth of his contact, and the surface swarmed in a parade of neat lines and colors. His personal slate caught the ping from the card, and when he acknowledged it, a scrolling document of dense legalese spooled onto his rig. He stopped it with a stab of a finger and swiped right to get to the end. A blinker box popped up, asking if he wished to mark the document. He pressed his thumb against the key, telling the slipware within the card that he had read and accepted the LATOS. He was ready to bind his profile to the ship's. Once marked, he and the ship were the same to every port accountant and registry within the Hanseatic Trade Foundation.

The card in his hand—the Passage Key—turned orange. It pulsed a few times as it compared the biometrics the card had just acquired to the stored data offered by his slate. The key flashed green one time—acknowledging both the bio match and the binding—and then went dark.

Maisi smiled at him. "Welcome to the family," she said.

Nome had already made his key disappear, and they all looked at Sheets. He showed his teeth in a feral grimace. "I'm going to read the fine print," he said.

"Fair enough," Maisi said. She nodded to Nome, who flicked a packet off his slate. It bloomed into a 3D render of local space. "We're due at Alshaita in about six hours," she said. "Nome's got us in the queue for the Venture

Gate, which will Interlink us just about anywhere in this quadrant of the Hub." She paused for a moment. "Now that we're done with the meet and greet, let's get on with the next bit of business, which is: we need a looker."

"A what?" Sheets grumbled.

"A face. A slick-talker, attention-grabber, and distraction-maker," Maisi said. "Someone who can get folks to look over *there* while we do things over *here*."

Sheets sat back in his chair. "Not my style," he said.

Nome acknowledged the truth in that statement with a quirk of his eyebrow. He crooked a finger at the rotating display, and a number of blue dots bloomed.

Maisi made a face. "That's more than a 'few'."

"I didn't want to limit our options," Nome replied.

Sheets laughed. "You got shit is what you mean."

Nome frowned, unhappy to be called out, but he did dip his head in Sheet's direction. "Best of a bad lot," he admitted. "Unless you want to range farther out."

Maisi ran a hand through her pale hair. "How much farther?" she asked.

Nome lifted his shoulders. "Outer spiral, if we're really desperate," he said.

"Like 'no filter, gimme the whole dataset' desperate?"

"Your search criteria was a bit . . . fusty."

"Fusty?"

"You are welcome to check my work on quantifying 'I've got a good feeling about this one' or 'Could definitely talk my panties off' into a reasonable algorithmic reduction matrix."

Maisi sighed. "Let down once again by the limitations of machine intelligence," she said. She waved a hand at the floating over-up. "Fine. Let's start with what's local. Leo, as the newest nestling, you pick."

"Me?" Leo put up both hands—palms out—dangerous distancing for a bunker, but it sent a clear signal.

"Or, talk the knuckle-jammer into signing and sealing," Maisi offered. "You won't be bottom rung. Job'll fall on his shoulders."

Sheets let out a gargling rumble at the fixer's dilemma. He knuckled the Passage Key on the table. "Ain't sealing it until you decide, little wrench," he said.

Leo didn't rise to the bait. By any scientific measure, he occupied less space than the ex-Fist, and during his time with the Liberty Security Fraternity, he had been called a number of names by the muscle meat who operated the heavy equipment, and like Maisi had noted earlier, survival among the hard-handers meant learning how to brush off the belittling endearments. A "wrench," however—he'd be happy to note—was always useful.

"Ayea," Leo sighed. He gestured at Nome's slate. "Let me see the summs."

Nome flicked over datasets for the dots, and Leo started to read the summaries.

Maisi watched him, a bemused expression on her face. Nome leaned back in his chair, finding the perfect balance that would simulate zero-G, and appeared to fall asleep. Sheets, after a few minutes of ship-board silence, covered his Passage Key with a broad thumb. The card lit up, and the hitter let out the rattling sigh that every living soul instinctively released when they were confronted with hundreds of pages of obfucascading legalese. Somewhere in his quantum belly bomb was a package that would sift, rinse, and render the LATOS in a single sheet bullet summary. Oh, this package alone—if it could be extracted and packet-parsed—would provide full recompense and rehabilitation (as per IECA Section 18.43.9) for every censused individual in two or three of the settlements on Cancarcosa that had been vaporized by the ASL during the Maricolasa Insurrection.

Allegedly, of course. CORE sealed all fiduciary and judiciary records following their humanitarian audit.

"Angabatay Marshalan," Leo blurted out, startling Nome who had mathed the estimated FR&R payout for the loss of life on Cancarcosa and was calculating full spec and total tonnage those funds would acquire. His chair dropped forward, the legs clattering against the deck. "Who?" he asked.

Leo tapped his slate, and one of the blue dots shifted green. "Angabatay Marshalan," he said. He tapped his slate again, and the dot exploded into a rotating ID. "One of the pop crooners of DreamBeam Cashisway. They were one of those flash cee 'n' vee collectives."

The other blue dots and the blinking system markers obligingly dimmed so as to not detract from the ridiculously handsome face that made eye contact as it slowly rotated.

"Oh my," Maisi said.

Nome made a face. "This is what I'm talking about," he said. "Is that 'Oh my' an eight or a nine on the TMPO scale?"

Maisi tilted her head. "Nine," she decided.

"That would have made a difference," Nome said, as if he still needed to justify why his data mining hadn't produced this result on its own.

"Well, good thing we had some retro spec quality assurance to fall back on." She tapped a finger against the table. "What's the hitch?" she asked—half to Nome, half to Leo.

Nome, swiftly retasking to the question at hand, found the scandal sheet in his summary package and flicked it onto the table display. The handsome face dissolved into a fuzzy video. Peeper drone footage. There was no sound and the image was shaky, but everyone at the table had seen enough feed footage from the judiciary theater around the Maricolasa Insurrection to recognize horrific humanitarian atrocities. In this instance, the drones were close enough to pick out individual body parts. "Fan action," Nome said. "Creepo got possessive. Wanted what wasn't his. Snatched half the group after a show."

Maisi frowned and flicked away the video. "That's a lot of blood for a snatch and grab. Did their security fuck things up?"

Nome scanned his slate. "Feeds are full of spicy theories, but official statements are . . . *thin*. Management layered up. They tagged outside assistance. An I & R team was brought in. House-sponsored."

"A fancy-grade Interdiction & Resolution team? Which House?"

Nome's hesitation was an answer in itself.

Maisi shook her head. "*Ay-challe*," she said.

Nome's reaction was—well, Leo hadn't flown with this crew long enough to know for sure, but he could read a room well enough to know the hacker was disengaging from the conversation. He thumbed his slate and slid through the summary package to find the details about the bloody resolution to the kidnapping. *House Bellephori*, he read. The I & R team had worn Bellephori colors.

He caught Maisi looking at him. "Family colors," she said, instinctively reading the question in his eyes.

He stared. "You're . . . you're blooded?"

"Only a little," she said. She waved a hand, cutting short any further discussion. "This Anglebaby—"

"Angabatay," Leo corrected.

"—this crooner," she continued. "He survived all the danger drama?"

Nome clipped back into the conversation. "Resuscitated," he said. "Brought back." His expression tightened. "Contractual grant."

"Of course there was." Maisi sighed. "I suppose they dusted him up and did a solo comeback tour?"

Nome shook his head. "Actually, no. He was . . . exempted and excused."

"Well, how refreshing. A compassionate lapse of judgement from management. So, if he's not sailing spinward on a nostalgia tour, where is he?"

"He pledged himself to CHAR—the Church of the Holy Absolute Resolve."

"Ah," she said. "Someone negotiated a way out if he vowed to never grace a feed screen again."

"Sensible read," Nome said.

Maisi summoned back the floating head. "Where?" she asked.

"CHAR monasterium on Balchar VII. It's a half-skip from here, actually. Place called—get this—the 'Spire of Perpetual Abasement for Eventual Reconciliation.'"

Maisi raised an eyebrow as she tracked the acronym. "Was the lot used for something else before CHAR came in and hung new drapes?"

"Not that I can tell," Nome said. "Scratch build."

"All right, then." Maisi directed her gaze at Leo. "Heya, nestling. Why this one?"

Leo found himself blushing. "Had a lady friend once who liked the songs."

The rest of the team stared at the fixer. "I—it was—" His fingers danced with belter slang. "She wasn't much for waiting," he said. "Once I got snatched . . ."

"Didn't mark her enough to keep her fixated during all those lonely nights," Maisi finished. "How many days were you going to make her wait?" There was a hint of a smile at the corner of her mouth.

"Two thousand, nine hundred, and eighty-four," he said.

"Not a lot of ladies who would wait one percent of that," she said. "No slight on you."

Leo gave her a gesture of appreciation.

"All right," she said. "Let's go save this pop star from a lifetime of . . . what was it?"

"Celibacy and austerity," Nome said.

Maisi looked like she had just thrown up in her mouth a little. She swallowed and grimaced. "That's a hell no one should have to suffer."

THE NEWEST ADDITION to the Trust Circle at the Spire of Perpetual Abasement for Eventual Reconciliation was always in the courtyard before the others for the morning solar salutation. Several of the brethren—less forgiving souls who persisted in clinging to a hierarchical understanding of how the worlds turned—had tried to catch him sneaking out of his cell, but they were typically spotted by the Night Masters and swatted with willow canes until they scurried to the courtyard. There, of course, waiting for them, his bent and broken face raised to greet the rising sun, was Penitent Pastroyalé.

It was the name he had adopted upon being taken into the arms of the Church of the Holy Absolute Resolve. He had had a different name prior, of course. They all did. In his case, his professional name had been "Angabatay Marshalan." It was, like "Pastroyalé," merely a series of letters someone had entered in a data field once upon a time. There were other names: "Shit-spewing sphincter of a hemorrhagic fever patient," for instance, given to him by DBC's road manager (an entirely unlike-able prick who enthusiastically embodied the worst clichés of the job description); "Molly," the pet name used by Drean, Bleu, and Candi-CanCan, the other Westies of the DreamBeam Cashisway; and "Bang-Bang Batay," a passing gift by one of the feed wringers during Dream-Beam Cashisway's first tour. The last one has stuck; he had signed so much swag with those looping B's that he could do it in his asleep.

A stinging slap across the exposed soles of his feet brought his mind into focus. "Your attention wanders, Penitent," the Dawn Master said, tapping his cane against Pastroyalé's hip. Letting him know that another slap was not out of question.

Pastroyalé did not flinch. He gave no indication of the physical rebuke. Nor did he show any reaction or emotional outburst when three of the brethren came to his cell for his nightly lesson. They whispered chapter and verse from the Holy Record as they laid hands on him, punctuating the nuance and subtext of the text with their fist and feet. Pastroyalé had not cried out. He did not complain. He suffered their abuse in silence. Such was his penance, to be accepted and internalized, over and over, *challe a' challe.*

The morning salutation would, depending on the Dawn Master's mood, last an hour or more after sunrise. During which time, the Blemished, those neophytes who had not realized their first Inchoate Incarnation, would remain prostrate and immobile on the mosaic tiles of the courtyard. Their bodies would be thoroughly bathed in the holy light that flensed all shame and degradation from puerile flesh. Only when their Master was satisfied with their suffering would they be allowed to rise and partake of their morning dollop of protein paste and recycled waste water.

This was, in every way, the most peaceful part of the day for Penitent Pastroyalé. His body was empty. His mind would empty. As his breathing slowed, he could feel something loosening inside. He imagined it was his spirit —that pure part of him that was without name or history. That part that had nothing, wanted nothing, and would be nothing. Each breath brought him a little closer. The simplest cycles: in for life, out for death. These are the breaths we take to enumerate our shame. Over and over, like serpents devouring themselves, until balance is restored and you give back that first breath you stole from the universe. Each breath was a step closer to the Holy Emptiness.

Pastroyalé had paid attention during his nocturnal initiations. He had learned the lessons. An earnest penitent cherished each breath. They were present during the transformation that occurred within the lungs. They were attentive when they exhaled, silently offering gratitude to be allowed such conscious immediacy during the sacred release. Pastroyalé had found a happy place during the beatings.

He was, in fact, closer to his first Incarnation than any of the Masters knew. It would come as no surprise to Pastroyalé, though. He had always learned choreography faster than any of the other dancers. Even their prick of a road manager had grudgingly acknowledged his gift for rapid kinesthetic assimilation.

"Master." One of the other brethren ruined the morning ritual with the squalid squawk of his voice. Pastroyalé came back to himself enough to hear the rustle of the Dawn Master's robes as the priest moved to punish the speaker. He heard the Master's cane slap against naked flesh—once, twice.

There was no third slap, and it was this violation of the ritual—more so than the brethren's breach of sacred etiquette—that hauled Pastroyalé back from his meditative consideration of the Eventual Reconciliation. His breath caught in his chest, and he fell out of the rhythmic embrace of nothingness.

There was a roaring sound, and his first thought was that it came from the chthonic emptiness of the Abyss—a stygian howl of abandonment. But he realized the source of any such sound would have to come from his own suffering, and for an instant, he marveled at the pain still locked within him.

"Inside!" The Dawn Master shouted over the rumble of a ship's burners, and these two sounds—the panicked shout of the Dawn Master and the resolute growl of a starship—brought Pastroyalé all the way back to reality.

He fell out of his abasement, banging his elbow on the courtyard tile. Looking up, he saw the oblong shape of an atmospheric flyer as the craft blocked the sun. Its stubby wings were limned with fire and its landing gear reached groundward like the outstretched claw of an enormous bird of prey.

Pastroyalé scrambled to his feet and followed the other brethren of the Church of the Holy Absolute Resolve as the penitents and their masters attempted to clear the courtyard.

The flyer, a flat-nosed assault transport, landed like a wallowing water beast. As the dust of its arrival dispersed, the back end of the transport sphinctered open, and a squad of visored goons charged down an extruding ramp. If Pastroyalé's contract for DBC hadn't excused him from mandatory martial service so that he could lip-sync bopalop trax and air-kiss feed fashionistas, he might have recognized the six by two forward lock-and-block formation of an assault squad: six ground-bumpers with tactical assault rifles, supported by a pair of heavy battery dragoons—wide-shouldered knuckle-draggers who waddled behind belt-felt, exo-mounted machine guns. "Rapid Rippers," so called because their incredible rate of fire could rip men, livestock, and basic infrastructure in less than half the time that it took to form that final prayer to a Deity who probably wouldn't respond to your plea.

The Dawn Master—still standing in the center of the mosaic pattern that graced the Courtyard of Involuntary Offerings—shook his cane at the approaching troops. "Your authority—"

His voice was cut off by an angry howl of bees. His midsection exploded, and a thousand points of light bloomed along the brickwork of the courtyard. Moistness spattered in a stomach-wrenching way.

As one, the penitents dropped to familiar positions,

abasing themselves before the awe-inspiring majesty of the All-Powerful.

Eventually, they heard the voice of God. "All right, maggots," it said. "Which of you ground-licking navel-suckers used to be somebody?"

SHE HAD THAT PRETERNATURAL ITCH—A flexing twitch around the crescent scar just inside her left scapula—ever since she breached the atmosphere of Balchar VII. When she cleared the airlock minders and popped the hatch on the flitter, that itch became a fully formed thought in her head: *something's off.* It wasn't the quality of the air—which was fresher and cleaner than the agro-copy churned out by the terrestrial-based marketing firm used by the Church of the Holy Absolute Resolve. Nor was the view an issue. It was—beyond the retro-historically machine-sculpted brickwork of the mosaic courtyard of the Spire of Perpetual Abasement for Eventual Reconciliation—breathtakingly picturesque. No, what set Maisi on edge, and what prompted her to toggle full feed back to the *Sparrow*—was the blood spatter and the guys with guns.

Blood is hard to hide on tile, even when you've laid a couple layers of tessellating geometric patterns. She didn't have much chance to examine the crime scene, though she was streaming a high-def feed back to the *Sparrow* for Nome to deconstruct. No, Maisi's focus was on the bangers pointed at her.

The three men standing in the courtyard wore austere robes befitting the brochures—dun-colored fabrics, solemnly-peaked hoods, belts of woven fiber—but the ancient slug-throwers they had in their hands ran counter to the Church of the Holy Absolute Resolve's mission statement of conspicuous celibacy and practical penitence.

Maisi showed her palms. "Salutations and salubriations," she offered. "It would appear that my unexpected arrival is unwanted and unwarranted. I am only too happy to recourse and . . ."

"Who are you?" demanded the guy in front. He had recently been struck in the face by a blunt object. The cuts hadn't scabbed yet, and the bruises were still ripening. It was altogether likely his attitude had little to do with her.

"Sally—" Maisi offered, reaching for one of her usual aliases. "Salliney Fortis-Morass, Field Correspondent for *The New Expression*. I'm, uh, I'm supposed to do a story for our . . ."

The priest raised his rifle. "We don't do interviews." Oh, now his attitude was turning in her direction.

Maisi maintained her hand position. "My mistake— well, someone at Home Desk, I mean. Probably that idiot Tryree. I told them CHAM doesn't sit for puff work, and he told me to shut my hole and hit my goal. 'Get some gab, Forty.' Fresh flush for the feeds, you know?"

The trio clearly didn't, and Maisi took the momentary pause afforded by her grift to give a cycle of attention to Nome, who was blathering all sorts of questions in her ear. "Why don't I make a call and . . ."

The short one on the left lowered his weapon. "CHAM," he said. "That's . . ."

The guy on the right was clearly the pleaser of the three. "We're CHAR," he said.

That was all Maisi needed. Never pass up the chance

to let someone explain their acronym. "CHAR?" she asked.

"Church of the Holy Absolute Resolve," the pleaser provided, a note of pride in his voice. "We are devotedly abasing ourselves in preparation for the Eternal—"

"We don't do interviews," the bruised one interrupted. "No Empty Utterances shall slip our lips."

The other two, chastised by the words of their sallow-faced friend, dipped their heads. Contrary to Bruiser's words, she could definitely see their lips moving. She couldn't hear what they were saying, though if she asked, Nome would wash her feed through a signal booster and isolate their words. *Leave them a little dignity*, she thought.

"Anyway," she said, smiling at the trio. "My meeting was supposed to be with someone from CHAM, the, uh" —she hesitated, waiting for Nome to pipe her something suitable—"the Crypto-Hydroponics Alliance," she said, repeating the phrase whispered in her ear. "That's right. The Crypto-Hydroponics Alliance. I'm doing an interview about agricultural subsidies on unmanaged systems. How, uh, free market forces can—"

"What's the 'M' stand for?" the bruised priest asked.

"The what?"

"The 'M,' he repeated. "In CHAM." He said it with a hard consonant.

"CHAM," she repeated. When she said it, the name had a much more sibilant sound. "The 'M' stands for, uh —" *Come on, Nome!* she thought frantically. *Don't leave me hanging like this.*

"*Managed*," came his voice in her ear. "*Crypto-Hydroponic Alliance, Managed.*"

She nearly rolled her eyes.

"*Stall them a little longer,*" the hacker whispered. "*I'm almost done with my analysis.*"

"*Peridot Scout Carbines. Small bore. Short range.*" The second voice in her head made the base of her jaw vibrate. "*Rounds for that weapon haven't been autofactured for at least twenty years. If they've actually got live ammo in those rifles, the cartridges have been hand-assembled.*" Sheets laughed, and the sound echoed up and down her spine. "*These guys don't look like they know how to work a machine press.*"

Maisi dropped her hands. "All right," she said. "Enough of this." That was mostly for the voices in her head. She made a note to tweak the audio settings on the *Sparrow* comm network. If they didn't get a compression filter on Sheets, he was going to rattle all their skeletons.

The priests were like those little statues you get at tourist traps. Little fellows with stretched faces, all acting out vastly different emotional reactions. You have the confused one, who doesn't understand why their credit key isn't working; the one who is in utter denial about how badly they've been oversold on this cruise; and the one filled with shame and dismay as it dawned on him how much it was going to cost for return passage.

The bruised priest—the dismayed one—took a step forward. *Sheets was right,* Maisi thought, noticing how he was holding the weapon. *These things aren't loaded.*

She gauged the proximity of rifle's dark socket. "I was hoping for more conversation and less aggression," she said, "but if it's another black eye you're looking for, I'm happy to oblige."

Her tone was all it took. Bruiser deflated. He lowered his weapon, and after a moment, the others did the same. The pleaser looked relieved, though the one on the left looked like he might still be up for a little tussle. Maisi gave him a hint of side-eye—denial could go either way, after all—but kept most of her attention on Bruiser, who seemed like he really wanted to get something off his chest.

"It wasn't supposed to be like this," Bruiser said.

"I know, darling," she said. "Why don't you start at the top and tell me everything . . ."

IN THE BEGINNING, there was only the beat. A steady pulse that was too quick to be the regular rhythm of a human heart. A persistent *tock-tocka-tock* that put a little skip in your step, and once you started skipping, it didn't take long for your breath to find its place within the pattern. Then, locked in step, breath in time, your hands started to move, didn't they? Patting and tapping. *Tock-tocka-tock hush slip-slap tocka-tock.* Do it with me now. *Do it to me now.*

That was their first single—"Hey Girl, Wanna Get Down With Me?" It barely blipped on the feeds across the Hub, which was the usual *par-far* for a fresh bit of *slick and pick*—the media tags and rags were always trying to stay relevant with the kids, *Moteria blessing.* The song found an audience on the spiral fringe, and a couple billion microtransactions later, the DreamBeam Cashisway found themselves fresh enough to shoot some actual Vee. And that—as history always shows—is what it takes to really capture people's attention.

Pastroyalé didn't want to watch the replay. This was a slice of his old life, the skin he wore before signing the Executory Exemption that released him into the slightly less abusive arms of the Church of the Holy Absolute Resolve. But he couldn't look away. He couldn't close his eyes and—*challe a' challe*—wish himself to lagoon splashing with baby turtles. No, this was memory, and memory was a cold-hearted bitch when it came to reminding you of the stupid shit you tried to bury.

There, on the left. The four Westies—Molly, Drean, Bleu, and Candi-CanCan—doing that *snap! & pop!* routine that made the girls and boys lose their minds. So much hip action. So many shoulder rolls. Early on, their choreographer had tried to get them to do this while singing, but no amount of advanced Valhadedic stretching and toning could give them the core strength and lung capacity to pull it off. That meant the focus pull during this verse would swing to the Easties, but the Westies weren't going to let the spotlight slip just because they weren't crooning.

The Easties, of course, didn't care for the upstaging, and the subsequent turf war of grandstanding, stage grinding, and rhythm nationing should have led to a furious immolation of the band on live stream, but the boys were more tightly bound than the media tags and rags gave them credit for, and this back and forth—this tag-team, hands up, feet down, *work it baby!* determination—made DreamBeam Cashisway explode.

Not literally. More—shall we say—*poptastically.*

He had been part of something that was more than family and only a little less than blood, which made the other memories—the ones he knew would follow—so hard to bear.

Pastroyalé tried to look away, but this was all in his head, and there was nowhere to go. He tried to shut out

the screams, but he couldn't cover his ears. He tried to beg
—*Stop it! Stop it! Make it stop!*—but he had no voice.

Which one of you used to be someone?

He hadn't said anything when the mercenary squad
leader asked his question. The merc made it easy for the
others to speak for him. *What about you?* he had asked
one of the brethren. When the man denied being of any
importance (they were, after all, still Blemished in the
eyes of the Holy Absolute Resolve), the man with the box
of bees made a mess of his chest.

What about you? the merc asked another monk.

This brother—one of the three who regularly beat
Penitent Pastroyalé, in fact—had pointed, singling out the
new neophyte. His reward for squealing on his faithful
family was a blow to the face with the butt of the mercenary's weapon.

So you're the one, the merc said, getting up close and
inspecting Pastroyalé face. Looking for some sign—some
mark—that would illuminate the significance of this individual. But Pastroyalé said nothing, and his face . . . well,
his face wasn't what it used to be, but that was all part of
the Glorious Realignment that brought one closer to the
Incarnations leading to Holy Emptiness and Eventual
Reconciliation.

MAISI CAUGHT Leo looking at her reflection in the
portside viewscreen. "Wondering where I've hidden the
hardware?" she asked.

His gaze darted back to his slate, where his fingers
were hesitating over a complicated data-dup join query—
a data diver he shouldn't be building, much less splicing

into the open-air network of the Uplift shuttle they were currently riding.

The tiny transport was on a tight-beam loop-lock between the Uplift orbital waystation and the egregiously overcompensatory luxury yacht that was parked geosynchronously over the largest urban sprawl on Alshaita III where it caused a partial eclipse during midday. The *Why Can't Wishes be Fishes?* was shaped like something that was most parts avian with a pinch of crustacean folded in. It was plated and polished in precious metals, of course, because this was a ship that announced itself on every possible wavelength.

Nome had pinged the HTF Registry for information on the yacht when the *Sparrow* had dropped into orbit around Alshaita III, and during that connection, he sliced through the Registry's security and slurped secure data about the ship. Tonnage, displacement, propulsion infrastructure, security network, armament, floor plans, Cipher ledger. He shed the data to the slates of the crew, and Leo had memorized a lot of it already. It was definitely a pretty prize. Not that they were planning on stealing anything.

While he was on the Registry's underside, Nome tapped a conduit, blew some bits, and wrangled a pair of invitations to a thing happening on the yacht. Before they showed, however, they had to make a quick stop at the Uplift. Maisi needed to do a little shopping.

The invitations said "fancy dress."

Leo allowed himself to be stapled into a bird suit. It was tight in the rear and across his shoulders, but the complimentary host said it made him look debonair, which was unnecessarily fancy talk for "not class, but not garbage either." Maisi added a sash, which drew an eager handclap from the host and a microscopic nod of approval from the draper.

She was poured into a sheath of silk and shine that was all smoke and mirrors. It shivered like water about to boil, and when she moved, it followed her like sunlight scorching the haze off a sandy shoreline. There was, in fact, nowhere to hide anything—certainly not any sort of physical hardware.

And speaking of things hidden, he had intended to do some digging after the staffer in the *Sparrow*'s ready room, but shortly after he had packaged and spliced his initial query, Nome had—uncharacteristically—shown up in the workroom. *Don't* was all the hacker said, and on his slate, Leo got an alert that the *Sparrow*'s network was—equally out of character—unavailable. "Unscheduled maintenance" was the explanation offered, and Leo understood that Nome bubbled them in a digital dead zone.

Canna bunker ken his kin? he had asked.

The hacker had offered a rare smile. *We ain't kin yet,* he said. *Ifen we go, izzano gen-blood, ayeo?*

Ayeo, Leo replied. The bunkers—the rank and file who crawled the conduits and capped the cables of the immense vessels that carried humanity between the stars —had their own clipped and compressed *linga*. Like all secret languages, it acknowledged a bond between all parties. *We watch out for our own.*

Nome knew what Leo wanted to know, but the hacker had black-boxed the fixer's curiosity. *Not now,* he said. *Maybe not ever. The boss's secrets are hers. We don't pry.* And with a final knowing glance, the hacker left him with a parting thought: *She won't ask about yours either.*

Aboard the shuttle, Leo stole another glance at his boss. She was the only one named on the ship's Passage

Key. Maisi Inviolux, Captain of the *Who's a Pretty Sparrow, All Aflutter in the Morning Sky?* and Field Lieutenant of Ansalaage's Ministry of Accordance, Recompense, and Solidarity. The rest of them—himself, Sheets, and Nome—were privacy-coded, a nice trick usually reserved for diplomatic couriers. There was no mention of House Bellephori, and again, without doing the dig, Leo had nothing to work with other than that conversational blip in the staffer.

It gnawed at him, not knowing. He was more curious than he should be, and it had gotten him into trouble on more than one occasion. The last had gotten him a ten-year sentence at a black-site extraction colony—a sentence he only served eight hundred and sixty-four days of, thanks to the enigmatic woman who was now his paymaster.

Leo knew better than to bite the open hand, as the bunker saying went, but at the same time . . .

"Been to a fancy dress party like this before?"

Leo pulled himself away from the madness-inducing prompt on his slate. "No—well, one time, I guess."

"You guess?"

"I was a plusser."

"Arm candy?"

"Maybe a little bit," he admitted. He noted what he was wearing—what *she* was wearing—and his stomach did a little whoopsy-turvy. Time was a circle that always came 'round to bite you again, *challe Moteria.*

"You're not candy," Maisi said, reading his expression. "You've the hard job tonight."

"I do?"

Her gaze wandered to the heads-up display that showed the shuttle's position, relative to the other objects in orbit. They were about to dock with *Why Can't Wishes be Fishes?* "You've got to be the sensible one," she said.

⋯⋯✶⋯⋯

THE REOCCURRING DISMAY of the pre-Incarnated penitent was waking and finding oneself still trapped in the flesh. Whatever transcendent vision you were having lost its magic when you realized it was nothing more than a dream. Waking was the hardest part of the path of the Holy Absolute Resolve; waking and remembering you were not free. And so when Pastroyalé had that moment of self-awareness, he reached for the Prayer Against Awakening and Awareness, the litany that provides solace and hope for those who have found themselves rudely pulled back from enlightenment. He didn't say it out loud; rather, he listened to it in his head, sensing and vibing with the rhythm of the words. It had a simple push-pull patter, one deeply ingrained in our linguistic psyches. One that we fell into without thinking—frankly, it was not far off from the core bopalop *tock-tocka-tock* of a modern dance trax.

There was a reason these prayers come easy to the tongue, that they fill the mind so readily. *Hear me, o Muse, and sing of—*

He was in a place he didn't recognize. It wasn't his cell at the Spire of Perpetual Abasement for Eventual Reconciliation. It wasn't one of a thousand different suites where he and the DeamBeam Cashisway transformed themselves from gravity-weary, star-dusted travelers into the shiny-dotted feed flashes they became for two shows daily—three, if they were resident in mechanized infrastructure that could flush and flood a full stadium of screaming DBC fans in less than two hours. No, he was someplace else, a room where the pixels were pulsing and the waves were wiggling.

It was a virtual ready room, a chamber of quantum disengagement where reality was in flux until someone ran a simulation. This one was between sesh—a blank slate, floating in limbo, waiting for someone to look and decide if they saw something in all this nothing.

Pastroyalé looked, and as the room registered his gaze, it warmed itself and sploomed buds and blossoms of fractalized fancy. He saw fireworks. He saw C-beams glittering. He saw . . . the opening animation from DreamBeam Cashisway's last tour, the revolving-evolving coin of many sides that showered each member of the band in a festival of flowers. The tessellating coin showed him Drean and Bleu and Candi-CanCan. And there he was—Bang-Bang Batay, all decked and dressed in white. His paint was immaculate. His hair was perfect. It was almost—no, it *was* too real.

He turned away, even though he had no head to turn, but they were still there, floating in front of him. The Westies of the DBC. The Fierce Four who danced like they were barefoot on molten steel, like they had stinging eels in their pants, like their spines were lightning rods that had just been touched by the fulminating fury of a Heaven on fire.

He tried to find the Prayer Against Awakening and Awareness, but his mind couldn't settle itself. He tried to hide, but where do you hide in a room with no edges, angles, or shadows? He tried to flee—to disperse, disassociate, disintegrate—but his heart, synched now to the *tock-tocka-tock hush slip-slap* of "Hey Girl, Wanna Get Down

With Me?", refused to go. He must stay. He must be witness. He must . . . participate.

It was then that Pastroyalé—though, truth be told, he was penitent no longer—it was then that Angabatay Marshalan realized the dream was not a dream. The room was not a room. The virtual dance party flashing and vibrating around him was of his doing. It was a nightmare snatched out of his head, a fever vision murdered and recreated by his own memories.

The band was back together because, in some corner of his brain, they were all still alive. The DreamBeam Cashisway Comeback Tour was being underwritten and over-performed by his subconscious.

And there was no way he could make it stop.

LEO KNEW money made him weak. What bunker didn't flush when currency went *ka-ching*? Shipboard life was— let's be polite—*functional*. You knew the air scrubbers were working because you could smell the farts coming off the man in the next rack over. You knew the hull hadn't been holed because your ears weren't bleeding. You knew you were going to live another day because your body wasn't going to die before expelling that toxic sludge you had for lunch. And so, a bunker's stoicism—his ham-hocked grip on notions like freedom and integrity— were easily assaulted by racking a stack of hard coin. And there was no blame among bunkers for letting your eyes go soft under the glow of gold. They all knew how cold and dark it was between systems.

Which is why he hadn't complained when Maisi had him slip into the bird suit. It was a nice suit—of course it was; Leo had seen the hit against the *Sparrow*'s Passage ledger. It was white and black, with tails and tassels, fine evening wear for an uplifted sort, the kind of man who didn't have grease in the deep grooves of his heels. He didn't know how to walk in it. Or how to stand nonchalantly without wanting to tug at the rear to keep it from crawling up the crack of his ass. And he certainly wasn't going to be able to crouch or crawl or run like hell when someone looked too closely and realized he didn't belong, among all this fancy flash.

He went to drink from his glass—laser-cut, hand-polished synthetic stemware that probably wouldn't break if you drove an assault tank over it—and found it empty. That wasn't good. He'd had two? three? already. The sparkling wine tasted like the grapes had expired with euphoric eagerness, crushed by soft-skinned and full-thighed virgins who were orgiastically experiencing the thanatostic transformation of the fruit as it squirted out its life juices between their supple toes. A waiter, nearly invisible in their active chameleon garb that allowed them to move unobtrusively through the sprawl of the freshly rich, incredibly rich, and stupidly wealthy, offered Leo a new glass. Without thinking, he took it, relinquishing his empty, and only after the waiter melted into the scenery, did he realize he shouldn't drink this—was it his fourth?

"Punch is pretty good, isn't it?"

Maisi materialized next to him. He wasn't sure how she did it. Her dress demanded your attention, and the attitude of her shoulders and the hitch of her hip made it clear there was no way you were going to get a better glimpse of the body underneath, which only made her more magnetic to the currency crew who were looking to score.

"You make them nervous," she said.

"What?"

She nodded at the sharp-dressed and sleepy-eyed fashionistas who were prowling on the periphery. Leo was reminded of the carrion dogs of Tunesfa IV in the way they were eager for blood but were all wary of being taken for a fool by a hidden blade. "Your jib confuses them."

"As it does me," Leo said.

She smiled. "It'll feel less false if you wear it often."

"I'm not sure mucking about the guts of some gear is a good idea if I can't bend over."

She plucked his glass out of his hand. "I'm sure you'll manage."

"Speaking of which, how much longer do we have to . . . ?"

"Drink with reckless abandon and look this good?"

Leo tried to give her a stern eying, but she wasn't having any of it. She finished the glass of champagne and handed the empty back to him. He took it without thinking, and upon noticing the impish gleam in her eye, realized he had reacted like hired help and not like a man about town.

She leaned close and put her hand on his shoulder. "It's all part of the play," she said, inclining her head toward the circus of carrion crawlers. "We're giving them what they want to see: me, strong and sexy; you, subservient and shackled. They'll decide you won't be a problem if they want to make a move."

A commotion in the crowd drew eyes, and Leo's concern about the circling rakes and rough-riders was sidelined by a flouncing flock of fops and fancy-makers. Their attire was garish, outlandish, and—in the case of the individual at the center of the swirl of satin and silk who stomped along in meter high boots and a cape that swelled behind him like a handful of preening peacocks on very short leashes—utterly nonsensical. Their host—who else could this mountain of make-believe be but the owner of this pleasure palace?—was magnetically drawn to Maisi in her sheath of silver smoke. "Revelations," the creature trilled, offering a hand beguiled in rings and things that glittered with all the dazzle of a sun going supernova.

Maisi pinched the tip of one of the extended digits and offered a modest curtsy. "Salubrations, your Munificence. Your extravagance ravishes me."

Their host made more bird noises, and Leo couldn't tell if the sounds were produced anatomically or if they came from sonic cinematics woven into the collar of the outfit. "Your devotion makes our hearts skip," their host sang. "Have you tried the puff pockets yet?"

Maisi curtsied again. "My attire precludes any appetite," she said by way of apology.

Their host stared down at her from their regal height, and even with their face obscured by their mask, it was easy to read a ravenous desire in the gaze. After a glance that lingered way too long, the mask turned toward Leo, and that insatiable hunger made the bunker's skin crawl. "Try the puff pockets," their host said.

Leo stuttered a reply, and then started when their host cut him off with a cackling *ka-kaw!* Something had caught their attention, and with a pirouette of peacockery, they were off, the flock of sycophants and scene-suckers flustering after them.

"Well, that was—"

Maisi wasn't listening. Her attention was on a figure

who had been revealed by the departure of the party's host and their entourage. His attire was crisp and knife-cut. His colors were diplomatically regal. He had a shock of white hair that reminded Leo of someone and his gaze was shrewd and predatory. His expression was . . . bemused.

"Hi, Daddy," Maisi said.

Vertavierta Lamiscullo Theodrosia Bellephor, the Eighteenth Viscount of Septimal Secariunda and an Honored and Appointed Diplomatic Agency of House Bellephori offered his blood relative a mere quirk of his upper lip in response to the overly familiar greeting. According to the stripes on his sash, he was not only a fully blooded House member but he was also a diplomatic representative of some stature. The sort of fellow one did not address in this manner (not publicly, at least, and quite possibly, not in private either), but even with the little Leo knew of Maisi's relationship with her family, this sort of insouciance was remarkably on brand for her.

For Leo, a spark of insight illuminated her comment made earlier on the shuttle. *You've got the hard job.* Illumination gave way to realization: She had known her father was going to be here . . .

Whoah! Who just drove you off the cliff and left you dangling? The author did. Is he really going to leave you hanging like this? Well, he's not that much of a—oh, look! A place to sign up for his mailing list, where he's got the exciting conclusion to "The Alshaita Uplift Job." There will be things blowing up. Promise!

markteppo.com/about/mailinglist.php

Pick Your Poison

1. *Wait. Did you say ghosts?* Head to "Mad Dog" by R.M. Olson

2. *I'm starting to forget...* Go read "Good as Gold" by Frasier Armitage in CROOKED V.2

3. *I read them all!* Congratulations! Keep going to learn more about the fabulous contributors to this anthology— and don't forget to check out the other volumes of CROOKED for even more sci-fi crime stories.

CONTRIBUTOR BIOS

MJ BLEHART

MJ Blehart has been writing fantasy and sci-fi/space opera all his life, the first when he was nine years old. Star Wars and Star Trek were some of the biggest influences in his youth.

He is a history aficionado. MJ has been a member of the Society for Creative Anachronism (SCA—a medieval re-enactment society) for over thirty years. As part of the SCA he studies and teaches 16th century rapier combat (fencing) and court heraldry, enjoys archery, and spending time with friends.

When not writing sci-fi and fantasy, MJ blogs regularly, exploring mindfulness and creating an amazing life. He strives to live a kickass life and consciously create his reality (and sharing that process to help others do the same).

MJ lives in New Jersey just outside of Philadelphia with his wife and their two feline overlords.

Facebook: @blehartmj
LinkedIn: Murray MJ Blehart
Website: mjblehart.com

PETER J. FOOTE

Peter got locked in a bookstore as a child and has been reading his way to freedom ever since.

As a blue-collar sci-fi author, Peter tells gritty and personal stories that resonate with readers and provide much-needed escapism.

Peter's first tales developed from Dungeons & Dragons campaigns that went unplayed and watching Babylon 5 on repeat. After having several dozen short stories published through various publishers, Peter has decided to try longer forms.

True to his Atlantic Canadian roots, many regional landmarks, businesses, and personalities are sprinkled within Peter's works.

Website: peterjfoote.com

K. GORMAN

K. Gorman is a Science Fiction and Fantasy addict from Western Canada who dabbles in different genres. In addition to being a fiction lover, she is also a history and culture nerd with a focus on China, Taiwan, and Japan. When she's not writing, one can find her devouring other author's stories, marathoning various sci-fi and fantasy franchises, or appeasing her ancient cat's need for laptime.

Website: kgorman.ca

ROBIN JEFFREY

Robin Jeffrey lives happily with her husband and their out of control comic book collection in the PNW. She is the author of the urban fantasy series *The Night*, as well as the author of the mystery series *The Cadence Turing Mysteries*. When not writing, Robin teaches writing workshops to local writers and writers around the world.

TikTok: @thesidekick_author
Instagram: @thesidekick_ig
Facebook: @RobinJeffreyAuthor
Website: robinjeffreyauthor.com

JESSIE KWAK

Jessie Kwak has always lived in imaginary lands, from Arrakis and Ankh-Morpork to Earthsea, Tatooine, and now Portland, Oregon. As a writer, she sends readers on their own journeys to immersive worlds filled with fascinating characters, gunfights, explosions, and dinner parties. When she's not raving about her latest favorite sci-fi series to her friends, she can be found sewing, mountain biking, or out exploring new worlds both at home and abroad.

She is the author of supernatural thriller *From Earth and Bone*, the Bulari Saga series of gangster sci-fi novels, the Nanshe Chronicles series of space pirate adventures, and productivity guide *From Chaos to Creativity*.

TikTok: @jessiekwak
Instagram: @kwakjessie
Website: jessiekwak.com

ARTHUR MAYOR

Arthur Mayor lives in the Twin Cities area of texlMinnesota. By day, Arthur is a mild-mannered special education teacher; and by night, a referee in the non-stop cage match between his two sons. Later that night, he writes stories.

Website: darkshadowycabal.com

R.M. OLSON

R.M. Olson writes fast-paced, feel-good science fiction featuring diverse casts, found families, and loads of action. R.M. has ridden the Trans Siberian railway, jumped off the highest bungee jump in the world, gone cage-diving with great white sharks, faced down a charging buffalo bull, and knows how to milk a goat. Currently they reside in Alberta, Canada with their four children, three cats, and a dog the size of a small bear. R.M. goes hiking and skiing more often than they probably have time for, eats more chocolate than is probably good for them, and reads more books than is probably prudent.

Website: rmolson.com

AUDREW SHARPE

Audrey Sharpe grew up believing in the Force and dreaming of becoming captain of the Enterprise. She's still working out the logistics of moving objects with her mind, but writing science fiction provides a pretty good alternative. When she's not off exploring the galaxy with

Aurora and her crew, she lives in the Sonoran Desert, where she has an excellent view of the stars.

Website: audreysharpe.com

MARK TEPPO

Mark Teppo divides his time between Portland and Sumner, and he tends to navigate by local bookstore positioning. He writes historical fiction, fantasy, speculative fiction, and horror, and has published more than a dozen novels. If he's writing a mystery, he's pretending to be Harry Bryant.

He also runs Underland Press, an independent publishing house.

Twitter: @markteppo
Instagram: @mark.teppo
Website: markteppo.com

HEATHER TEXLE

HEATHER TEXLE is the award-winning author of the *Reliance Sinclair* science fiction series who finds inspiration in quirky, weird, and I-can't-believe-that's-true things. With a lifelong passion for learning, Heather is fascinated with the creativity and ingenuity of the human spirit. She also adores a good conspiracy theory.

After graduating college, Heather moved to Minnesota where she attained her law degree and continues to live with her husband and two cats, Mew and Spots. Despite once being stranded in the Gulf of Mexico on a burning cruise ship, she loves to travel and can often be heard muttering "I miss Scotland" on cool, rainy days. Her debut novel, *On Impulse*, won the 2023 Minnesota Author Project contest for Adult Fiction.

Facebook: @Heather Texle
Website: heathertexle.com

Thank you so much for reading!

If you enjoyed this anthology, please let others know by leaving a review or telling a friend. As a scrappy crew of authors, we depend on word of mouth to connect with new readers.

Looking for more great sci-fi crime reads?

Don't miss the stories in CROOKED V.1 and CROOKED V.2.

Head to jessiekwak.com/crooked